P9-DEI-308

Viking
Unchained

Sandra Hill

BERKLEY SENSATION, NEW YORK

THE BERKLEY PUBLISHING GROUP
Published by the Penguin Group
Penguin Group (USA) Inc.
375 Hudson Street, New York, New York 10014, USA
Penguin Group (Canada), 90 Eglinton Avenue East, Suite 700, Toronto, Ontario M4P 2Y3, Canada
(a division of Pearson Penguin Canada Inc.)
Penguin Books Ltd., 80 Strand, London WC2R 0RL, England
Penguin Group Ireland, 25 St. Stephen's Green, Dublin 2, Ireland (a division of Penguin Books Ltd.)
Penguin Group (Australia), 250 Camberwell Road, Camberwell, Victoria 3124, Australia
(a division of Pearson Australia Group Pty. Ltd.)
Penguin Books India Pvt. Ltd., 11 Community Centre, Panchsheel Park, New Delhi—110 017, India
Penguin Group (NZ), 67 Apollo Drive, Rosedale, North Shore 0632, New Zealand
(a division of Pearson New Zealand Ltd.)
Penguin Books (South Africa) (Pty.) Ltd., 24 Sturdee Avenue, Rosebank, Johannesburg 2196,
South Africa

Penguin Books Ltd., Registered Offices: 80 Strand, London WC2R 0RL, England

This is a work of fiction. Names, characters, places, and incidents either are the product of the author's imagination or are used fictitiously, and any resemblance to actual persons, living or dead, business establishments, events, or locales is entirely coincidental. The publisher does not have any control over and does not assume any responsibility for author or third-party websites or their content.

VIKING UNCHAINED

A Berkley Sensation Book / published by arrangement with the author

PRINTING HISTORY
Berkley Sensation mass-market edition / July 2008

Copyright © 2008 by Sandra Hill.
Cover illustration by Don Sipley.
Cover design by Rich Hasselberger.
Interior text design by Stacy Irwin.

ISBN: 978-0-425-22295-9

BERKLEY® SENSATION
Berkley Sensation Books are published by The Berkley Publishing Group,
a division of Penguin Group (USA) Inc.,
375 Hudson Street, New York, New York 10014.
BERKLEY SENSATION and the "B" design are trademarks belonging to Penguin Group (USA) Inc.

PRINTED IN THE UNITED STATES OF AMERICA

10 9 8 7 6 5 4 3 2 1

This book is dedicated to all the military men and women serving our country, especially those serving in Iraq and Afghanistan. And to the families who support them . . . in particular the spouses and parents who write and tell me that the humor in my books makes the waiting easier.

While many of my books involve tenth-century Vikings, I am continually amazed at how much society has changed, but also how much stays the same. It seems that there will always be those brave, dedicated men and women willing to put their lives on the line for a greater good . . . whether they be Viking warriors, Saxon knights, or modern-day Navy SEALs, Marines, Air Force, or whatever military branch.

God bless them all!

Prologue

Five years ago . . . not your regular Welcome Wagon . . .

Lydia Denton shifted the paper grocery bag to her left hip
and used her right hand, holding the carryall with her aerobics customer files, to punch in the security code on the
front door of her San Diego beachfront home.

No sooner did the door start to open than a male hand
grabbed her wrist and yanked her into the darkness, the
door slamming behind her. The grocery bag and carryall
fell to the floor, spilling their contents, as he pressed her
up against the door, his nude body telling her loud and
clear what he had in mind. A yelp of distress, followed by
"Wait!" barely escaped her lips before he rasped out,
"Don't talk," and a hot, hungry mouth covered hers with a
kiss that was devouring in its intensity.

He was like a madman, his mouth everywhere, sucking

her nipples into hard points through her T-shirt and bra, licking her neck, nipping her shoulder, and always coming back to kiss her senseless, his tongue a demanding weapon of erotic torture. And his hands . . . oh, God, his hands! She could not keep track of their fast-moving foray. Cradling her face, lifting her by the buttocks to ride his hips, then skimming up her thighs, under her short denim shirt, to grip the sides of her bikini briefs and rip them apart. Within seconds, without warning, he plunged inside her. Steel-hard and thick, pulsing with arousal.

She moaned.

His eyes were closed, his neck arched back, the cords standing out in emphasis of the control he was trying to maintain. His lower body did not move. But then his eyes fluttered open and he said, so low she could barely hear, "Help. Me."

Without hesitation, she complied. With one hand cupping his nape, she used the other to reach down and touch herself where they were joined. Instantly, she began to climax around him. Wild, grasping convulsions of her inner muscles, milking his hardness. Only then did he begin to move. But no long slow strokes from him. No, he was fast and furious, hitting her clitoris every time he thrust in, causing her to have a never-ending orgasm 'til he impaled himself deep in her and cried out his own release. Even then, she continued to spasm around him.

It seemed like forever before he raised his head from her shoulder and grinned. All he said was, "Babe."

That was enough.

To him, she said, "Dude," and grinned.

That was enough, too.

Same show, second act . . .

He carried her, his penis still curled up inside her, her legs still straddling his hips, down the three shallow steps leading into the living room. It was somewhat lighter here, the full moon shining through the plate glass windows facing the ocean.

"I thought you weren't coming back 'til tomorrow."

He grunted and said distractedly, "Mission accomplished early." No wonder he was sparse on words. The brute was doing something strange to her ear with his tongue. Deliciously sexy, but strange nonetheless.

"Where did you learn to do that?" she inquired, squirming against his belly.

"We were hiding in a Kuwait safe house with nothing to do but listen to Cage ramble on with his usual nonsense. He told us about that trick." Cage was a fellow teammate in the SEALs, known for his Cajun blarney. "Do you like it?"

She tried to laugh, but it came out as a gurgle.

"I'll take that as a yes."

Easing himself out of her with a grimace, he laid her across an upholstered ottoman, one of those low pieces that serve a dual purpose as a coffee table, and knelt between her legs.

"Raise your heels to the edge, baby, and spread wider," he ordered as he sat back on his haunches.

She did.

"Hold yourself open, sweetheart."

She did that, too, her fingers spreading her private parts. No questions. She would do anything for him. This was her husband of three years, the man she loved beyond life itself.

"You're wet."

"No kidding!"

"Does that mean you missed me?"

"Like crazy."

"Good. Cage said something else? Wanna know what?"

Is he crazy? He wants to have a conversation about Cage? Now? "Do I have a choice?"

He pinched her belly lightly. "He claims he knows how to have a tongue hard-on."

"And you believe him?"

He shrugged. "I'm just sayin'." He leaned forward and tasted her. One quick lick.

"Dave. Wait. I can't. I'm too sensi . . . aaaaaaaah!" Turns out she could. Turns out she wasn't as sensitive as she'd thought. Turns out Cage wasn't too far off base, no pun intended.

Before she could say "Wowza!" or "Oh. My. God!" he flipped her over and took her from behind.

She wasn't sure if it was her or him who screamed this time.

Third time around, and much later, following a quick meal of grilled cheese and tomato soup and then two glasses of wine out on the deck, she sitting on his lap, he made love to her in the bedroom. This time, he took things slow. Very slow. Mixed in with the wicked things they did to each other, and the wicked words that slipped easily from both their mouths, they said out loud and expressed bodily how much they loved each other.

Then they fell asleep in each other's arms.

Baby, baby, baby . . .

The next morning they slept in. She stared down at this beautiful man, all six-foot-three of hard muscles, his arms thrown over his head, his breathing soft. His black hair was a little long for his preferred "high and tight," a military cut she usually didn't like, but on him it was sexy as hell. But then, even his breathing was sexy to her.

His beeper and a Glock sat on a bedside table. In the closet, three rifles and a collapsible machine gun were stored. One specially made kitchen drawer with a combination lock held a fully stocked backpack that included, among other things, a KA-BAR knife, night-vision goggles, Kevlar gloves, another weapon, a backup secure satellite phone, plastic cuffs, a length of thin rope, a black balaclava, and prescription pills, whose purpose she had never wanted to know.

She leaned over him, carefully.

On closer scrutiny, she noticed the dark circles under his eyes and new bruises on various parts of his body. She recalled from last night the weariness and despair that had clouded his remarkable gray eyes, as was the norm these days when he returned from a live op. He'd made some kills this time, she could tell. And horrible as these terrorists were, as noble as the SEAL cause was, killing took its toll on a man eventually.

She wished he would quit. Or take a long vacation. But, since 9/11, the demand for SEALs was unremitting in the war on terrorism. The tangos, as SEALs called the terrorists, were everywhere and their ranks growing.

Dave was thirty years old, and he'd been a SEAL for seven years, but no one seemed to notice, except her. Where would it end? Where would he end?

An hour later, after showering and setting the big traditional homecoming breakfast she'd prepared in the warming oven, she carried a tall glass of iced orange juice into the bedroom.

His eyes opened slowly as she walked into the room and sat on the edge of the bed. He took the glass from her and drank thirstily, down to the last drop. Then he pulled her down on top of him, giving her a quick kiss on the mouth. "Hey, babe! Tsk, tsk, tsk! You showered without me."

"You were sleeping like a baby."

"A baby, huh?" He tugged her hips against his morning erection.

"Braggart," she accused.

"It's only bragging when you have nothing to back it up." He waggled his eyebrows at her.

Later, when they were sitting in Adirondack chairs on the deck, soaking up the sun, she said, "Honey . . . ?"

"No."

"What do you mean, no? You don't even know what I was going to say."

"Yeah, I do. You have that baby look in your eyes."

He was right. Lydia desperately wanted to have Dave's baby. Yeah, she was only twenty-five, and she had a full-time job she loved as an aerobics and yoga instructor, but at heart all she wanted was to be a mother, especially a mother to Dave's child. "Why . . . why can't we get pregnant now?" She bit her bottom lip to still the tremors.

He squeezed her shoulder in comfort, but still he shook his head. "Not now. I'm already losing my focus, worrying about you. A baby could be dangerous to my concentration, as well as a target for terrorists if my identity were known." In fact, Dave had not wanted to marry her, at first, for this very reason. It was why their home was sealed tighter than a drum, with every type of security device know to man. He squeezed her shoulder again.

"When?" she asked softly.

"Once I quit the teams."

"And that will be . . . when?"

"Don't push me," he snapped, then immediately apologized. "I'm sorry, babe. It won't be much longer, I promise."

But his promise was not to be fulfilled.

One month later, Dave set out for a new mission, once again to Iraq. His words as he went out the door were, "Love you forever, babe."

Her words to him were, "Back at you, hon." Except hers were accompanied by tears.

Who was she kidding? He had tears, too.

Three weeks after that, a Purple Heart–decorated warrior was buried in Arlington National Cemetery. Lt. David

Denton, U.S. Navy SEAL, had died in an ambush by al-Qaeda terrorists.

Life really does go on . . .

For three months, Lydia was a zombie. Her grief was a living, breathing animal of crushing hopelessness.

She'd quit her job. She rarely left her house, where the blinds were drawn. Many times she forgot to eat or bathe. She put her cell phone on permanent voice mail.

No one knew the extent of her depression. No one had ever felt this bad before, no matter what they said. Time would not heal. Time was her enemy.

Dave was never going to come back.

But then, ninety-three days after his death, she discovered that he *was* coming back. Oh, not him personally, but a part of him. She was pregnant.

Five months later, a black-haired, gray-eyed Michael Denton came into the world.

And gave Lydia a reason for living.

Chapter 1

Even eleventh-century Vikings get the blues . . .

Thorfinn Haraldsson was going to kill his brother Steven for bringing him to this place.

They, and a dozen other men, were lying on pillows scattered about the floor of a Baghdad residence, eating fruit and sipping at some potent beverage that smelled like camel piss. "Holy Thor! Grown men were not intended to contort their bodies and eat lying down," he grumbled.

"Then do not eat. Watch." Steven half-reclined against an enormous cushion with his hands linked behind his neck, a mocking twinkle in his eyes.

Eight women—not just Arab, but blonde- and red-haired wenches and one black-skinned Nubian—were twirling about in sheer scarves, their breasts and buttocks bouncing in a manner intended to be tempting but which only seemed foolish to him.

His opinion must have shown on his face.

"What? The sap does not rise for you whilst watching them entertain?"

"Do you jest? 'Tis a pointless exercise, really. By Odin! If a houri wants to tempt a man, all she has to do is stand afore him naked." *I love my brother, but he is a lackwit.*

Steven laughed.

At the same time, a young girl, no more than fourteen, with black-kohled eyes and rouged nipples, clearly visible since she was naked on top, knelt down betwixt the two of them, and began popping grapes and sugared dates into his halfwit brother's laughing mouth.

When she tried to do the same to Thorfinn, he turned his head and stood. The girl scurried away in fright at his scowling face.

"Now why did you do that, Finn?"

"Steven! She is young enough to be your daughter." *Plus, she has youthling spots on her face and baby fat on her middle.*

"And so?"

"'Tis . . .'tis craven." *And she smelled like onions.*

"Craven is good when it comes to swiving."

He threw his hands out in disgust. "Stop acting like an untried boyling with a constant thickening of his cock. You are twenty and seven years old, for Thor's sake." *And I must needs bite my bottom lip or burst out with laughter. You are the only one who keeps me sane.*

"And you are thirty, Finn, but you act like a graybeard.

Nay, not a graybeard, because even they enjoy women." Steven stood and matched his stance, hands on hips. His words were biting, but they were said with a teasing smile.

The two of them were of the same height, with the same long, black hair, and eyes a peculiar shade of silver gray, but the resemblance ended there. Steven's countenance was ever joyous and Thorfinn's grim. The youngest sons of Viking nobles, Jarl Harald Gudsson and Lady Katla of Norsemandy, the brothers owned and lived on estates in the Norselands, Amberstead and Norstead.

"Steven, I like women, and I sure as stars enjoy swiving, like any man, but once grown, a man gets more discriminating. The sap does not have to rise at the least swaying hip." *In truth, my sap has gone gummy these past few years, with good reason. Women . . . one woman in particular . . . have colored for all time my view of the fairer sex as devious and untrustworthy.*

"By the runes! You are far too serious," Steven said with a grin. "I had no intention of bedding the girling. A mature woman awaits me back at our camp, warming my bed furs."

"Mature?"

"Yea. Fifteen."

He shook his head at his brother's hopelessness.

"Didst know that the eunuchs teach the harem girls how to pleasure a man by practicing with a marble phallus?"

That got his attention . . . and brought on many an explicit mind picture. "I have ne'er heard such."

"See, there is something I can teach my big brother."

I seriously doubt that.

"I bought two of them."

Here it comes. He lays the groundwork for one of his jests.

"Do you want one?"

Do not ask. 'Tis a trap. Still, he was curious and took one of them in his hand, amazed at the smooth heat it threw off. "Whatever for? Are you starting up a harem at Amberstead?"

"A harem? Hmmm. There is a thought." He tapped his closed lips pensively with a forefinger.

Thorfinn could not be angry with his brother. In truth, if not for Steven, he would go insane at the bleakness of his life. "You will give Father Bart another attack of heart pains." Vikings practiced both the Norse and Christian religions, and Father Bartholomew traveled betwixt Amberstead and Norstead, dispensing his priestly services, *tut-tut-tut*ting whenever he heard references to the Viking gods. Personally, Thorfinn thought they were one and the same. Father Bart considered Steven a libertine and told him so on every occasion, clutching his chest in exaggerated distress as he did so.

"No harem then." Steven grinned, caressing the marble column in his palm. "They are sex-play trinkets."

Thorfinn's jaw dropped open. His brother never ceased to amaze him. Then, jabbing Steven with an elbow, Thorfinn laughed. "Come, let's us walk off this camel piss. We must needs talk."

"Should we not first express thanks to our host?"

Thorfinn glanced over to the stout Caliph reclining on a low divan with three half-nude females feeding him dates dipped in honey and fanning him with large palm leaves. "Methinks he will not miss us." *Besides, he asked me earlier if I would rut with his second wife, who is barren. Not that Steven needs to know that.*

With a silent signal to the half dozen of his *shiphird*, or "ship army," in attendance to rise and follow after them, Thorfinn and Steven walked companionably out into the street and headed toward the outskirts of the city where their tents had been erected.

Despite the lateness of the hour, the streets were alive with activity. Light was provided by torches on tall spikes. Camels *gr-onk*, *gr-onk*, *gr-onk*ed their nasal cries. Exotic music wafted from various buildings . . . discordant, twanging melodies. Braziers cooking lamb and vegetables on long sticks were offered to passersby, for a price, of course. Merchants, bowing low with obeisance, cajoled them to buy their wares from open and closed stalls. "Master, come smell these spices from the Orient."

"May Allah bless you with many children . . . a certainty if you give your wife these fine silks from Miklagard."

"Amber from the Baltics, sweet Frankish wines, fresh dates and figs."

"Ah, such fine virile young men! Surely, you need a female slave or two to warm your blood." Yes, even men, women, and children were for sale. He had to drag Steven away from that one after seeing through an open curtain a nude slave girl performing a sex act on another nude slave girl.

He stopped several times to make purchases, which he ordered delivered to his campsite in the morning. Saffron and tea. Several ells of fabric, which he would gift to his mother. Salted meats and fishes; the sailors left on his longship had been complaining about the hated old cheese known as *Gammelost* and roasted camel tongue, a delicacy the Norsemen failed to appreciate.

Steven bought an ointment that purported to enhance male pleasure in the bedsport.

"I would be damned afore I would put some unknown substance on my manpart. For all you know, it might shrivel it down to a nub," he told the lackbrain.

His brother stopped, aghast, and tossed the ointment aside.

Several of his men dropped off to visit houses offering sexual favors. Of any kind! Acts were described aloud in explicit detail, along with their prices. He would not admit it to Steven, but he was not sure what some of them were.

Steven guessed his thoughts, though, and said, "I have no idea what that last one is either."

Once they got back to the campsite, he went into his tent and brought out two mugs of mead he had brought from Norstead. Made by kinsmen of his at Ravenshire, the beverage was warm, of course, but still better than that camel piss.

Sinking down next to Steven onto a sea chest, he said

right off, "I am going home on the morrow. Two months I have been gone, what with bad weather-luck and all. I cannot neglect Norstead any longer." *Time for me to admit defeat.*

Surprised, Steven said, "Thank you, Odin! My prayers have been answered. And your wife?"

Thorfinn's wife, Luta, had deserted him five years ago when he had been off a-Viking, a springtime custom for all good Norsemen. She had taken with her their infant son, Miklof. She had not left alone. Even worse, accompanying her had been that slimy sly-boots Gervaise of Jorvik, a young, wealthy Saxon merchant, a man he had once called friend.

Thorfinn had been in a rage at first—still was, in many ways—especially when he had learned that the trading vessel taking them on one of Gervaise's trading trips had sunk in an ocean storm. He no longer cared whether Luta had died, or how. After all, she had broken bond with him in leaving. But his baby . . . ah, he had loved Miklof the instant he came squalling from his mother's womb. Thorfinn's heart would ne'er recover from his loss.

But then, several months back, an Arab trader named Ahmed had reported seeing Luta and Miklof in a Baghdad marketplace. The detailed description he had given came too close to the mark for Thorfinn not to investigate. Steven, ever irksome, had insisted on accompanying him on this two-month wasted venture. So far, neither Luta nor Miklof were to be found in the Arab lands. Ahmed must have been mistaken.

"Someday you will understand, brother. Leastways I

think most fathers feel the way I do. Losing Miklof . . ." He had to stop speaking for the lump choking his throat. "Losing Miklof was like losing a part of myself. I have not been whole ever since." He blinked repeatedly to stem the tears in his eyes. *Tears! What kind of man am I who weeps like a woman? I have got to stop this madness.*

Steven gazed at him with compassion. "Everyone has demons, Finn."

He arched his brows. "You, too?"

"Of course."

He could not imagine what, so merry of heart was his brother. Clearing his throat, he said, "One thing is for certain. If I ne'er see a camel again . . . or sand, for the love of Thor . . . it will be too soon. I vow not to complain about the Vestfold cold again. Man is not meant to bake his skin."

"Well said! Does that mean you have finally given up this bloody search?"

He nodded. "I will try on the morrow to find that one last woman I was told about. If she is here with my Miklof, I will take him back with me. If not, I concede defeat. They must be dead."

"Praise the gods!" Steven looped an arm around his shoulder. "Mayhap now you will regain your sense of humor. You have been much too dour of late. Betimes I think you have forgotten how to smile."

"And methinks you smile too much."

They both smiled at each other.

"Be ready at dawn to go back into the city. We launch our longships afore noon."

"As you wish, master."

He shook his head at his brother's flummery. "One more thing: do not dare go back into the city to buy any slave girls."

The flush on his brother's face told him that was just what he had intended. *Gods, will this nightmare ever end?*

You can do WHAT with a pole? . . .

The last strains of "Do the hustle . . ." rang through the room, accompanied by the rhythmic pounding of athletic shoes on the hardwood floor, the wheeze of panting breaths, and Lydia calling out, "One last time, ladies. Cooling down. Lunge-slide and clap. Slow and easy. Lunge-slide the other side and clap. Do the hustle, forward, and clap, do the hustle back, and clap. Lunge-side again. Right. Now left. Knee lifts. And scissors. Now one last hustle. That's it. That's it. Now slooooow down."

Turning to the twenty ladies in the advanced aerobics dance class behind her, Lydia smiled. "Good workout."

Even though it was only noon, this was the last class of the day for her . . . a perk of being the owner of the Silver Strand Studio, the premier aerobics dance and yoga facility here in Coronado. One of the reasons she'd bought the club two years after her husband's death was so that she could be her own boss . . . so that now she would be home when her four-year-old son, Mike, got home from nursery school.

Her class members followed her lead in slowing down to recover, this time to the slower beat of Rascal Flatts' "I Melt." They checked their pulse rates as they moved.

"I am sweating like a warhorse," Madrene MacLean complained. Madrene, the blonde-haired, statuesque wife of one of the SEAL commanders over at the naval base, hated exercise and didn't mind telling everyone so, but she was trying to lose the last of the baby fat from a recent pregnancy. And to tone up her very impressive breasts, which she disdained but which always earned her a second look from men *everywhere*.

"That's the point, Madrene. No pain, no gain," Lydia said. "If you don't sweat and ache and pant, then you're not working hard enough."

"*Hmpfh!* There are a few people back in the Norselands that would find humor in that philosophy. Deliberately making oneself sweat and ache! Life is hard enough, they would say." Madrene was using a Silver Strand Studio towel to wipe off her brow and neck as she talked. Madrene was always saying weird things like that, referring to Vikings of old and Dark Age "Norselands," as if she had personal experience with both. Plus, she talked in a quaint manner sometimes, using words like "mayhap," or " 'tis" or " 'twas." Or, even more interesting, "bedsport."

"Stop complaining," Madrene's sister Kirstin Magnusson said, as she too mopped her brow. "Now you won't feel guilty when you have crème brûlée for dessert at lunch today." Kirstin, three years younger than her sister at thirty-two, was a newly hired professor of ancient studies at San Diego State University. Kirstin shared her sister's long, platinum blonde hair, but whereas Madrene was buxom, Kirstin was flat-chested. Both of them were stunningly beautiful.

"As if I would e'er feel guilty over food!"

"You're coming to lunch with us today, aren't you, Lydia?" asked yet another member of this very interesting family. It was red-haired Alison Magnusson, who was married to Madrene and Kirstin's brother Ragnor; she was a Navy physician affiliated with the SEAL teams. Alison's brother was Commander MacLean. Lots of convoluted family connections here. "We're celebrating over at the Del." The Del she referred to was the famous Hotel del Coronado, known for its red-roofed, castlelike appearance and for the famous people who had stayed there over the years.

"Of course," Lydia answered. Mike was going to a birthday party straight from nursery school today and didn't have to be picked up 'til three. "And crème brûlée sounds *veeeery* tempting."

They drove together in Alison's Mercedes sedan. On the way and while walking into the Del, there was talk, talk, talk. These women did know how to talk. Not that they shut Lydia out, but mostly she just chose to sit back in fascination. *So, this is what big families are like.* Lydia was an only child of Minnesota dairy farmers. Dave had been the only son of a nearby couple who raised beef cattle. While her parents had been loving, she had always felt lonely . . . still did, even with her darling Mike. And it looked as if he was going to be an only child, too.

Once seated in the Sheerwater Restaurant in the Del, with its spectacular view of the Pacific, they started off with one of the Del's signature margaritas—watermelon today.

"To tube tying!" Madrene raised her stemmed glass in a toast.

Everyone tapped glasses with her, even Lydia, who had to ask, "Tube tying?"

"Yea, 'tis true. I had my tubes tied on Monday."

Lydia choked on her drink. *Oh, good Lord!*

Madrene smiled widely, then took a long drink, licking the salt off her top lip. "Do not missay me. I love children. I have three of them. Two-year-old Ivan, fifteen-month-old Ranulf, and now three-month-old John. Methinks that is enough."

I'll never complain about being tired with one little boy again. "I wasn't being judgmental," Lydia inserted quickly. "Believe me, I'm all for women's rights and birth control. I was just . . . surprised."

"I know that, dearling." Madrene squeezed her hand. "Ian was supposed to get one of those vasectomy things, but he walked around half-green for the past sennight; so, I took pity on the lackwit. But believe you me, I intend to profit from that favor. I'm thinking, a tractor."

Kirstin and Alison laughed.

This woman is nuts. "A tractor?" Lydia was having trouble following Madrene's train of thought.

"My husband is a commander of SEALs, but I yearn to be a farmer. In fact, my father gifted me a farm in the Imperial Valley as a bride-gift. Someday, when Ian retires, we will become farmers, although every time we visit, Ian gets a rash. I think he does it apurpose to thwart me."

Somehow, Lydia could not picture Ian MacLean giving up the teams to become a farmer. On the other hand, Madrene appeared to be a very strong-minded woman. Instead of voicing that opinion, she told Madrene, "My parents are dairy farmers in Minnesota. I couldn't wait to get away. It's grueling work."

"Oh, I know good and well how grueling the work is. My father had a large farmstead afore coming to this country. I ran the household 'til my first marriage, and then again after my marriage failed."

There had to be a story there, Lydia decided, but one she wouldn't ask about right now. She hadn't realized that Ian was Madrene's second husband.

Ian had trained for SEALs with Lydia's husband, Dave, but he married after Dave's death. So Lydia had never socialized with them and barely knew Ian well enough to say hello, even though he and the other teammates had come to Virginia for Dave's funeral. She'd met Madrene through the aerobics class.

"Back to Madrene having her tubes tied. You have to understand that where we come from"—Kirstin exchanged a secretive glance with Madrene—"women do not have this kind of choice. Well, men either. Birth control was nonexistent back then . . . I mean, back there, except for early withdrawal, which is highly unreliable. Besides, most Viking men are too prideful of their male parts, not to mention lustful, to give up any part of the sexual experience. It's not unusual for women to have ten children or more. In fact, our father has bred fourteen children, twelve of them still living." Kirstin seemed to realize belatedly that she had spouted out quite a bit of information. Probably the college professor in her. "Sorry. It's a sore subject with me."

Fourteen children? Lydia forced herself not to arch her brows in shock. "Where is it precisely that you're from?"

"The Norselands," Madrene replied.

"Norway," Kirstin said at the same time.

Pink color rose in both their cheeks.

I feel as if there is a whole other conversation going on here below the surface. Surely, there is birth control in Norway. "Do you have children?" She addressed both Kirstin and Alison.

Kirstin shook her head. "Nope. No children. No husband. I'm thirty-two years old, which is totally over the hill back in our . . . um, country. But here . . ." She shrugged. "I'm still hoping for Prince Charming to come riding over the horizon on his fair steed. Or Harley. Hey, I'll even accept a broken-down pickup truck for the right guy. In the meantime, I enjoy my job."

"No children for me, either, though I do have a husband." Alison blushed just mentioning her husband, and Lydia could understand why. Lydia had met Ragnor Magnusson one day when he came to pick up his wife at the studio. Some kind of computer genius, he was pure, one-hundred-proof hunk. "We didn't want to have any children 'til we decided exactly where we wanted to live. Then when we were ready, nature wasn't. But we're still trying."

An awkward silence followed, but not for long.

"Since you and I are the only single ones here, maybe

we should hit the Wet and Wild one night," Kirstin suggested. The Wet and Wild was a singles bar that catered to military personnel, especially SEALs, from the nearby base.

"Oh, I don't know." *Another Navy SEAL? I don't think so!*

Madrene narrowed her eyes at Lydia. "Have you been with any man since your husband died?"

Lydia bristled at that intrusive question, but then relaxed, knowing Madrene meant well. "There's a landscape contractor I know . . . but, really, we're just friends."

"How long has it been . . . since Dave's death?" Alison put a hand on hers in understanding.

"Five years." She gulped. "But it seems like yesterday. I know, I know, I should be getting past this . . . this . . . grief, but I still feel raw." Truthfully, since Lydia had never viewed Dave's remains before his burial—the explosion presumably making him unrecognizable—she'd always sustained an unspoken hope that he was still alive . . . a POW, or involved in some secret government operation, and that someday he would knock on her door and say, "Honey, I'm home." *Pathetic, pathetic, pathetic!* She turned to Kirstin. "Yes, I would like to go out clubbing sometime, but the Wet and Wild would not be my first choice. With all due respect"—she glanced at Madrene and Alison—"I don't need another military man in my life."

The waiter arrived, cutting off conversation for a bit.

As an appetizer, they all opted for blue crab bisque with sweet sherry and tarragon. For an entrée, Madrene chose grilled salmon with braised fingerling potatoes and a shaved fennel, green bean, and wilted lettuce salad. Alison picked the mushroom ravioli in vodka sauce, and for Lydia and Kirstin, it was black and blue Angus burgers, heavy on exquisite Roquefort blue cheese, with caramelized onions, lettuce, tomato, bacon, and cheddar, served on warm-from-the-oven kaiser rolls. Then, for dessert, coffee and crème brûlée for all. Not quite the fare you would expect from body-conscious women, but then they'd worked hard today.

They were on their way back to the studio parking lot, where their cars were parked, when Lydia told them, "We're starting a new class next week that you ladies might be interested in." She grinned and paused for a *ta-da* moment. "Pole dancing."

"Are you serious?" Kirstin's jaw gaped open.

"Oh, yeah! A good pole dance works all the muscle groups at one time."

"Plus, there's the naughty factor." Alison waggled her eyebrows.

Alison and Kirstin giggled, but Madrene frowned in confusion. "What is pole dancing?"

Once Lydia explained, Madrene snorted, "*Pfff!* As if I need to do aught but look at my husband to turn him lustsome!"

"I don't know. I think it might be fun," Alison said.

"Me, too." This from Kirstin. When Madrene and Alison both looked at Kirstin questioningly, she said, "Hey, if a little pole dancing will attract Prince Charming, I'm game."

They all laughed at that. The image of some knight on a white charger coming on to a woman pole dancing was just too funny.

"Leastways, where would I get a pole to dance for my husband?" Madrene continued to harp.

"How about that support pole in your basement?" Kirstin suggested.

"Now I must go down into the basement, amidst the furnace and storage bins, to entice my husband?" Madrene asked mockingly, but Lydia could tell that she was interested.

"I could use the flag pole in our backyard," Alison said.

"Your neighbors would appreciate that, I wager," Madrene scoffed.

"Don't be such a killjoy," Kirstin said. "Oh, look. Ian's here."

They were just pulling into the parking lot. Ian and the three children were standing on the grassy area behind the building near the water. Ian didn't see them yet, and what a picture he made! Holding the baby in one arm, cuddled against his chest, he laughed as the two little boys chased each other around his legs, the toddler comical in his staggering gait. Ian glanced up then and saw Madrene approaching. The light that came into his eyes was priceless.

A searing, crushing pain seized Lydia's chest. *It should be Dave and our children. It should be Dave giving me "the look."*

She stayed in the car, windows open, while the others piled out.

"I was called back to the base; so, I brought the kids over here," Ian said after giving Madrene a quick kiss of welcome.

Kirstin and Alison waved as they made for their own vehicles, with Kirstin calling out, "Remember. Girls' night out. Soon."

As Ian walked Madrene and the children back to the van, Lydia heard Madrene say to her husband, "What would you think of me pole dancing?"

Ian stumbled, then stopped stock still. Turning slowly, inch by inch, to look at his wife, he merely grinned. That was answer enough.

Lydia drove off then to pick up her son. And for the first time in a long time she wept for all she had lost. She felt so very lonely.

Maybe it *was* time to move on.

But no military man ever again!

Chapter 2

When the Norns of Fate come calling . . .

Thorfinn was a strong military man, but he was unprepared for and outnumbered by the six Arab men who attacked him on the way back from Baghdad the next morning.

The woman and child he had sought turned out to be a false lead once again. No surprise there. It had been ludicrous, really. The woman was blonde, like Luta, but she had a hooked nose and weighed as much as a small horse. The child was a girl, not a boy. And the husband, who had been away from home, was Arab, not Saxon.

He had sent Steven and his men on ahead after their wasted trip back into the city whilst he had stopped to speak to a horse breeder who betimes traveled to trading posts in the Norselands . . . Hedeby and Birka, in particular. The man promised to come as far as Norstead on his next trip. Steven should have the two longships ready to launch by the time he got to the harbor.

But then the unbelievable happened.

He was caught off guard when he was some distance from the city, but not yet close to the river where the longships were anchored. He did not see the men coming at him. He *did* hear a noise behind him that saved him from the spear which merely lanced his shoulder, not his heart, as intended.

Nimble-footed, despite his size, from years on the exercise and battlefields, he danced back, at the same time drawing his battle sword from the scabbard at his side.

Luckily, it was his favorite pattern-welded sword, "Skin Biter," an especially powerful weapon. All swords were strengthened by quenching the hot metal in liquid ... water, honey, oil, wet clay, or in this case, blood.

Unluckily, there were six of these miscreants to his one, and they were weapon-heavy, brandishing lance and bow and knife as well as sword.

In Arabic, he asked his attackers what they were about afore he gave them a sample of the flavor of his wrath. They did not appear to be thieves. Mayhap they had mistaken him for someone else.

One of them, seemingly the leader, snarled out something about how Thorfinn had befouled their sister-by-marriage when he gazed on her beauteous face.

Ah, the woman he had just visited. Beauteous she was not with that huge nose and splotchy skin, but no matter. Arab men took a harsh view of their wives' faces being seen by other men. And these were six outraged brothers of the husband.

He apologized for his mistake. "I did not mean to give offense."

The leader said a foul word in Arabic.

So be it!

In one swift movement, he gritted his teeth with unleashed fury, crouched, then lunged with sword held high in both hands. Coming down hard, he cleaved the first man from head to heart. Blood spurted everywhere, dimming his vision and stunning the brothers.

He fought valiantly after that, but made no more kills even after an hour of swordplay. All of them had wounds, though none mortal. A warrior must needs hit a foeman in the fat line, the area betwixt neck and groin, in order for the injury to be fatal, but these men were weapon-skillful, and his stamina was wearing down.

Bloody hell! It appears that I will be in Valhalla this day. Ah, well, my demise must have been destined; no doubt the Norns of Fate have been busy on my behalf.

In the distance, he saw some white objects floating down from the sky. Mayhap it was the Valkyries come to escort him to Asgard.

At first he wished his brother was there, fighting at his side, but then changed his mind. He did not want his brother to make that final journey with him . . . not yet.

The only sounds now were the clash of swords, the loud panting of seven men's breaths, himself included, the occasional curse in Arabic or Norse, and a raven over-head heralding that someone would die this day.

One of the men slipped in the blood on the ground, and Thorfinn was able to swing his sword in an arc, lopping off his head. Not a pretty sight but not unknown for a seasoned warrior.

The head lopping enraged the remaining five brothers, who came at him as one.

The side of one of their swords hit his head. *Ooooooouch!* He staggered backwards, dazed. Through his pain-ridden, blurred vision, he saw a group of men tossing the white objects off their backs . . . the selfsame objects he had seen floating from the sky. Was this a death-dream? They wore strange garments of mottled pale brown colors that nigh blended in with the desert sand. Who were these men who seemed to be coming to his rescue? For a certainty, they were not of his *hird*, or his brother's.

He gasped when recognition hit him. *Praise the gods and bring on the mead*, 'twas his cousin Torolf, whom he had not seen for four years and who was supposed to be living in a far-off land. *No matter! I will welcome help from any quarter.*

"To the death!" he bellowed. Then, to his self-shame, fell back in a stone cold faint.

Hey, Cuz! Long time no see! . . .

Lt. Torolf Magnusson, better known as Max, raised a hand to halt the small team of five SEALs behind him, then scanned the bizarre scene in front of them. "Holy crap!" about summed it up.

Some distance ahead of them stood a lone man, about

six-three, wearing a belted, short-sleeved, suedelike leather tunic over matching narrow pants. Etched gold bracelets, two inches wide, glinted on his upper arms. Ankle boots were cross-gartered up to his knees. His black, shoulder-length hair had two thin braids framing a face of chiseled fury. In his hand was a broadsword, which he was wielding with great expertise against the six Arabs.

He looked like a freakin' Viking warrior of old. And Torolf ought to know, being of Norse background himself.

As they watched, the "victim" raised the heavy weapon with two hands and chopped one guy in half, through the skull, between the eyes, giving him a permanent cleft in his chin, all the way to his belly. The body fell in a puddle of blood. One down, five to go.

"*Mon Dieu!* Did I just see what I think I saw?" asked Justin LeBlanc, even as they began to run in a leapfrog fashion toward the kill zone, SEALs working in pairs, covering each other's advance. One crouched and covered his partner's six 'til he moved forward and passed him, over and over. "Me, I thought I'd seen it all, but this takes the Mardi Gras cake. Talk about!" LeBlanc, or Cage, was a Cajun from Southern Louisiana and a longtime SEAL.

"I think I might just hurl, and I have a strong stomach." This from Sylvester "Sly" Simms, who ought to have a belly lined with steel. The black dude had grown up in one of the worst blood-gang neighborhoods, blood being the key word.

They were getting closer, but still not noticed, thank God. For a long time, they stayed hidden, letting the Norse Rambo duke it out with the five remaining Arabs. Were these Arabs the ones Torolf and his team were after? Probably.

The nitwit should have run like hell in the beginning instead of trying to face off a small mob. But then, to everyone's amazement, said nitwit raised his broadsword high, then swung it in an arc, lopping off the head of another one of the assailants. Two down, four to go.

"Holy shit!" Sly did gag then. In fact, Torolf would bet they all had bile rising in their throats at that gruesome sight.

"Who the hell is this guy? A freakin' gladiator?" asked JAM, or Jacob Alvarez Mendozo, who had once studied for the priesthood.

"You got the wrong country, pal. He's a Viking," Torolf said, more than a little impressed with the guy's strength and expertise with a sword.

"Oh, crap! The Viking bullshit again!" Cage jabbed Torolf's upper arm playfully, a reminder that the men had heard more than enough from him about his Norse background.

Torolf's small squad was in Iraq, attempting to jimmy the works of some al-Qaeda tangos who were about to buy Russian nuclear arms from an Iranian intermediary. And these numbnuts fighting the lone Viking numbnut were presumably those al-Qaeda terrorists. The whole mission, which was supposed to be hush-hush with a quick in-and-out, was about to go FUBAR, if they didn't stop this berserk, sword-wielding idiot from screwing up the works.

But then everything changed as Torolf got his first good look at the face of the victim who staggered at a sharp blow delivered to his head. Pale silver eyes connected with his for a second.

"Oh, my God!" he murmured. It was his cousin Finn . . . Thorfinn Haraldsson, to be precise.

Why was that kinship curse-worthy?

Because Finn was an eleventh-century Viking warrior.

Stubbornness . . . a genetic Viking trait . . .

"Put the friggin' uniform on before I friggin' bop you over your friggin' head with your own friggin' sword."

Torolf was trying to argue some sense into his hard-headed cousin, to no avail.

Finn just arched his brows at the threat. Apparently, *friggin'* was a word he could understand, in context.

Really, all Torolf wanted Finn to do was put on a helmet and jumpsuit so they could help the moron get out of this very dangerous place. The other four Arabs had been dispatched to their Maker. The perimeter would soon be swarming with tangos, he would guarantee it. How was Torolf going to be able to explain who Finn was when he was wearing an outfit that screamed, "I am Viking. Hear me roar"? Not to mention his carrying a big-ass sword that would do Genghis Khan proud. *Jeesh!* Those gold armbands in themselves were enough to raise questions.

Oh, yes, General, sir, he mimicked in his head, *I just came from eleventh-century Baghdad. The sultan gives his regards. And this yahoo is Finn the Dark, a head-lopping Viking warrior.*

"Do you dare try to bop me, whatever in bloody hell bopping is, and I will have to hurt you." Finn was casually swabbing at the blood from his wounds and splatters from his victims with a T-shirt one of the SEALs had tossed his way, as if he had all the time in the world.

"What? Ya gonna lop off *my* head, too?"

"Mayhap. By the by, last time I saw you, you were drooling over that shrew Hilda Berdottir."

"Be careful what you say about Hilda. She's my wife now."

Finn's lips twitched with humor. "Better you than me."

"You never had a chance with Hilda."

"Since when do women have a say in who they wed? That choice is best left to men and their superior intellects. If I had wanted her, believe you me, Hilda would have been my wife. 'Tis the trouble with this world, women are getting too uppity."

"Oh, God! The women of America are going to love you." Merrill "Geek" Good, another SEAL, made that remark as he passed. It pretty much reflected all their sentiments. Finn was a chauvinist just waiting to be cut off at the snout by some raging feminist.

"Look, much as I would like to continue this tea party, we don't have much time," Torolf said. "Put this jumpsuit on and let's get out of here. There's a chopper coming in for us any minute. Yep. There it is."

"What is a ch . . ." Finn's words trailed off at the *thwack-thwack-thwack*ing noise in the distance. His eyes widened. "That is the biggest bloody damn bird I have e'er seen."

"You idiot! It's the chopper. It'll take us out of here."

Finn laughed as he stood and put his sword back in his side scabbard. "That bird is going to land, let you climb on its back, then fly you away? Who is the idiot here, cousin?"

The rest of the guys had been searching the tangos' bodies for documents while he'd made sure his cousin was okay, then stood here arguing with him. He understood Finn's confusion, but, dammit, their mission was over, and they needed to get out of Dodge. The team had radioed Cent-Com first thing, and special forces in the city were already on the way to a certain warehouse in Baghdad where the arms were being stored. Omar Jones, one of his teammates who was half-Arab and could read the language, had found an address in one of the tango's pockets, as well as the names of some contacts who would soon be rounded up.

"Fare thee well, Torolf. Thank you for your help, but I must needs get back to my longship. Steven and my *shiphird* await me there. He will be worried at my delay. And give Hilda my regards . . . or not. Ha, ha, ha."

Torolf rolled his eyes. *Oh, Hilda is gonna love having Finn around again.* "I got news for you, buddy. Steven is definitely going to be worried because it's possible you might not ever see him again."

"*What?* Do you threaten me?"

Torolf saw Cage creeping up behind Finn and read his silent signal to keep Finn talking to divert his attention. "It's not a threat. It's a fact of life."

"You make no sense."

"I probably don't, but there's no time to explain now."

Quickly, Cage put a choke hold on Finn from behind and pinched a nerve in his neck, which immediately immobilized the big guy. He and JAM jumped right in to help Cage catch Finn before he hit the ground. He had to weigh about two hundred thirty or forty pounds. They got the jumpsuit and helmet on him somehow. It required four of them to carry the dead-weight body at a run toward the hovering chopper, then get him into a harness and up into the air. But soon they were all strapped into bench seats, including the unconscious Finn, and the Blackhawk took off.

Not a moment too soon, they saw. Battered vehicles and trucks were careening down the highway, coming to the rescue of their dead al-Qaeda friends. He hoped to God that Al-Jazeera didn't get photos of the head-lopped guy or the body-cleaved guy. Not the greatest PR for Uncle Sam's brave and bold.

The six SEALs grinned at each other and cheered as one, "Hoo-yah!"

"Me, I'm pretty sure your cousin ain't gonna be cheerin' once he wakes up, *cher*," Cage told him.

"Not to worry. I plan on wearing body armor." He laughed. "Or else I'll sic Hilda on him."

His fool cousin was an ill wind beneath his Viking wings . . .

Thorfinn awoke groggily from a hazy sleep.

The first thing he noticed was that he was strapped in at the stomach to a strange padded chair . . . straps which he immediately tried but was unable to untie.

The second thing he noticed was that his lackwit cousin

Torolf was likewise strapped into a chair to the left of him. Had they been captured by those Arab curs?

The third, and most alarming, thing he noticed when he turned to the right was a small glass window. Staring outward, he saw what appeared to be clouds. He was disoriented at first. How could he be seeing clouds below him, instead of above him? Then the clouds parted and he saw, way below, an ocean. *Way* below!

"Son of a bloody whore!" His head pivoted to take in his surroundings. He was in some kind of enclosed space with many rows of chairs holding people, mostly men, in similar attire . . . fabric made of splotchy mixes of brown and sand colors. Uniforms of some kind, he presumed. All of them strapped in.

"Are we prisoners?" he whispered to Torolf. *Best I keep my voice low, to avoid notice.* He saw none of the Arabs who'd attacked him, but they must be about somewhere. Then the red welt marks on his wrists caught his attention. "I have a vague memory of chains being there."

"What? No. Those are from handcuffs we had on you before. Man, you were behaving like a maniac when we tried to calm you down. Took four men just to get your pants off and cammies on."

"Huh?" Puzzled, he stared down at the belt restraining him to the seat and back at Torolf.

"Oh, that. We're in a plane."

He frowned and glanced outside again.

If he were a screaming kind of man, now would be the time. "Am. I. In. That. Flying. Bird?" he demanded of

Torolf, pausing after each word, for fear he might heave the contents of his stomach.

"Not *that* flying bird . . . not the one you saw yesterday. A different flying bird," Torolf told him, laughing like an idiot.

"Yesterday? Holy Thor, my head hurts."

"No wonder. That tango gave you a good whack on the noggin'. Then Geek had to knock you out."

"What is a tango?"

"Bad guy. Terrorist."

"Then why not just say bad guy?"

Torolf, ever the lackbrain, just grinned.

"Where in bloody blazes is my sword?"

"In cargo . . . um, storage. You'll get it back once we land."

He did not like to be without his weapon, but that appeared to be the least of his problems. "How could a day have gone by?"

"Actually, a day and a half. Drugs."

"Huh? Explain yourself."

"We gave you some happy pills to make you sleep. Even with the handcuffs, you were no bundle of joy, believe you me. We had to get you immobile so that the authorities wouldn't ask too many questions. They think you're shell-shocked. So make sure you act dazed."

"That will not be difficult. I *am* dazed."

"See? I'm just looking out for you, cousin."

"Are you saying that you chained my hands together, then fed me some potion to make me lose consciousness?"

"So to speak."

"I am going to kill you," he said, struggling to escape his belt.

"Be still. I'll explain everything later. And, by the way, your name is Jake Lavin, if anyone asks."

"Jake? You named me for a privy?"

"Jake is short for Jacob. Good ol' Jake bought the farm in Afghanistan, but he has no family to claim his body, and we sort of commandeered his name. Just for the short-term. 'Til our boots hit the ground in Coronado."

"Bought the farm? Boots hitting the ground? What tongue do you speak, Torolf?"

"English. And, really, you should call me Max like everyone else does."

"'Tis like no Saxon English I e'er heard, *Max*."

"This is Uncle Sam's English."

"We have no Uncle Sam." He shook his head with bewilderment. "Where are we going?"

"California."

"Cowl . . . what?"

"America."

"How far is that from the Norselands?"

"As the bird flies, more than ten thousand miles, give or take." At his continuing look of confusion, Torolf explained, "Under good weather conditions, resting on land at night, at one hundred nautical miles per hour in a long-ship, I'd guess two to three months."

"I am going to kill you."

"Yeah, yeah, yeah!" Torolf stood.

"Where are you going?"

"To the head."

"Me, too," he said quickly. There was no way he was going to let his cousin out of his sight. "Whose head?"

"Privy." Torolf continued to grin at him like an idiot. "And you are not going to the privy with me like a sissy girl. I'll be right back."

Only belatedly did he realize that Torolf had insulted him.

So it was that Thorfinn was sitting, locked in his chair, when a voice came out of the ceiling. The bird, no doubt. "Fasten your seat belts, folks. We have a little turbulence up ahead."

The flying bird began to dip and shake. Whilst he held on to the chair arms, white-knuckled, with his stomach nigh up to his throat, Thorfinn made a mental list of how he was going to kill his cousin when he returned. All he knew was it was going to be slow . . . and painful.

After the flying bird settled down, he scanned the area around him, his scrutiny stopping at a woman seated on the other side of a narrow corridor that separated the rows of chairs. Wearing a white uniform, including braies, she had short, red, curly hair and her lips were painted red. She must be a loose woman. Mayhap from the Arabs' harem, and, truth to tell, he had more than enough of harems after his recent sojourn in Baghdad.

His assumption was proven true when she smiled at him, then winked. The universal invitation to bedsport.

"Not now." He had no interest in bedding the wench, but there was no need for rudeness; so, he added, "Mayhap later."

Her red eyebrows arched at him in question.

"My belly is roiling too much to swive you right now."

"Whaaaat?" the woman screeched and was undoing her belt restraint. In truth, she looked as if she might attack him, and not for sex.

The man on her other side chortled, and Torolf stepped up quickly, apparently having overheard. "Uh, Millie, don't be offended. My friend here doesn't understand the language or the customs of our country."

"Hah! I need no interpreter to understand the look the wench gave me," he argued.

"Wench? Wench? I was just being friendly," she protested to Torolf.

"There is only one thing I need from a woman, and it is not friendship," he continued. "Bedding and birthing, those are women's roles."

"Is he for real?" the woman asked Torolf.

"Unfortunately," Torolf answered. "Millie, I'd like you to meet my cousin . . . Jake Lavin. Jake . . ." Torolf scowled at him. "This is Army Captain Millie Donovan."

"Army? She is a soldier? What kind of soldier wears white into battle? She must be Frankish. They are dimwitted when it comes to warfare."

Torolf groaned.

"I knew Jake Lavin," Millie said, narrowing her eyes, "but he was short and had blond hair."

Thorfinn was no lackbrain . . . leastways, not all the time. "I am a different Jake Lavin."

Torolf nodded his approval.

He cared not a whit for his cousin's approval.

"Like I would be interested in a man who wears beads

in his stupid braids!" The woman continued talking to Torolf. He assumed she was referring to him.

Torolf groaned again, knowing Thorfinn could not let the insult lie, like a rotten lutefisk on a Frigg's Day feast table.

"Everyone knows that warriors must needs wear war braids on either side of their face to keep their hair from blinding them in battle," he explained haughtily. "Mayhap you are not really a soldier, if you do not know that."

Another groan from Torolf.

"Uh, why not just cut your hair, ding-a-ling?" the barmy woman asked with a smirk.

"Because I am a *Vik*-ing, not a dingle-ing, as you said. The beads are there to denote class in Norse society. Mine are fine crystallite."

"La dee da! Vanity, thy name is man . . . or rather, Viking man. And, *jeesh*, don't be offended. The braids are adorable."

"Adorable? My braids are not *adorable*."

"Where do the SEALs get these idiots?" The woman laughed and turned away from them.

"Vanity? Does she say I am vain?" he asked his cousin. "I am not an excessively modest man, but I am not vain."

Torolf was shaking his head, as if he were a hopeless lackwit.

"The One-God's biggest mistake was giving Eve a tongue," he grumbled.

"A woman's tongue has its uses on occasion," Torolf remarked under his breath.

He ignored Torolf's statement, though it had merit. "That is what happens when women are let out of the keep. Attila the Wench." He pointed at the woman who was blathering away now to a soldier on her other side. "They get uppity. Best to keep them in the scullery, stirring the stew pot, or on their backs in the bed furs, for a man's pleasure."

"Oh. My. God! I give you one day in America before some female castrates you with a butter knife."

"I have to piss."

"Shhhh."

"Do not *shhhh* me. Where is the privy?"

"Down the aisle, at the back . . . never mind, I'll take you." Leaning over, Torolf showed him how to undo his chair restraint. Then he shoved him ahead down the narrow corridor.

"Do not push me, or you may find yourself riding a cloud."

People were staring at them, some snickering.

"Crap! I'll never live this down. I'm taking my little cousin, who's as big as a grizzly, to the bathroom."

"I do not need a bath," Thorfinn said over his shoulder. "I need a—"

"I know, I know. Here . . ." He opened a door which opened into a small chamber, which might very well suit a dwarf, but a man his size could scarce get his leg inside. Even so, Torolf crammed both of them inside.

"Which one is the privy?" he asked, pointing to two porcelain bowls, as he struggled with the odd metal fastening on his braies.

"Oh, good Lord! Don't piss in the sink. That's for washing your hands."

"How was I to know that?" When he was done, Torolf pressed a lever and water washed his piss away. Thorfinn's eyes bulged at this amazing phenomenon. If he had any more piss in him, he would have pissed again, just to watch it disappear in a magic waterfall.

"Wash your hands, and let's get out of here."

But he was not to be rushed. He turned the water lever in the sink on, dipped a forefinger in, then sniffed it.

"Now what?"

"I just wanted to make sure it wasn't piss from the privy bowl." He proceeded to turn the water levers on and off, then used the soap dispenser several times, tasting it once to confirm it was actually soap. He had ne'er seen liquid soap afore, except for that scummy substance under a block of hard-used soap. And none of it smelled like flowers.

When they finally began to exit the privy chamber, there were several people standing in line. One of them, a short man whose hair had been shaved nigh bald, sneered. "What the hell were you two doin' in there so long? Didja give new meaning to the Mile-High Club?"

Without understanding the specific words, Thorfinn could tell what the man implied . . . that he was a cod-sucker. He bared his teeth and was about to lift the whore-son off his small booted feet when Torolf jumped in front of him and said, "Back off, Riley. Finn . . . I mean, Jake suffered a brain injury. He forgot how to flush a toilet."

"Oh, yeah, and what's he to ya, Magnusson?"

"I'm his . . . uh, babysitter."

Chapter 3

Her trip down the dating highway sure was twisted . . .

"I like to have my toes sucked. Do you have any problems with that?"

Lydia's spoon stopped midway between her bowl of clam chowder and her gaping mouth. This was her fourth blind date in the past two weeks. Who knew a seemingly house-trained pediatrician could be so crude . . . or lacking in good sense? They'd just met for the first time an hour ago, for heaven's sake.

Taking her silence for assent, he munched, loudly, on a bread stick and inquired, "What do you like in the sack, honey?"

To be honest, it was all about context. If Dave had asked her that question, and his feet had been clean, not like they'd been after a full-day SEAL workout—*pee-you!*—

she probably would have said, "Sure." Or at least laughed, and then told him something equally outrageous that she'd have liked him to do. Like the time she'd suggested . . .

She shook her head to clear it of unwanted memories.

When she'd decided a month ago to get on with her life, after her lunch with the Magnusson women, she'd never envisioned dating being such an ordeal.

Her first date in almost ten years had been with a sales rep for the exercise clothing company whose products she sold in her aerobics studio. Blond-haired and cute in a surfer boy kind of way, even though he was twenty-eight years old, he must have figured she was desperate for sex, being an ancient thirty and widowed for five years. He'd put the moves on her before they'd even left her house for their movie date, and he wouldn't take no for an answer. Turned out she was more physically fit than he was, she'd learned when she wrestled him to the floor in her hallway and threatened to cut off his balls with Dave's KA-BAR knife if he didn't remove his obnoxious self, pronto.

Her second date had been even more distasteful. Brian, an Internet computer genius, had taken one look at the photos of Mike on her mantel and bowed out. "Sorry. I didn't know you had a kid. Instant families aren't my cup of tea." If she had a chance for a do-over, she'd have had an instant response: "Sorry. I didn't know you had a comb-over. Bald men aren't my cup of tea."

Her third dating disaster was probably her fault. She should have known that a guy as good-looking as Jeff, who dressed like a *GQ* model and wore clear nail polish, was gay. He'd been in need of a female front to fool his homophobic family in L.A.

And now there was Bill.

"Listen, Bill," she said, putting down her spoon. "Before I would even remotely consider sucking any of your body parts, I would have to know you a lot better. Has anyone ever told you that your dating skills leave something to be desired?"

Clearly offended, he bristled and said something so obnoxious she was forced to stand and dump her bowl of clam chowder all over his pristine white shirt and Gucci tie. Which was a shame. It was really good soup.

Was America ready for another dumb man? . . .

"I am tired of being a prisoner," Thorfinn complained to his cousin Torolf three months later as they sat, boots propped on the metal rail of the balcony of what he had come to think of as his dungeon—an apartment overlooking the ocean in Coronado, California.

An apartment was a keep divided into dozens of living units, piled one floor onto another to an ungodly height. Even with three sleeping chambers, their keep was cramped with him, Torolf, his witchy wife Brunhilda, their son Styrr, and a mangy dog called Slut.

Slut, who was sleeping at his feet, raised her head and growled agreement over the prison conditions. The lustsome dog was no more happy than he was with being confined to the keep; in her case, Slut was unhappy staying inside when there were so many willing and ready male dogs in the neighborhood, as evidenced by their nightly howls, dog talk for, "Come see what I have for you, dearling."

"This is not a prison, Finn. Stop your damn complaining." Torolf took a long swig of mead, rather beer, and belched.

He followed suit.

"How's the tutoring?"

For twelve sennights now, Thorfinn had been instructed, up to ten bloody hours a day, on how to acclimate himself to this new time and country. It had taken him the first two sennights just to accept that he had, in fact, traveled through time. And another four sennights to learn the language . . . English but not like any Saxon English he had ever heard. Then it was history, geography, math, and the most modern of all inventions: computers, for the love of Thor! His mind still reeled with shock.

"The tutoring is boring, difficult, unbelievable, tedious, beyond mind-numbing. And Blade Jackson has stinksome garlic breath."

Torolf grinned at him. "It's *Blake* Jackson, and he's no worse than the other four tutors you ran off with your incessant complaints and insults."

"That last one . . . the woman . . . *did* have a nose so big it could be the prowhead on one of Uncle Rolf's longships."

"You didn't have to tell her so."

"Why not?"

Torolf just rolled his eyes at him.

"I like your friend Geek. He has been most helpful." Merrill "Geek" Good was a Navy SEAL teammate of Torolf's. He had been working with Thorfinn this past week whenever his military duties allowed.

Until Thorfinn figured out how to return to the past, he had decided to join the elite warrior group. In truth, fighting was all he knew. He had already had his first interview with the commander, who conveniently happened to be wedlocked to his cousin Madrene.

Torolf nodded. "Geek is a good guy, but, man, you need all the help you can get, and Geek can't work with you full-time. So, I suggest you use both of them . . . Blake *and* Geek. If you want to try out for SEALs, you need to be believable. At the least, you have to be able to fill out the freakin' forms."

"I am more than ready."

"In your opinion."

"Who else's opinion matters?"

Torolf sighed deeply. He did that a lot around Thorfinn, when he was not muttering curses under his breath. "Look, you've got to pass the ASVAB test."

"Arse-what?"

"Not ass, ASVAB. It's a multiple aptitude test."

"Well, that explains it."

Torolf did the swearing-under-his-breath exercise. "Presumably no study is required for that test, but still Geek thinks you need to study to the test. Once that's over, you should be able to handle the physical requirements of the PST."

"Another test!" He groaned.

"You'll need to be able to swim five hundred yards in less than twelve and a half minutes."

"I was born swimming."

"Do forty-two push-ups in under two minutes followed by a two-minute rest. Then fifty sit-ups in under two minutes, followed by a two-minute rest. Then six pull-ups, followed by a ten-minute rest. Then run one and a half miles in boots and long pants in less than eleven and a half minutes."

Thorfinn could feel his face heat up. "What a lot of foolishness!"

"Gotta do it, buddy."

"If you can do it, I can do it."

Torolf did the eye-rolling exercise again. "And you better cut that damn hair. Hilda says it's clogging the drains after you take a shower."

"I will cut my damn hair when I start SEALs. Not before. And Hilda should talk! Her hair is longer than mine. Really, Torolf, how could you have married such a shrew?" How a man of seeming intelligence like Torolf could have bound himself to a waspish female like Hilda was beyond Thorfinn's understanding.

"You provoke her. Besides, if you want a shrew, that would be Commander MacLean's wife, Madrene. My sister. Hilda is nowhere near as bad as Madrene. We like to say she drove my father out of the Norselands with her nagging."

"On that I must agree. Still, can you not tame your wife better? She tortures me with her black looks of condemnation, and her sharp tongue, and her overall annoying presence."

"You torture her right back."

"That is neither here nor there."

"I love her."

"*Pffff!* I wish you joy of her."

"Have you learned nothing about women's lib in your tutoring sessions?"

Turning in his chair, Thorfinn yelled through the open doorway to Hilda, who was feeding Styrr in the scullery. "Didst wash my codpiece?" he inquired arrogantly, just to watch her back go stiff and to make a point with Torolf.

Torolf choked on his beer, and Thorfinn had to clap him on the back, hard, 'til he calmed down.

Meanwhile, Thorfinn saw Hilda bare her teeth at him, pausing in the midst of ladling pea soup out for three-year-old Styrr, who was wearing as much of his food as he ate. And who could blame him? The mushy green concoction resembled baby shit. In truth, he tried not to look at Styrr very often or be around him; he reminded Thorfinn too much of his own lost son, whom he had never got to see at this age.

"Your jock strap, your jockey briefs, your tunic, your braies, and every other blessed item of your clothing are in the washing machine, you lazy lout," Hilda yelled back at him. "I still do not understand why you cannot wash them yourself."

Jabber, jabber, jabber. "I do not know how."

"You do not want to know how."

Jabber, jabber, jabber. "There is that. 'Tis women's work." He smiled at her.

She did not smile back. In fact, she was muttering

something about half-brained, pain-in-the-arse, full-of-themselves men.

"See," he told Torolf, "that is how you put a woman in her place."

Slut raised her head and growled at him.

Torolf just shook his head as if they were both lackwitted, he and the dog.

When lunkheads pound away . . .

"Get rid of him."

That was Hilda's message to her husband when she crawled into bed that night after finally getting a fussy Styrr to sleep.

"I'm trying, sweetling," he said, as he raised the sheet and opened his arms to her.

She raised her eyebrows at his nude body, then snuggled up against him, resting her face on his chest. He kissed the top of her head and tugged her closer.

"I just wish he would have stayed at Blue Dragon."

"Hah! Two days at the vineyard, and even my father could not put up with him. He offended every female in the region, and the men did not appreciate him ordering them around. As if he knows anything about growing grapes!"

"Well, I forewarn you, husband. I am leaving two days hence for Hog Heaven. I must needs take care of some matters at the center." Hog Heaven was the unlikely name for a motorcycle/RV park where Torolf owned a trailer. It had been where he and Hilda had fallen in love, and it was where Hilda had established a sanctuary for abused women, aptly called The Sanctuary. It was named after another sanctuary she had run years ago in the Norselands.

"How long will you be gone?"

"It could be two days, or more. I'll tell you this, I am not taking the lunkhead with me."

Torolf laughed. "Just so you're back by next Monday. We go boots up on the next mission then."

Hilda remained silent for a few moments, trying to stifle her fears. She knew it was Torolf's work, that each of his missions was dangerous. She also knew that one of these times he might not come back.

He kissed the top of her head again, sensing her dismay. "We should be tolerant of Finn. You and I both know what a shock it is to finally accept time travel. Even after all these years, since I was sixteen, I can't truly believe it happens. But more than that, Finn has had a hard time of it, with his wife leaving him and taking his baby."

Hilda nodded. "I can understand his wife leaving him. Any woman would. But the baby . . . even I can see how he grieves for the lost child. And, truth to tell, half the time methinks the lunkhead says outrageous things just to get a rise out of me."

"A dry sense of humor?"

She shrugged.

"Maybe we could find a woman for him," Torolf suggested.

Hilda raised her head to stare at him with astonishment.

"Maybe not," he said with a laugh. But then he tugged her down for a real kiss, mouth to mouth, arousing. "By the gods, it's hot in here."

"What? The air conditioner is on, and you're nude." At his grin, she added, "Oh." And lifted her nightshirt over her head, exposing her body, which was also nude.

"Oh, dearling," he whispered and began to make love to her in the heated fashion she liked most. When he had aroused her to a fever pitch, and himself, as well, he began the long, hard strokes that would lead to their mutual peaking.

But a loud pounding erupted on the wall behind the headboard of the bed, and a male voice shouted, "The lunkhead can hear you."

Torolf looked at her in the dark and repeated her earlier comment back at her: "Get rid of him."

Like father, like son . . .

Mike was suspended. From preschool!

Lydia sat on the beach with her son that weekend and tried to explain why it was inappropriate to punch the lights out of a little boy, a fellow classmate, who'd made the mistake of saying Navy SEALs were buttheads. Apparently, Joey's father was a marine.

"Fighting is not permitted, Mike."

"Never?"

"Never." She didn't entirely believe that, but she wasn't about to attempt an explanation of the exceptions to a four-year-old boy.

"Betcha my dad would say it was okay." His chin went mulish, just like Dave's had when he'd given in to his stubborn streak. In fact, he was a miniature version of Dave with his short hair and gray eyes. "Sometimes," he added.

Lydia's heart about broke when Mike mentioned Dave. She knew he missed having a dad, and she worried that the hole in his life would only get bigger the older he got.

She squeezed his shoulder, and they both watched the surfers, who were out in force this morning. It was a beautiful day, it was a beautiful beach, and she was fortunate that Dave's insurance had paid off the mortgage of the house so she could stay here. Although the house was modest, any waterfront property was worth a mint . . . way out of her price range.

"How can I let you go to Nana and PopPop's farm once school lets out next week? I need to be able to trust you, Mike. No more fighting."

"Moooooom! I hafta go. PopPop said I kin ride a horse this year."

Her parents, Mary and Travis Hartley, owned a dairy farm in Minnesota, called Mill Pond Farm, where they also raised some chickens, turkeys, and goats, and boarded a half-dozen horses. Dave's parents, Julie and Herb Denton, raised beef cattle nearby on Green Meadows Farm. Usually, they took turns with Mike, one week at each place with get-togethers in between. A kid paradise!

"A pony," she corrected.

"That's what I said. *Pleeaaaasssse!*"

She knew she should punish him, but withholding this much-awaited trip would be punishment for the grandparents as well as for Mike. "Okay, if you behave, you can go, but there will be no TV for the next seven days, and that includes DVDs."

He started to argue, then stopped himself. Smart kid! Instead, he jumped up and hollered, "Last one in is a loser!" He made an L-shape on his forehead with a thumb and forefinger.

"You're on." She jumped up and raced after him. Of course, he won, having had a head start.

Her heart swelled with pride as he dove into an oncoming wave and swam to the smooth waters on the other side of the breakers. Mike had taken to the water practically since he could walk. Like a seal.

Like his father.

In that moment, Lydia decided to stop looking for a replacement for Dave. There was none.

But then she recalled a conversation she and Dave had had one time after they'd made love, knowing he was leaving on a mission the next day. He'd told her that if something ever happened to him, he wanted her to find someone else. When she'd avowed that he would be the only one for her, he had growled and promised, "Well, then, I would just have to send someone for you."

"From beyond the grave?" She had laughed.

The eeriest premonition swept over her then, a premonition that something was about to happen . . . something related to Dave.

Curb your enthusiasm . . .

"Now, remember what I said. Keep your mouth shut."

Thorfinn, who was sitting in Torolf's solar sharpening his sword, raised his head and glared at his cousin with indignation. "Why should I keep my mouth shut?"

"Because every time you open it, *I* get in trouble. Listen, Hilda's stuck at her women's shelter at Hog Heaven—"

What a country! Imagine naming a village Hog Heaven! And there are not even any actual pigs there. "Hilda takes exception to every blessed thing I do. The harpy is always accusing me of making a mess. Tell me true, Torolf, what is so wrong with cutting my toenails in her scullery with a paring knife?"

Torolf shook his head at him, something he did overmuch, and continued, "I don't feel like cooking. And, no, we are not ordering pizza again, either."

"We could go to that burn-your-tongue place."

"We're not going to Hot Wings Palace, either. We're going down to the Wet and Wild for dinner, some beers, and a little friendly conversation. Try to behave yourself."

"Dost insult me, Torolf? Thor's Teeth, you do! I am not a boyling to be chastised so."

"Sometimes you act like one."

"And what will you do if I *misbehave*? Tie me to a bed again?"

Torolf's cheeks filled with color. "I only did that for one day and that's because you were going off half-cocked."

"You did it for two days," he corrected, "and that does not count what you did on the ground in Baghdad to get me in that flying bird." He thought a moment. "Did you just tell me I have half a cock? Another insult?"

Torolf laughed. "That's just an expression that means you were out of control. Only the gods . . . or God . . . knows where you would have run off to when you learned where you were if I hadn't restrained you."

"Well, at least then you would not have to *babysit* me."

"Are you ever going to forgive me for that remark?"

"I want to go home . . . back to Norstead."

"It's out of my hands, buddy."

"I do not like it here."

"I don't see why not. Other than Steven, you have no compelling reason to go back. Your brother will take care of any loose ends at Norstead."

"That is not for you to decide."

"Think about all the modern marvels. Cars, airplanes, motor boats, electricity, running water, indoor plumbing, guns, Wal-Mart."

Thorfinn waved a hand dismissively. "All well and good, but I am lost here. I have no place."

"I thought you were resigned to joining the military, whether you make SEALs or not."

"Of course I am resigned to fighting. What else would I do?"

"I'm losing patience with you, Finn. You're not the first person who has time-traveled and you probably won't be the last. There are thirteen in my family alone, including my brothers and sisters and two uncles. Then Britta and Hilda, of course. And a few of my SEAL buddies that you met back there."

"Are you sure this is not just some other world created by the gods . . . Loki, the jester god, mayhap?"

His cousin shook his head. "It takes time. For some, it takes longer than for others to accept what has happened, but you will. Eventually. That's why we've kept you pretty much in seclusion so you can learn the skills to blend in here."

"But how does this . . . um, time travel happen . . . and why?"

"I don't think there's any logical explanation. Not today. Maybe sometime in the future. We've all decided it's just a miracle performed by God, possibly in cooperation with the Norse gods."

"Huh?"

Torolf punched him in the upper arm. "Exactly. So, are we on tonight for the Wet and Wild?"

"Will there be women there?"

"Yes. Why?"

"My enthusiasm is on the rise." *And I am bloody damned tired of pleasuring myself.*

"Your enthusiasm? Oh, shit! That's what my brother Ragnor used to say when—"

"Yea, the male sap is running." *And running and running.* "Mayhap I can find an equally enthusiastic wench to tup. I have not engaged in a good swiving in more than six months." *I should have taken a woman when I had a chance back in Baghdad.*

Torolf groaned and put his face in his hands.

His cousin did that betimes when Thorfinn said something exceedingly wise. Leastways, that was his opinion.

So he continued, "Especially since you told me about birthing control in this country. Praise the gods, I do not have to fear being wedlocked to some woman just because we shared the bed furs." *Someone like Hilda, gods forbid.*

"I don't think there's anything to fear in that regard. Modern women are not going to jump with joy at the prospect of being *wedlocked* with you."

"Why do you say that? I am handsome, or so women have said. I have much wealth . . . if my arm rings and sword are worth what you say they are. And I have talents."

"Talents?" Torolf choked out.

"For bedplay, of course."

"Mercy!"

"Best I go change into my tunic and braies if we are going out."

"No, no, no. You look just fine in jeans and a T-shirt, but, please, could you put your hair in a ponytail or something? Those war braids and crystal beads attract too much attention. And do not even think of bringing that frickin' sword with you."

"All these orders . . . you exceed yourself, cousin."

"Yeah, well, somebody has to put you straight. Another thing, you walk in the wrong neighborhood and some two-bit mugger is gonna kill you for those gold armbands alone. Do you have any idea how much they're worth?"

"How much?"

"A half a mil each, give or take a hundred thousand or two."

"Is that a great deal of coin?"

"That is a hell of a lot of coin. You could buy a small country."

"Why would I want to buy a small country?"

"Aaarrgh! Would you just make an effort to fit in?"

"Torolf, what has happened to you? Have you no shame in denying your Vikinghood?"

"Vikinghood? That's a good one. No, I'm not ashamed of my heritage, but I don't have to shout it out."

"Then why do you not own even one longship?"

He did that shaking his head exercise at him again. Then he exhaled with a *whoosh*. "Here's the deal, Finn. I'll take you out tomorrow and give you another driving lesson if you promise not to call any woman a wench tonight, or ask her if she wants to be tupped, or brag about your . . . um, talents."

Thorfinn thought, but only for a moment. In truth, he got the better of the bargain, in his opinion, since he harbored a fascination with Torolf's shiny black jape.

A woman? Or a shiny, black, horseless cart which moved at exciting speeds?

No contest!

" 'Tis a deal."

Chapter 4

Hooking up was a little like fishing . . . for men . . .

"The Wet and Wild? Oh, no, I don't think so," Lydia protested.

She and Kirstin Magnusson had just finished dinner in a small Coronado cafe and were sipping their second glasses of wine when Kirstin suggested they wind down their evening at the hangout, which catered to Navy guys and gals from the base, including SEALs.

"Why not?"

"It's a singles bar, isn't it?"

"Not really. A lot of singles hang out there, but married folks stop off after a billet, too. They serve food, and there's a band on weekends."

"I've already told you about my bad dating experiences.

I don't need to add a military man to the sad mix. Besides, I've given up on dating."

"Hey, we've all had dating nightmares. That doesn't mean you give up. I told you about the guy with the penis piercings. And the jerk who expected me to pay for our dates . . . for *both* of us. And the one who talked about his yacht and it turned out to be a bass boat. Worst of all was the guy who kept smirking at me and saying, 'Who's your daddy?' I mean, Toby Keith can get away with that crap, but a stockbroker in a bow tie? I don't think so!"

"See? That's what I'm talking about."

"You gotta lick a few warts to find a prince, honey."

"Yeech!"

"You're too young to be so jaded."

Lydia just shrugged. Kirstin was thirty-two, only a few years older than she was. The difference was, Lydia'd had the best. It was hard, if not impossible, to settle for less.

"Who says we're looking to hook up with men tonight anyhow? Can't we have a girls' night out, enjoy a drink, dance a little, without men being involved?"

"Well, yes, but—"

"Besides, your son left yesterday for his farm vacation; so, lack of a babysitter can't be an excuse."

"But—"

"Okay, truth to tell," Kirstin sighed deeply, "there's this guy, and I don't want to appear too obvious going by myself, and if I just happen to show up with a friend—"

"Enough said!" Lydia laughed. She could recall a time

when she'd managed to accidentally bump into Dave. A lot. Later, he'd confessed to doing the same thing. Ah, the games of love! "I'll go with you, but I don't want to be stuck there without a car if you do hook up."

"We can both drive."

It was Lydia who sighed now and finished the last of her wine . . . for fortification.

She had a feeling tonight was going to be a colossal mistake.

Little did she know.

Down on the farm . . .

On the way to the tavern, Lydia pulled out her cell phone to call her son. Taking into account the time zone, Mike and her family should be just finishing dinner, which was part of a fixed schedule on the farm. If her dad didn't get his meal by seven, after the evening milking, he was grumpy the rest of the night.

"Hello."

"Hey, Mom," she said. "How's it going?"

"Oh, just wonderful, honey. You know how much we enjoy having Mikey here with us. I still say you should move back home, and—"

"Not now, Mom. That subject is a dead horse."

"*Tsk, tsk, tsk!* Speaking of dead horses isn't a joke."

Lydia had to smile. She could just picture her mother, with the old-fashioned wall-phone at her ear. Oh, not the crank kind, but out-of-date, nonetheless, with its finger dial. On the farm, nothing was thrown away or changed unless it was no longer useful. Her mother even recycled Ziplock bags.

Yep, Mom would be standing in the kitchen, which had been painted yellow and had tie-back white ruffled curtains as long as she could remember. And a big pine table and side benches.

"Is Mike behaving?"

"Of course. He's been helping his PopPop milk, and he's been a special helper to me collecting eggs. Here, he wants to talk to you."

"Hey, Mom, did you know a cow's boobies are called tits?" He giggled, and Lydia just knew he would be imparting this bit of information to his kindergarten classmates in the fall.

"I knew that, sweetie. Have you seen Grandpa and Grandma Denton yet?"

"Yep, they came over this mornin'. Grandma hugged me so hard I could hardly breathe, but Grandpa jist shook my hand. They wanna go to the fair with us when you come."

"Oh, boy! You know how much I like the country fair."

"Itchy entered his pig, Ester. Betcha he wins a prize." Itchy was the ten-year-old son of Lanny Brown, the longtime hired hand. He was given that nickname when he'd gotten a particularly bad case of poison ivy.

"Is Nana going to enter her pie this year?" Nana was the name given to her mother, so as not to be confused with his other grandmother.

"Yep. Me and PopPop picked two buckets of huckleberries. I ate so many I thought I was gonna pee blue. But

I didn't." How like a little boy, to be disappointed over the color of his pee!

"Let me talk to PopPop now, and you behave for them, and for Grandma and Grandpa when you go there next week. Do you hear?"

"I will."

"I love you bunches, sugar pie."

"I love you more bunches, sugar plum," he replied, making a kissy sound into the phone.

She clicked off after talking to her father, who related some of the activities related to the ceremony for Dave, including the fact that the local newspaper did a big spread, even mentioning her and her Silver Strand Studio in Coronado. A very patriotic piece. Lydia hated the publicity, but knew that it made Dave's parents proud, and that was the most important thing. And, frankly, a similar article that ran in the Coronado paper, as well as *Stars and Stripes*, would probably garner her more business.

As she pulled into the parking lot, waiting for Kirstin to catch up, she realized that she was in a good mood, looking forward to a good time. And that was a new stage for her in her grieving process.

Maybe I'm finally healed.

Vengeance is mine, sayeth some people . . .

"Assalam Alaikum."

Jamal Udeen glanced up from his computer to see his

brother Saluh entering his apartment in Detroit, Michigan. *"Wa alaikum assalam wa rahmatu Allah,"* he replied. "And to you be peace together with God's mercy."

Jamal turned back to his work at the computer, knowing why his brother was here once again. It was a rude measure of hospitality to ignore a visitor, but then Saluh pressed the bounds by entering his dwelling un-bidden.

"Mother sends me," Saluh said right off. "She is worried about you."

Jamal rolled his eyes. "Can you not speak for yourself?"

"All right, then. I am worried about you." A physician at Our Lady of Hope Hospital, where he had done his internship, Saluh, at forty, was his older brother by ten years. There was a large Muslim population here in Michigan, including their extended family, which had given Saluh the opportunity to come here for an education those many years ago.

His mother and two younger sisters moved here after his father's death in Iraq three years ago, despite Jamal's harsh condemnation for their choosing to live amongst the enemy. They did not share his hatred of the American special forces for the explosion five years ago, calling it an accident. He knew better.

Jamal had arrived only a few months ago. Saluh's house was crowded, with his mother and sisters, along with his own wife and four children, but family was always welcome. It was the Muslim way. Jamal was considered a black sheep, living alone in this tiny apartment

as he did, but he had plans. Once completed, he would
return to his homeland.

"Have you been taking your medication?"

"Of course." Actually, he'd tossed out the antidepres-
sants a month ago because they made his brain fuzzy.

Without invitation, Saluh pulled a chair over to sit by
him in front of the computer. When he saw what was on
the screen, he gasped. "Jamal! Surely you do not continue
these thoughts of revenge."

"Allah says if anyone transgresses against you, trans-
gress likewise against him."

"You twist the Koran to meet your own needs."

He shrugged. "The American infidel caused the
death of my wife Aisha, Baasim, who had just learned to
walk, and my unborn child. He must pay. Collateral damage, they called it." He made a spitting gesture. "I call it
murder."

"But he is dead, Jamal. He died in the explosion, too."

"Then he must lose a wife and child, too." He pointed
to the screen, where there was a newspaper article, taken
from a Coronado, California, newspaper, about a woman
named Lydia Denton, widow of Navy SEAL David Denton, and mother of four-year-old Michael Denton. Apparently, there was going to be some kind of honorary
celebration for Lieutenant Denton in his hometown in
Minnesota soon, on the fifth anniversary of his death . . .
the same date as Aisha and Baasim's demise.

"Jamal! What are you planning?"

"I, Jamal Udeen, declare a holy jihad to avenge my
family."

Hooking up with women . . . isn't that painful? . . .

Thorfinn was sitting at a table in the Wet and Wild tavern, sipping at excellent beer, popping salty nuts into his mouth as they awaited their meal—pizza, after all— whilst listening to the conversation betwixt Torolf and his Navy SEAL comrades. Like men in all countries, once the mead flowed, they discussed women: how to attract them to their bed furs, what to do when there, then how to get rid of them.

Along with Torolf, there were Geek, JAM, and Cage, men he had met several years back when they'd come to the Norselands to fight the evil villain Steinolf. So, though no one mentioned it, they knew or suspected he was a time traveler if, in fact, that was what he was. What strange names people had here, though! Like JAM and Geek and Cage. On the other hand, there were strange names in his country, too, he supposed. Like Svein Fork-beard or Cnut No Nose.

Torolf was the only married one amongst those present. But then, he ever had been a lackwit.

Missing was Slick, the SEAL with a shady background who had procured all his false identification papers in the name of Thorfinn Haraldsson of Lock Haven, Pennsylvania—black hair, gray eyes, six foot, three inches tall. Also missing was Pretty Boy, another SEAL he had met before; he was no longer a SEAL since he'd married Britta, a Viking warrior woman of some renown, and moved far away. Pretty Boy was now a cow-boy, according to Torolf. Thorfinn didn't bother to ask what that meant, though he thought it amusing that the full-of-himself man had gone from being one animal to another, seal to cow.

"More and more I'm beginning to believe that women are like phones," Geek said.

The others grinned at Geek because he had the innocent face of a boyling. What could he really know about women?

But Geek blathered on, "They like to be held and talked to, but push the wrong button and you get disconnected."

The others groaned. Thorfinn just stared at him with confusion.

"So, we have Viagra and other male-enhancing drugs here," JAM said. "What did they use in your . . . um, country when the flagpole flagged?"

Oh, good gods! Thorfinn knew what Viagra was, having watched Torolf and Hilda's TV box; it was a blue pellet for men whose manparts would not rise, or would not stay risen a sufficient amount of time. He raised his eyebrows at JAM, the questioner, since he was a man who claimed to once have been a priest, or studied to be a godman. Then Thorfinn responded, "Mayhap our flagpoles ne'er flagged."

"Hah! Flagpoles always flag sometime, *cher*." This from Cage, who spoke with an odd, drawling dialect, unlike the odd American dialect.

"Well, they had aphrodisiacs throughout time," according to Geek, whose sharp brain never stopped working.

"Probably something disgusting, like ram or goat

testicles." Cage made a face at Thorfinn, as if he would ever eat such distasteful food, though he did, in fact, know some half-brained Viking men did. No doubt his brother Steven had tried it at least once.

"Lots of other things, too," Geek went on, "like Spanish Fly, which is no more than ground-up beetles, and can be toxic, if misused."

Yea, I am going to grind up bugs and eat them, just so I can last longer in the bed furs. When stinksome Gammelost *becomes a king's delicacy!*

"Then there are oysters and figs, which are supposed to resemble and smell like a woman's yee-haw." This from Torolf, the idiot.

Thorfinn did not need to be told what a yee-haw was. "And you have told Hilda this . . . that her nether parts smell like oysters?" Thorfinn asked Torolf.

"What? You think I have a death wish? Besides, I never said it was true, just that some people make that claim. *Shiiit!* Don't you dare repeat that to Hilda."

Thorfinn just smiled at his cousin.

"I read that Aristotle once advised Alexander the Great not to let his soldiers drink mint tea before going into battle because of its aphrodisiac powers," JAM said.

"Lustsome men do not make good warriors?"

"Apparently not." JAM waggled his eyebrows at him.

"You are all idiots," Thorfinn proclaimed.

"Time for some hooking up, boys," JAM said then, flexing his fingers as he motioned his head toward a group of three women who were approaching their table.

"Hooking up?" he asked, but no one answered as the

other men pulled out chairs for the women to join them. Torolf flashed him a warning look. Hah! It would be a cold day in Nifhelm afore he took his cousin's advice on good behavior.

"We know these women from the military base." Torolf leaned over and imparted this information to him in an undertone. "They're female soldiers. In fact, female SEALs in a rigorous program called WEALS."

He made a clucking sound with his tongue. "What is it about some females who e'er try to be men?"

"*Shhhh!*"

The women wore those *den-ham* braies, which were so favored in this country by both men and women, though he must admit they looked far better on the women since they delineated their thighs and buttocks and flat stomachs. On top, they wore tight armless and neckless *sherts*, which left naught to the imagination about the shape of their breasts, even though none of them had gone through that watering device at the door which produced some greatly-to-be-desired effect called a "wet T-*shert*." Even without being dampened, on one of them, a tall Nubian, the nipples were apparent. *Were all women in this country wanton?* he wondered. *If so, how nice for the men!*

He noticed that Torolf, respecting his marriage vows, pulled his chair back, distancing himself from any one female, though conversing with all. He admired him for that. Not that fidelity had done him any good when he'd been married.

"Ladies, this is my cousin Finn from . . . um, Norway.

Cuz, this is Terri Evans." He indicated a petite woman with red hair and mischievous green eyes; then, "Donita Leone," who was a tall, slim Nubian with ebony skin and tight black curls like a cap . . . and the nipples, of course. Finally, there was "Marie Delacroix, who is a Cajun like our Cage here," whatever that meant, indicating a dark-haired woman with chestnut-colored eyes. All of the women were well-muscled.

He stood and was about to say that it was his pleasure to meet the ladies when Torolf jerked him back to his chair and said, "My cousin doesn't talk much."

While a tavern wench took orders for drinks from the ladies, Torolf told him in an aside, for his ears only, "Terri used to be a gymnast. That means she can twist her body in lots of intriguing ways." Torolf rolled his eyes meaningfully.

What a lackbrain! But then, he considered what those twisted positions might mean in the bed furs and reconsidered his opinion of his cousin.

"Donita there was an Olympic swimmer . . . you know, like the Greek games of old. Later she had a job diving from a high board through a circle of fire into a pool of water at circus events."

He gave Donita a considering scrutiny. He was a Viking, and Vikings admired feats of bravery, whether they be from men or women. Mayhap she would be the one enjoying his "enthusiasm" this night.

"And Marie was a Marine; they are fierce fighting men . . . and women, too, second only to SEALs. Her father died in the Twin Towers on 9/11. Remember that terrorist attack I told you about? She joined WEALS to enact just retribution."

He nodded, fully understanding how a person would want vengeance for such a cowardly act.

The little red-haired woman sidled her chair closer to his and gave him a slant-eyed glance . . . the universal signal of male-female interest. "From Norway, huh? Don't suppose you know Britta Asado."

He frowned, then realized she referred to Britta Asadottir. "Yea, I have made her acquaintance. Methinks she wed the seal, I mean, cow named Pretty Boy."

"Huh?"

"He means cowboy," Torolf interpreted for him.

Thorfinn glowered at his cousin. "That is what I said."

The woman continued, "Britta was in training for the WEALS at one time, you know."

How would you like to tup? He nodded. "She was a warrior back in the Norselands, too."

"You talk funny."

Dost prefer top or bottom? "Nay, you talk funny."

She smiled at him.

I could have her on her back in the bed furs in a trice, if I choose. Oddly, he did not choose. She was comely, as were the other women at the table, but he could claim no "enthusiasm." *Mayhap I need one of those magic blue pellets.*

But then, he smiled to himself. Nay, it was not that. More the stress of being in this time and place, and the wariness to watch his every step. Even if those steps were in the bed furs.

After answering her questions tersely and asking no personal questions in return, she finally realized that he was not going to mate with her. She muttered something to Torolf about his "brooding cousin," and wondered, "Is he gay?" Which was silly, of course. *How could I be brooding and gay at the same time?* With a final glower cast his way, she turned to the man on her other side, Geek, who proceeded to expound on some invention of his called a penile glove. He must remember to ask Torolf about that, later.

Meanwhile, he leaned back in his chair, ankles crossed, and observed his surroundings. The music, if it could be called that, was so loud he could scarce hear what the others said around the table. And the lyrics! The musicians sang something about a man telling his wife that she wasn't much fun since he quit drinking. He pondered the words for a few moments. 'Twas true. A little mead made a nagging wife tolerable; a tun of mead made the homeliest maid pretty. The downfall of many a man.

The men and women were dancing together, and what dancing it was, too! Arms wrapped around each other as they undulated their body parts. Then Cage got up to dance with the Cajun woman, Marie, and Thorfinn's eyes about popped out of his head. In rhythm to a pounding beat of a song about "Hot, Hot, Hot!"—must be about California, since the climate here was sweat-producing even without exertion—they scandalously emulated bed-sport in their motions. He bucked his hips against her backside. She nigh rode his extended leg. Foresport, it definitely was.

He turned to Torolf and asked, "Is this a brothel?"

His cousin laughed and said, "No. Why do you ask?"

"The last time I saw a man and woman engaging in sex in front of others was in a Miklagard brothel."

"They aren't having sex. They're just dancing."

Thorfinn was about to argue the point, but his attention was arrested by a woman who had just come in, on the far side of the tavern. Two women, actually, but it was the black-haired one who caught his attention. In fact, the other one, the blonde, was Kirstin Magnusson, Torolf's sister and his cousin.

She was not young, the dark-haired wench. She might even match his thirty years. Definitely not a young maid.

Her hair was piled high atop her head, making her appear even taller than she already was, with loose strands framing her face. She wore *den-ham* braies and a sleeveless, collarless *shert* like many of the others here, but on her they somehow seemed more . . . alluring.

Some men approached Kirstin and the woman, offering them drinks. The woman laughed at something one of them said, causing his back to straighten with displeasure. How odd! Then his attention moved to her mouth. It was wide and full and painted crimson, to match her red *shert*.

He groaned as a lurch of enthusiasm hit his groin. At the same time, the fine hairs stood out on the back of his neck.

Torolf gazed at him with alarm. "What . . . what's wrong?"

"I do not know."

Torolf turned his head in the same direction as his stare, then said, "Oh, it's Kirstin." He waved at his sister, motioning her to come to their table.

"Not her. The other wench."

Torolf groaned at his use of the word *wench*, but then stiffened. "No, no, no. Not Lydia Denton. Do not go setting your sights on her."

"Why not?"

"She's a friend of the women in my family, and I'd like to keep it that way."

Now it was Thorfinn's turn to stiffen. "Dost think I am such a dolt as to offend every woman I meet?"

Without hesitation, Torolf said, "Yes."

"I can be charming when I want."

"Are you kidding? You are the most insulting man I've ever met. Hell, you wouldn't know charming if it hit you in the face. Do you even know how to smile?"

He decided to ignore his cousin's insults and concentrated instead on the black-haired woman. Lydia, his cousin had named her.

Lydia sounds much like Luta, he thought of a sudden.

He attempted to see better across the room, and, in truth, there were some similarities. Height. Slender build. Nose and chin. But, nay, this woman had a definite bosom, whereas Luta's chest had been flat as a round of unleavened manchet bread. And Luta had been blonde.

Still, there were common characteristics and a similar name. Most important, there was an ominous tightening sensation in his gut that he often experienced just before battle . . . a signal of something big about to happen.

Is it possible that Luta time-traveled, too?

Of course not! What a fanciful notion!

But then, he gasped as an even more fanciful notion hit him, this time in the chest, causing his lungs to contract and his breath to be cut short.

Is it possible that Miklof is here in this land?

Is that the reason for my time travel?

Is this woman . . . Lydia . . . the key to all I hold dear in this world?

For the first time in what seemed like forever, he smiled. Life was suddenly worth living again.

Chapter 5

When old loves become new loves . . .

Lydia and Kirstin were laughing so hard they could barely speak.

The two ensigns who'd been hustling them had gone over to the bar to replenish their drinks when Lydia and Kirstin took one look at each other and burst out laughing.

"They're sooooo young," Lydia said, swiping under her eyes to make sure her mascara hadn't smeared.

"Yes. And that's great, isn't it? You know what they say about younger men and older women, sweetie?"

"But Lanny wanted to know if I have an Xbox. At first I thought he was referring to my sexual parts. I know, I know, I'm behind the times. But really, do thirty-year-old women play video games?"

"Hey, the guy who was talking to me . . . Elliott . . . implied that his package is larger than average. As if that's the first thing mature women are looking for?"

"Isn't it?"

They both burst out laughing again.

All of a sudden, Lydia felt a prickling at the back of her neck. It was the sensation her grandmother used to describe as "being tickled by the devil."

Her head shot up and immediately she saw the tall . . . very tall . . . man approaching her from the far side of the tavern. Why he should have caught her attention, she wasn't sure. He wore jeans and a black Aerosmith T-shirt, both of which showcased a very fine body. Other than his height, he was not her type at all. With gold bracelets on his upper arms—probably brass—he had long, black Fabio hair, and, good Lord, were those beads in the braids framing his face, which was dark and brooding. *He's probably gay. My luck.*

Noticing her stare, Kirstin said, "Oh, look, it's my cousin Finn. He's new in town. That must mean . . . yep, there's Torolf and his buddies." She waved at her brother, seated at a round table with a group of men and women. "Should we join them?"

"Sure," Lydia said, "but first I'm going to the ladies' room. You go ahead." She gave one last glance at the tall man who was now stalled in the middle of the dance floor, where he was shoving people aside in his haste to get . . . somewhere. Torolf, no longer seated, was trying to tug him back to their table.

This stranger scared her, she realized, and she couldn't

figure out why. Maybe it was the liquor. She'd had two
glasses of wine during dinner, and she was halfway
through her second screwdriver. Time to slow down before she did something she might regret, like pole dance
in public. *Like that would ever happen, drunk or sober!*

She went into the ladies' room, and after having peed
and repaired some straying strands of hair from her top-
knot, she pressed a wet paper towel to her heated face.
Her heart was racing, and her skin felt both clammy with
coolness and hot with dryness. Was she getting sick? Or
was she having a delayed reaction to the alcohol? Hands
trembling, she reapplied her lip gloss and left.

Only to see the tall man with the Fabio hair leaning
against the opposite wall, arms folded over his chest,
waiting for her. None of his separate parts registered with
her . . . not the long hair, height, muscles, somber, almost
angry expression. It was his eyes.

Silver gray.

Dave's eyes.

Could it be . . . was I right all along? Dave isn't dead?

No, it can't be. It's just wishful thinking on my part,
she argued with herself.

But he looks so much like Dave, she thought—*and not
just his eyes. His height. Body build. Even the way he
leans against the wall. It was all so . . .* Dave.

Only his face was a little different.

That was when a crazy thought took hold of her. *If he
was hurt in the explosion, he could have had plastic sur-
gery. And maybe . . . maybe he'd been a POW or covert
operator all these years.*

The fantasy of it was so sweet that it hurt.

"Are you . . . my husband?" she asked softly.

He recoiled, as if she'd struck him. "I do not know . . . I might be."

That was all she needed to hear.

"Oh, my God! What have they done to you?" she murmured, then threw herself into the man's arms, kissing his neck and face and lips. "I have missed you so much, baby. So much!"

He didn't respond, at first. In fact, he acted as if he was in shock.

Well, she was, too.

Looping her arms around his neck, she leaned back to stare into his face. Not Dave's face, but that didn't matter. Not too much, anyway.

"Dave?" she said at the same time he said, "Luta?"

Both of them shook their heads.

"I am Thorfinn . . . or Finn."

"I'm Lydia."

Lydia was confused, but she didn't want to dwell on her confusion. She wanted to bask in the joy of being with Dave again, even if it was this weird reincarnation of Dave.

"Kiss me," she urged in a raw voice.

"You do not like kisses," he remarked, cocking his head to the side. Then, tentatively, as if unsure now, he added, "*Luta* does not like kisses."

"I do." She leaned up on tiptoe, placing her mouth a hairsbreadth from his. *I'll know if it's him if I kiss him. No one kisses like Dave.*

He hesitated only a second, then hauled her up tight into his embrace and kissed her as only Dave could. A mind-blowing, hungry kiss that went on and on and on. Alternately gentle and fierce. Coaxing and demanding. Always hot.

All the frozen places inside her melted by degrees.

It's him. Oh, my God! It's Dave.

When they finally came up for a breath, he stared at her. Her belly was pressed against his erection, her breasts against his chest. The muscles in his shoulders bunched under her hands. They were both panting.

"Where is my son?" he asked, his face going harsh and angry.

"Mike? You know about Mike?"

"Of course I do. I was there when Miklof came out of your womb."

"You were?" Lydia was lightheaded with wonder to know that Dave had been there in spirit throughout the hard labor. She had sensed his presence.

"Where is my son?" he repeated.

"On vacation. With our parents, actually."

He frowned. "In Norsemandy?"

She shook her head. "No. Minnesota," she told him hesitantly. *Normandy?* Maybe Dave had some kind of amnesia. That would explain a lot. "I'm going to pick him up in two weeks. They're going to erect a statue in the town square to mark the fifth anniversary of your death. You'll have to tell them to call it off."

"All that damn tutoring, and I can scarce understand half of what she says." He seemed to be speaking to himself, but then he looked down at her again. "What in bloody hell is going on here?"

"I have no idea. All I know is you're back, and I love you." She kept touching him. His face. His shoulders. His lips. His silly hair.

"I do not want your love. I want my son."

"We're a combined package, buster, as you well know. And stop kidding about not wanting my love. You love my loving you."

Ignoring her words, he ordered, "Take me to your keep where we can talk, in private."

"Keep?"

"House. Dwelling."

She nodded, bewildered and ecstatic at the same time.

As they walked out of the tavern, she put an arm around his waist and leaned her face against his chest, inhaling his delicious male scent. Dave's scent. A knot rose in her throat.

It has to be Dave. It just has to be.

Even a Viking knows good sex when it lands in his . . . um, lap . . .

This was one of the strangest experiences of Thorfinn's life, second only to the strange time-travel nonsense.

He was in a woman's house . . . a woman who appeared to be Luta, but was not Luta. Or was she? He was not sure. There were similarities. Height. Facial features. But the hair color was wrong, and for a certainty this woman wanted him with a red-hot passion. She could not stop touching him, whereas Luta had merely tolerated his presence, never mind her initiating any intimacy. Mayhap she had had numerous lovers over the past five years and she had learned passion. That would be the least of her crimes.

He glanced around whilst she flicked levers on flameless torches about the solar. Lamps, they were called. It was an attractive room with soft cushioned chairs and low sofas, and with the ocean visible through massive windows, but he was not here to enjoy the comforts of her home or the view. Wooden shelves held dozens, maybe hundreds of books. Other than the church, only kings or very wealthy men had books where he came from, and then only one or two. Across the room, he saw framed pictures on the fireplace mantel, some portraying a small boy. Fearing disappointment, he would need to get his nerve up afore going over to examine them.

"Where have you been the last five years?" she asked dreamily.

Hah! More like, "Where have you *been, you faithless witch?"* Biding his time as he tamped down his wrath, he merely replied, "Looking for you."

"Oh, that's sweet. You could say I've been waiting for you to find me, honey."

Sweet? Me? "We must needs talk," he said. *Lest I cut out your lying tongue.*

"Later, honey. First, I want to make love. I haven't had sex since you left."

'Twas not I who left. Lest you forget, wench, you went off with your lover and my baby. And do not try to foist

that false story of celibacy on me. Not with the way you are nigh drooling over me.

Noting his resistance, she tugged on his hand. "C'mon, sweetie. Let's go to the bedroom. I want to kiss you all over, to prove to myself that you're real, not a figment of my imagination."

"Oh, I am real," he said, and a very real part of his body lurched to attention. To say he'd gotten his enthusiasm back would be a vast understatement.

"You look so different, like a stranger, but only on the outside." She giggled like a girling. "It will be like the first time we made love."

Did she really just put her hand inside my braies? He tried to snarl out, "I am angry with you," but it probably came out as a gurgle.

"Because of the baby?"

"Most definitely about the baby." *And your faithlessness. And your deceit.*

"It wasn't planned, if that's what you're thinking."

"And that excuses your perfidy? Truly, your gall is amazing. When I think . . . what are you doing?" *Oh, good gods. What is that lacy harness over her breasts? Does it serve some purpose? Other than causing my heart to nigh explode?*

"Taking off my clothes. If we're not going to the bedroom, we can do it here."

"Have you no shame?" *Whatever you do, do not stop.*

"Not where you're concerned, honey. What's the big deal, anyhow? We've already done it on every surface in this house. The floor, the couch, the deck, the kitchen table, the countertops, the washing machine, the dryer, the shower. Remember the time we made love under a beach blanket in broad daylight?"

We did? The mind images she painted caused his cock to harden and lengthen even more. Meanwhile, she removed her shoes, *shert*, and braies. "Stop! Have you become a harlot?"

She raised her arms, releasing her hair from its ties, letting the ebony waves puddle over her shoulders and back and chest, but not too far in front because her breasts were clearly visible as she slipped out of her scandalous, almost transparent undergarments and stood before him, totally nude and not a bit self-conscious.

"I'll be anything you want me to be, honey." She leaned back against a wall, one knee bent, her arms raised over her head. A pose of seduction. "Is this harlot enough for you, big boy?" she purred.

Holy Thor!

This could not possibly be Luta.

Could it?

She appears to want my lovemaking.

Could her lover have done a better job than me in teaching her an enthusiasm for the bedsport?

Her breasts are different. Bigger. With large nipples.

Mayhap nursing changed them.

But Luta claimed no desire to suckle the babe. She said she would get a nursing mother to perform that odious task.

Did she change her mind?

And her woman's fleece is thick with dark curls, whereas Luta's had been pale.

These thoughts flicked through his brain, which felt fuzzy and disoriented. 'Twas like swimming through a pool of honey, trying to get his bearings.

"Do you have a condom?" she asked in a low, husky voice.

He nodded, pulling one of the birth control packets Torolf had given him out of his back pocket.

"Will you undress, or would you like me to undress you?"

"Uh . . . ," he said, as what was left of his brain turned to porridge and his cock practically did a handstand. The bone-melting anger was still there, but it was being overcome, for now, by waves of excitement. The intensity of her passion swirled around them both.

His brain said, *Halt! Something is not right here. We need to talk.*

His cock said, *Talk later. Enjoy now.*

His garments were half off when he noticed the tears welling in her blue eyes. "What? You have changed your mind?" *How like a woman!*

She shook her head vigorously, which caused her breasts to jiggle, which caused his blood to nigh hum.

Enthusiasm, thou art fickle.

"I'm just so happy to have you back, even if you don't exactly look like Dave."

"Who is Dave?" he asked as he continued to disrobe. *Who in bloody hell cares?*

"You," she said, studying him.

"I beg your pardon."

"Oh, I know you don't look exactly the same, but your

eyes are identical, and you know what they say about the eyes being windows to the soul?"

The wench is barmy, he concluded, immediately followed by, *and I could not care less.*

Should I tell her I am not this mythical Dave?

Not if I want my enthusiasm sated this night.

Before he had a chance to approach her, she launched herself at him, her arms clutching his shoulders, her hands making quick work of sliding the condom on him. Then she buried her mouth in the crook of his neck, and her legs locked around his hips. She smelled like flowers and feminine arousal.

"Wait . . ." he started to say.

But she wiggled her hips, and he found himself embedded in her sheath up to the hilt, her inner muscles spasming around him with a welcome that was both torture and pleasure. *I am in heaven. Or is it Asgard? Who cares? This. Is. Bliss.*

His knees almost gave way, and he backed her up to the wall. *Please, knees, do not give way now.* With his elbows braced on either side of her head, he pressed his belly against hers, forcing her to remain still. *Aaahhhh . . .*

"Sorry," she murmured, a blush blooming on her cheeks.

Now she was embarrassed? *Will I ever understand women?*

"It's just that I've missed you so much. And it's been so long since I've had sex."

It has been a long time for me, too. Six bloody months.

"How long?"

"You know when the last time was, honey. Remember? Out in the surf, during low tide. Like that scene from the movie *From Here to Eternity*. Almost five years ago."

Five years! No wonder she is so lustsome.

A thought came to him, unbidden. He had meant to sate his brutish urges on her body, bend her to his will, but her kisses bestirred him mightily, and it was possible she was the one bending him to her will. *A lady availing herself of a man's charms? Now, there is a twist I could like.*

He began his long, slow strokes then, relishing the way she picked up his rhythm . . . like old lovers, which they were not, no matter what she claimed. It was the first time he'd engaged in sex with his cock sheathed in a membrane, and he decided he preferred to be bare. Still, she felt so good. Like a hot silk glove, tight and slick. *Do not let go yet. Think of something other than my raging enthusiasm. Think of lutefisk.* Sex had never been this intensely pleasurable for him, even covered as he was.

She peaked with a gasp of appreciation when he touched that place betwixt their bodies, the nub usually hidden by woman folds but openly exposed now by her widespread thighs. *That was good, but mayhap if I put my lips on her breast and suckle her nipple . . .* This time, she peaked with an unending wail. The third time . . . and he had been thrusting into her tight grasp the entire time . . . he peaked with her, and it was uncertain if he or she was the one who groaned loud and long, "*Aaaaaaah-hhhhhh.*"

At the end, she said, "I love you so much."

And his heart clenched in an odd fashion, despite his resistance to her charms. He did not want the wanton's love.

Everything was a haze of sexual ecstasy after that. One episode moving into another, almost without interruption. She was insatiable. He was insatiable.

They sank to the floor, and she rode him as if he were a destrier and she the battle knight. If he closed his eyes, he could pretend that this was Luta, but his brain was increasingly telling him it was not so. Which brought him both joy and sorrow. If it was her, that meant his son was alive. If not, Miklof was dead.

How they got to her sleeping bower was unclear to him later. What was absolutely clear was the way in which she kissed and licked his entire body. His *entire* body. With throaty endearments of adoration. For the love of Frigg! Luta—or Lydia or whoever in bloody hell—was accomplished in the bed arts. In the dark, he could pretend she was anyone. Likewise for her, he supposed, as she paid homage to his body as no one ever had.

And he surprised himself when he reciprocated, bringing her to more peaks, using his tongue and teeth as instruments of sexual torture in places his tongue and teeth had ne'er been before. His thrusts were so hard they moved across the bed and almost fell off.

She tongued the inner whorls of his ears, and he nigh exploded with enthusiasm.

He flipped her over and took her from behind, her face on the bed, her buttocks raised high, one of his favorite positions, one Luta would have never allowed.

She actually screamed when her last series of inner spasms hit, causing him to roar out his own lengthy peaking.

Afterward, he fell into a deep sleep, facedown, arms and legs splayed on her soft mattress. He did not recall having felt this kind of complete physical satiety in all his thirty years.

"I love you, darling," he heard as he drifted off to sleep.

Oddly, the words soothed his tortured soul.

Chapter 6

Listen to the lion . . . uh, Viking . . . roar . . .

He is not Dave.
Or he might not be Dave.

To her horror, Lydia came to these conclusions as dawn light began to spread over her bedroom, and the giant male specimen slept, sprawled out on his back, taking up all the space on the bed. Just like Dave. But not Dave.

Like a pendulum, she switched back and forth to opposing viewpoints. His eyes were identical to Dave's. And she'd felt a shock of recognition the second she'd seen him. And he kissed like Dave.

If not Dave, is he Dave reincarnated?
Or a man sent to me by Dave?
Or just wishful thinking?

Like dominoes, thoughts turned over in her head.

He used a condom. Still, good thing I'm still on the pill. Those damn menstrual cramps.

I just made love with a total stranger.

I did that . . . THING to him.

He did that . . . THING to me.

He said his name is Thorfinn. What kind of name is that?

But wait, didn't Kirstin say this was her cousin Finn? So maybe he's not an ax murderer or serial killer or pervert.

And always she kept coming back to her original idea . . . that maybe Dave hadn't died in the explosion. That he'd been injured, requiring facial reconstruction, and that the government had taken advantage of his changed appearance to utilize him in some hush-hush mission . . .

But, no, Dave would never have allowed her to suffer all this time, not knowing.

Unless . . . he'd had amnesia!

His eyes were closed, and those had been the most compelling reminder of Dave. Truly, his very unusual silver gray eyes were identical to Dave's. And his body was similar, too. Long. Lean. Muscular . . . not just arms and legs, but hard ridges of abdomen and stomach. And his penis, well, yeah, it was impressive. But his face was different and that silly long hair with the beaded braids! And did he really think wearing brass armbands made him look macho?

On the other hand, maybe Dave really is dead, but he sent this man, and the eyes are a signal to me.

How can I be sure?

I need time, she decided, *time to figure out what's going on. I can't let him leave me yet . . . I have to keep him here.*

Going into the kitchen, she used the combination to

open Dave's Navy SEAL operative drawer for the first time in five years. She hadn't been able to face disposing of the contents before. Scrambling among the pager, gun, KA-BAR knife, night vision goggles, Kevlar gloves, satellite phone, length of thin rope, and black balaclava, she came to what she had been looking for: a package of disposable flex cuffs, the lightweight, extra-strong handcuffs used by police and military today.

I must be losing my mind.

Going back into the bedroom, she saw that her Dave, who was not Dave, still slept soundly, thank God. Quickly, but gently, she cuffed both wrists in one double cuff to the headboard, and each ankle to opposing lower bedposts. At one point, he moved a bit, scaring the spit out of her, then went back to sleep with a soft snore.

A half hour later, she was in the kitchen, having her second cup of coffee, when she heard his roar of outrage.

Tears of a Viking . . . oh, my! . . .

He was a captive.

In all his thirty years, many of them engaged as a farfamed warrior, Thorfinn had never been captured by his enemy. But he was now, and the enemy was a woman.

He let out a roar of outrage as he fought against his restraints, to no avail. Both wrists and ankles were locked to the bed with some thin black ties. Not rope, but just as strong.

Almost immediately, the wench appeared in the doorway.

"Good morning." *Come closer, you evil witch.*

"Now, don't be mad," the idiot woman said.

Mad? How about stone-cold furious? "Now why would I be mad?"

"I just want to ask you some questions."

I am the one with questions. Like where the bloody hell have you been the past five years? And where have you hidden my son? And who taught you to do that trick with your tongue?

"Just a few polite questions."

"And you needed to tie me up for that purpose?"

She nodded. "I was afraid you would leave before I could ask all my questions."

She was right there.

"So, just bear with me for a few moments. Okay?" The whole time she spoke, the wench avoided looking below his neck.

She swives the sap right out of me, all night long, and now she plays the modest maid. Hah! I am not buying the act, m'lady harlot. "Let. Me. Loose," he said through gritted teeth.

"Not yet."

"When?"

"After I get some answers."

"Like?"

"Who are you?"

"Thorfinn Haraldsson."

"Finn?"

"Some call me that."

"Did Dave send you?"

"Dave?"

"My husband."

"You have a husband, and you tup strangers from taverns?" Thorfinn had a policy of never engaging in bedsport with married women. "Am I expected to pay for your freely offered services?" *It will be a cold day in Nifhelm afore you see any of my coin, you traitorous wench.*

Her face bloomed with color.

Interesting . . . that she can blush.

"My husband is dead. I mean, last night I thought you were him. Dave, I mean. You have identical eyes, and there are some other similarities, but, really, you're not the same, are you?"

"You think your dead husband sent me to you?" *Likely excuse to swive one and all.*

"Yes." Her face brightened with hope. "Did he?"

Pathetic, lackwitted woman! But best he not be too open with her . . . till his restraints were loosened. "Mayhap."

You would have thought he'd told her there was a sack of gold awaiting her pleasure, so joyous was her demeanor now.

"Release me now."

"I don't know . . ."

"Heed me well. If you do not release me immediately, I am going to throttle you when I am free." *Or should I tup her a time or two first?*

"I don't think you would do that. Dave wouldn't let you."

He rolled his eyes. "A dead man is going to control my hands? Have you gone addleheaded?" *Not that I care.*

"Probably." No matter who he was, Lydia decided she had no night to restrain him. She left the room and came back with a metal scissorlike device, which she used to cut through the restraints. While he was pulling them off the rest of the way, she left the room again. He used the opportunity to find her bathing chamber, relieving himself in the toilet, then taking a shower. When he returned to her bed-chamber, one towel wrapped around his waist and using another to dry his body, she was just setting down a metal tray on a side table. On it was a large glass of orange juice, a delicious beverage he'd never tasted until coming to this country, and two slices of toasted bread spread with butter.

"When you're done, you can call a taxi to take you home," she offered politely.

"Do you want me to leave?"

She hesitated, then shook her head. "I don't blame you if you want to go, though. I haven't handled this well, I know." She turned, about to leave.

"Wait!"

Stopping, she glanced back at him over her shoulder. She was wearing short braies . . . very short braies, which ended mid-thigh on long legs made golden from the sun, as was the skin on her bare arms and face. He had learned whilst staying with Torolf that folks in this country favored tanned skin on their women, as compared to milk-white complexions, which were revered in his country and time. In any case, the long, supple legs on this woman, tanned or not, were very attractive, especially when he got mind-images of how they'd looked yestereve wrapped d his hips.

Another thing he'd noticed the night before. She had no hair on her underarms or legs, unlike most dark-haired women. Did she pluck it out like a harem houri? *What else can you do like a houri?*

Today, she wore no lip or cheek rouge, nor eye kohl. Her face looked scrubbed and, well, passing fair. Hah! In truth, she was beautiful.

"I saw some framed portraits on your mantel . . . of a small boy," he said. "Bring them to me."

"Why do you want to see pictures of Mike?"

"Because he is my son."

She gasped. "Why do you say that?"

"For months I have wondered why I have been sent here, and now I know. Leastways, I think I know. My son has drawn me here."

She was staring at him as if he were the gold at the end of a rainbow once again. Then she went out and returned with three frames, all of which she set on the mattress beside him where he sat. Taking the frames in his hand, one at a time, he studied the images. First, a baby with scraps of dark hair, very much like he recalled Miklof having soon after his birth. Then there was one of a toddler, now with more dark hair, and finally, one which must be more recent. "How old is he here?"

"Four, soon to be five. It was taken earlier this year."

He nodded. That would be about the right age. "He has gray eyes."

"Yes. Sometimes Mike's eyes are bluish gray, and at others, a true silver gray."

He did not need to say, "Like mine." The conclusion

sat betwixt them, a living, breathing entity. "You call him Mike."

"Yes. That's his nickname. For Michael."

Thorfinn knew that nicknames were shortened names given to people, just as some in his country and time called him Finn, instead of Thorfinn. And, yea, Mike was a logical one for Miklof, he supposed. "Tell me about him."

"He's adorable. A scamp, but an adorable scamp. He walked and talked earlier than most kids. When you touch the bottoms of his feet, he giggles. He likes to play rough boy sports, but then he can sit still for an hour or more if I read stories to him. His favorite is *Trolls, Dragons, and Other Scary Beasts*. He swims like a fish, and his skin gets brown as an acorn in the summer. He has gone to preschool, but next year he goes to kindergarten. He can't wait. He's on my parents' farm right now, as I told you last night. My dad got him a pony and he's teaching him to ride. He'll go to your parents' neighboring farm next week. That is, if you really are . . ." Her words trailed off. She must still be thinking he was her dead husband again. Which was no more demented than his thinking she was Luta.

But that was neither here nor there.

He'd always thought he would be the one to teach his boy to swim and to ride his first horse. He would have liked to see him take his first step. Or hear him giggle. There were so many firsts he had been deprived of these ~~ve years. And what did she mean about his parents' ~~ His parents did not farm.

"You have tears in your eyes," she informed him. In truth, she had tears, too.

"I have missed my son sorely." *And all because of you.* Unashamed of his eye dew, he did not bother to swipe it away. Instead, he continued to study the pictures.

And then she said the one thing that tore at his heart. "He misses you, too."

I'll be your sex slave if you'll be mine . . .

He needed to disconcert the woman, who was clearly alarmed at his inquiring about his son. Soon she would be kicking him out the door . . . or trying to. "Did you plan to make me your sex slave?"

Her mouth dropped open, and she appeared to be speechless. "No. Of course not. What makes you say such a thing?"

Uh, dost really need to ask that question, oh, thick-headed one? "Mayhap because you lured me to your lair. Distracted me with numerous bouts of sex. Then chained me to your bed. You said you did it because I look like your dead husband, but methinks you were just looking for a sex slave."

"You . . . you . . . you . . . ," she sputtered.

"Not that I have e'er been a sex slave afore, nor had the need of one myself. But I have heard of such."

"Don't be ridiculous."

"So you say." He shrugged. Then he stood, dropped the towel around his waist, and lay down on the bed. "Just so I am back by a week from next Frigg's Day." That w when he took his Navy SEAL test. Not that he would tell her that. Best not to give the enemy too much information. "I'll have to tell Torolf to cancel my tutoring lessons in the meantime."

"Tutoring? For what?"

"My English is not so good." *That is an understatement.*

"Why didn't you put your clothes back on after you took a shower?"

He declined to tell her that he was getting perverse pleasure over her discomfort at his nudity. She looked everywhere *except* at his manparts. Which was amazing, considering everything she had done to said manparts the night before. "Take off your garments."

"Whaaat? Why?"

"What kind of a sex slave would I be if I swived you fully clothed? I am a man. I like to see what I am doing. And what you are doing."

"Stop talking about sex slaves. I never wanted a sex slave. Why do you use those ancient words?"

"Why do you avoid what I tell you to do?"

"Did you wear those fake gold armbands in the shower? Be careful or they'll rust."

Now she was being rude. He drew himself up straight. "These are pure gold. Gifts from my mother when I first went a-Viking and from King Olaf for a successful mis-
~~sion~~ against the Saxons."

~~"Ha~~. If those were real gold, they'd be worth a

irrelevancies! He inhaled deeply for patience.

"Anyhow, we need to talk. So get dressed, please."

Talk is the last thing I have in mind for your mouth. "I can talk without my clothes on, talented fellow that I am. And I tell you now, if you ask me again who I am, I may very well heave the contents of my empty stomach."

"Oh. You're still hungry?"

I thought you would never ask. "How brilliant of you to notice! What did you think that rumbling noise was?"

"You. Growling."

He arched his eyebrows. "Sarcasm ill-suits you, m'lady." *And, yea, I will be soon growling if you do not hop onto the bed and prepare to be swived.*

"Likewise, m'lord."

Huh? Best I try a different tactic? "I want my son."

"Too bad. Mike is away for two weeks—"

"Two sennights! If you think I will wait that long to see my son after all these years, you have an oar missing in your longboat." Thorfinn had learned to make those types of word comparisons from Torolf, who was always saying someone was "two bricks short of a full load," or "a loaf missing a slice or two."

"Listen, buster, you aren't getting within a hair of my son until I find out exactly who you are. If you're not Dave's reincarnation, or sent by Dave, you will never see him."

He girded himself not to say something rash, like that she would be the one not seeing her son again once he laid hands on him, but even in his fury, he recognized that he was in no position to make threats. "If you think I am going to be interrogated whilst I lie here naked, enthusiastic as a raging bull, and you fully clothed, or partly clothed in those scandalous garments, you are more barmy than I already thought."

"I'm wearing shorts and a tank top. There's nothing scandalous about that."

"Scandal is in the eye of the beholder. And bare feet! Didst know that in some cultures a woman's foot is considered a temptation greater than a bared breast?"

"You're making that up."

"Why would I? You are the one wearing wanton attire."

"Wanton? I'm not wanton. In fact, I never bring strange men home."

Really, I am in no mood for false modesty at this late date. He arched his eyebrows at her, taking her measure with a full-body survey. "Women always protest their chastity, even as they wiggle their arses in a man's face."

"I never wiggled . . . just for the record, I'm not a slut."

"Dost think I care." *In fact, wantonness is an asset to be desired, in some women.* "But just so we are clear, you invited me, then swived me up one side and down the other, head to toes. If that is not wanton, I do not know what is."

"Uh . . . you mentioned feet. You're not into toe-sucking, are you?" Rosy patches bloomed on her cheeks as she asked that outrageous question.

He pretended to consider her question. "Nay, methinks *that* bedsport exercise would not be to my taste . . . lest you mean that you would be sucking another body part of mine whilst I sucked your toes. Yea, there might be some attraction in that . . . um, position." *And, after all, I did pare my toenails this week.*

"Oh!" she huffed with indignation. "I didn't mean that *I* wanted . . ." She clamped her mouth shut, but he could tell she wanted to say something biting to him. Instead, she waited 'til her temper tamped down and asked, "Are you Dave?"

His only response was a snort.

"Did Dave send you?"

Dave, Dave, Dave. I am sick of hearing about this Dave person.

"Where do you live?"

If you only knew!

"Why did you follow me to the ladies' room last night? Did you feel that same zap of recognition that I did? Why did you come here with me?"

He bit his bottom lip to keep from answering her last question in crude terms once again. But he thought them, and those thoughts must have shown on his face.

She grimaced, then made her face go blank. "You said your name was Thorfinn. Do you prefer Thorfinn or Finn?"

He still did not answer.

"Okay, Finn it will be. Thorfinn is too much of a mouthful."

I can think of something that was not too much of a mouthful for you.

"I'll be right back."

And she was gone, afore he could tell her all the things he wanted to do to her.

Chapter 7

Getting to know you . . .

He followed her to the solar, where she tossed his clothing at him. Afterward he went into her scullery, where she was preparing a meal for them both . . . ham, eggs, more toasted bread, and a hot beverage he recognized as coffee, a bitter brew which he had come to like.

While they were eating, she said, "My husband, David Denton . . . Dave . . . died five years ago in Baghdad. An enemy ambush."

I was ambushed in Baghdad, too, though that fact is probably irrelevant. Still . . . hmmmm.

"Dave was a Navy SEAL."

Another SEAL! The world is overflowing with the arrogant lot.

"We have a son, Mike, who is more than four years old, as I told you before."

As my son would be now.

"I loved Dave so much."

Luta nigh hated my guts.

She gulped visibly several times and fought against tears. "Dave had silver-gray eyes, as does Mike. An unusual color unlike any I've ever seen before until . . ."

". . . me," he finished for her. *I think I have fallen down the barmy hole.*

She nodded. "It's not just the eye color, though. When I saw you across the tavern, even before I could see your eyes, I got goose bumps. I sensed something about you."

He realized now where this conversation was going. Pushing aside the tray with the half-eaten food, he said, "I am not Dave."

"I know that, and yet . . . there's something. Don't you feel it?"

The only thing I feel is a growing vexation with your incessant jabbering. "No, I do not feel *it*, whatever *it* is. However, I will concede this. I am here in this . . . um, country . . . under unusual circumstances which I cannot explain, even if I wanted to. Let us just say that I was drawn here, to this time and place, for reasons unknown to me."

"Damn!" She frowned. "Every time I think you're just a stranger and I need to get rid of you, you say or do something that makes me second-guess myself."

Chirp, chirp, chirp. She is like a bird that will not stop chirping. "What did I say this time?"

"That you felt drawn here. That might mean . . . that Dave sent you here."

He rolled his eyes.

"Okay, if you're not leaving right away, you can go for a walk on the beach, or there's a TV and DVD player in the living room. Check out the DVDs. You might enjoy movies like *Braveheart* or *Pirates of the Caribbean*. Have you seen them?"

"Seen who? Of course I have seen pirates. Any Viking who rides the high seas has met a pirate or two."

She blinked in confusion. "Never mind. If you need something, just yell. I have to go somewhere and think."

"Somewhere?"

"The basement. To dance. I have a small studio downstairs. I don't work today . . . on a Sunday. I always think more clearly when I dance, and you've given me tons to think about. Besides, I have some new dance moves to work out before tomorrow." She stopped short when she realized she was blathering with nervousness.

"I do not understand what you say by half."

"I'm not making much sense to myself either."

After she departed, he muttered to himself, "My brain burns with questions, and the wench goes off to dance."

The demented wench was dancing with a maypole . . .

After an hour, Thorfinn decided he had had enough.

He was allowing himself to be all twisted up inside over a woman. His comrades-in-arms back in the Norse-lands would laugh their bloody heads off. And his brother Steven would never let him forget this happenstance.

On top of all that, he was bored. After his walk on the beach, which was like any other beach in the world, Thorfinn attempted unsuccessfully to start the TV. Then he visited the bathing chamber, where he thoroughly examined the showering stall, the running water, the toilet, and all the objects in a mirrored cabinet above the sink. *What is lavender douche anyway?* He'd pulled out every drawer and opened every closet, including a room which must be his son's sleep bower, decorated as it was with stuffed animals and stars on the ceiling.

The witch was still below stairs. Dancing, no doubt, if the music he heard was any indication. Barmy as a bell tower!

Well, she would be doing a different type of dance soon. He'd given her privacy long enough.

He walked slowly down the stairs, letting the loud music lead his way. Son of a troll! The music was so loud and raucous, the closer he got, it was a wonder her ears did not bleed. His for certain were starting to ache. Some wailing about boogie woogie woogie, whatever that was.

Then he saw her.

Oh. My. Gods!

After being ambushed by Arab villains, riding a bird in the sky, time-traveling to the future with all its unbelievable inventions, being made captive by a woman, he'd thought he could no longer be shocked.

He was wrong.

Lydia was dancing. With a pole. A floor-to-ceiling pole

that was surely a phallic symbol. Mirrors covered an entire wall. Holy bloody hell! Mayhap he had died and gone to Valhalla after all, and Lydia was a Valkyrie, whose sole purpose was to appease the hungers of dead warriors. Of course they were supposed to be virgins, but that was of no matter to him, especially after the far-from-virginal performance this lady had put on for him thus far.

With hair piled atop her head, she wore a one-piece black garment that hugged her body like a second skin. There were stirrups at her bare feet. Her arms, neck, and shoulders were exposed. The curve of her breasts was clearly delineated. For the love of Frigg, he could probably see the dimples in her buttocks if he looked close enough.

And she was sweating. Who knew a woman's sweat could be erotic? Certainly, not him, and the evidence was standing out from his body like a bloody banner. In truth, he was not certain he had ever seen a woman sweat before lest she were a peasant doing hard labor in the fields or scullery. And being aromatic then had definitely not been lust-producing.

He watched from the doorway as she danced, not knowing she was being observed. She strutted around the pole. She climbed it, then arched backwards, arms dangling, held only by the strength of her thighs straddling the pole. She lunged up to grab the pole at a height above her head, climbed even higher, using hands and thighs, then spun downwards in a spiral fashion.

If one viewed the pole as a representation of a penis . . .

and he did . . . her dance moves could only be construed as sexual foreplay. And he was construing, for a certainty.

Another thing was certain. She would be entertaining him later by dancing with the pole. Naked.

Without missing a move, the song changed to lyrics about not being able to get any satisfaction. Well, he was going to give her satisfaction; that was another for-certainty.

"Greetings, Lydia," he said loudly enough to be heard over the music.

Startled, she lost her grip on the pole and fell to the floor, no doubt bruising her buttocks. She stood and began to back away.

Big mistake.

She was soon trapped against the mirror wall, betwixt his two extended arms, braced on either side of her head. "I thought you might have left."

"Obviously, I have not." *Has there ever been a woman with lips so rosy red . . . and kiss-some?*

"What are you going to do?"

Guess. "Suffice it to say . . . never drop your sword to hug a wild boar."

"That makes no sense. Besides, I was just going to come up."

"So you say! Methinks you hoped I would leave if you malingered long enough."

"True enough. Actually, I was going to call your cousin Kirstin."

He arched his eyebrows. *Her nipples are hard, I can*

see. Is it because I excite, or is it due to my earlier fondling?

"I recalled, belatedly, her telling me that you were her cousin when we first saw you in the Wet and Wild, and I thought maybe she'd have some idea how I could . . ." She let her words trail off, realizing she was doing herself no good.

"So, you knew I was kin to Kirstin and Torolf when you brought me here." *That hole you are digging gets deeper and deeper, wench.*

"You have to understand. Something about you reminds me of my husband—"

"The dead one?" *Is there more than one?*

"Yes, Dave is gone, but your eyes are the same."

Here we go again. "Lots of people have the same color eyes." *Is your heart beating as fast as mine, vixen?*

"No, not like yours . . . and Dave's and my son Mike's."

Her mention of the boy caused him to grit his teeth to prevent himself from throttling her.

"I'm so confused."

You are not the only one. "And that is an excuse for your wanton behavior? For kidnapping me?" *Not that I am really complaining. Not anymore since I have benefitted so well.*

"I did not kidnap you. I just . . . um . . . uh . . . temporarily restrained you." She gave him a little hopeful smile.

You will have to do much better than that, sweetling. Gods! Where did that come from? Now I grace her with endearments? He shook his head to clear it and said, "Notice my lack of amusement."

"We need to talk—"

I do not think so. Lest it is sex talk. "The time for talk is long past, m'lady, lest you mean to talk with your body again."

He was already barefooted; so, 'twas easy to shrug out of his braies and *shert.*

Face blooming with color, she continued, "Before we talk, I would appreciate it if you would put your clothes back on."

He glanced down at himself and his rampant "enthusiasm." Then drawled, "My nudity did not bother you afore." *I know when a woman likes my body.*

The blooming color in her cheeks deepened. "Well, it does now. It's not appropriate." She licked her lips with nervousness.

"M'lady, I would like to know how you expect me to swive you with my manpart covered."

"I don't expect any such thing."

Even as his mind boggled at her typical female ill-logic, he slipped the backs of his fingers under the strap of her garment, pleased at her hiss of outrage. Or was it arousal? Her skin felt warm and very soft. He watched in fascination as the fabric sprang back when he tugged it outward. "What manner of garment is this?"

"A leotard. It's worn for . . . what are you doing?"

"Taking it off."

"Why?" she nigh gurgled.

She cannot be so thick-witted. Can she? "Mayhap to

even the playing field." He glanced down at his own nude body for emphasis, then tugged her garment down to her waist, thus trapping her arms at her sides. *What a gift from the gods is a woman's body!* She was tall and slim, but her breasts were full and rose-tipped with big nipples. *She is definitely aroused,* he concluded with satisfaction. He also noticed that her breasts were high for one who had born and mayhap nursed a babe.

"I refuse to do any . . . playing."

"That is not up to you, wench." *Especially after showing me how well you play.*

"And stop calling me wench."

By the runes! I am going to enjoy taming this one. "Where did you get the idea that you have any control over my actions?"

"What are you going to do?"

Ah, smart she is to ask that question. "Plenty."

She whimpered.

Whimpering is good. "Methinks you would make a good love thrall."

"Thrall?" she choked out.

"Slave," he said. "Yea, instead of me being your love slave, you will be *my* love slave."

He held her eyes with his as he sank to his knees, tugging her garment off and to the floor. Still holding her gaze, he ran his fingertips from the outside of her ankles, up her bare legs to her thighs and hips, waist, and underarms. Then, without warning, he moved up and took one breast in his mouth, sucking hard.

She groaned, and her body folded itself down so that she was on her knees facing him.

"Who are you?" she murmured, placing her hands on his shoulders, as he continued to suckle her.

The answer to your maiden dreams? "Your master," he murmured back, moving his mouth from the one wet, erect nipple to the other.

She shook her head. "Your eyes . . . they tell me . . . something. There's a message in them."

He glanced upward from her breast. "That I want to swive you?"

She shook her head some more. "Somehow Dave is involved."

Dave, Dave, Dave, he wanted to chastise her, but the time for talk was over.

She was trembling with need.

He was trembling with need.

And so it was that he played master to his slave on the floor. Up against the mirror. On her back. On his back. All with a pounding rhythm that seemed to go on endlessly.

But, a long time later, he panted for breath and had to wonder who was the master and who was the slave in this particular bedsport.

The things a woman will do for love . . .

Lydia was in a state of pure shock as she sat at her kitchen table, sipping a cup of black coffee from a mug which read, "Dancers Do It with Rhythm." What an understatement!

Her visitor or captive or captor or whatever you wanted to call him . . . Finn . . . had allowed her to put her leotard back on, hinting that if she didn't follow his orders, he would put restraints on her, as she had on him. He was only teasing.

But that wasn't what had her in shock . . . or only partially. And her dancing had done nothing to clear her mind.

She was behaving in a totally bizarre manner. Bringing a stranger home with her. Engaging in sex . . . numerous times. Never once protesting the things he asked her to do . . . in fact, initiating some of it herself. Continually seeing him as some reincarnation of Dave, or a messenger sent by Dave, or Dave himself, for heaven's sake. She was finally going off the deep end. She didn't even know what he did for a living.

Maybe her behavior was as simple as a reaction to five years with no sex. Or maybe it was a delayed reaction to Dave's death, not that she hadn't reacted before.

Her kitchen, dining area, and living room were all one open-air plan. So, Finn could easily be seen sitting on the sofa, back to her. If she were braver, she could creep up on him with a baseball bat and conk him over his thick skull. A skull which was covered with that long hair with those two ridiculous beaded braids framing his face. Men should not have prettier hair than women, she'd always contended. Barefooted and bare-chested, he wore a pair of Dave's old gray jogging pants. That was another sign of her shock . . . that she would have allowed him to root through the storage box in the basement, which hadn't been touched since Dave's death.

Finn continued to peruse a photo album and all the framed photographs he had taken off the mantel and spread out on the coffee table, not bothering to look up as she walked over. She sat down on the ottoman and picked up the wedding picture, where Dave's tanned skin was a sharp contrast to his dress whites. His dark hair had been trimmed into its usual high and tight. The lines that later bracketed his mouth and eyes from repeated violent live ops had been absent then. He gazed down at her with a big goofy smile and dancing eyes that promised loveplay later. And she, in white gown and veil—*Was I really that innocent and hopeful?*—stared up at him as if he were her everything. Well, he had been.

"Why do you weep?"

Her head jerked up to see Finn staring at her.

Setting the picture down, she swiped at her eyes. "I miss him so much."

"Dave?"

She nodded.

"And that is why you have engaged in bedsport with me as if I am your long-lost love?"

She nodded again, ignoring his sarcasm.

"I am not Dave."

"I know that now." *I think.* "Still . . ."

He cocked his head in question.

"Still . . . I can't get rid of the notion that there's some connection. You mentioned Baghdad. Did I tell you that Dave died in Baghdad?"

"You may have said something. How long ago?"

"Five years."

"Five years . . . *pfff!* The lackwit event that drew me here took place a mere three months ago."

"Now see, I could accept your story, but then you talk with a foreign accent, English but not English, using words like *lackwit* or *sweetling*. And you drop little bombs like the fact that you were *drawn* here. What do you mean by *drawn*? Like an angel?"

He grinned, something His Somberness rarely did. And—*be still my heart*—he had a wonderful, crooked grin, accented by one cute dimple. "No one has ever likened me to an angel. The devil . . . now that is another story."

"Then what did you mean?"

"I cannot explain right now. Suffice it to say, my means of getting here was unusual and against my will."

"You don't see anything peculiar in our coming together?"

"Oh, these are peculiar matters, indeed." He held up a baby picture of Mike, taken in the hospital soon after his birth, and said something which totally knocked her for a loop. "This, m'lady, is *my* son, Miklof."

The big gruff Viking had tears in his eyes.

Chapter 8

Being a love-slave master is such hard work . . . not! . . .

"Come here," he said, motioning her toward him with the fingers of his free hand.

"No. I don't take orders," the foolish wench said as she stood and dug in her heels.

"More is the pity!" *Hell and Valhalla! I am going to enjoy this.* He reached out suddenly, grabbed her hand, and yanked her hard. She flew toward him, landing across his lap. With a slap to her bottom, he set her on the cushioned pallet-type furniture beside him.

She gasped and glared at him.

"I must needs explain my situation to you . . . well, part of it . . . and see if you can make sense of all this insanity."

Straightening her back, she gave him her full attention.

She was a beautiful woman; he had to give her credit there. Long hair like ebony silk down to her shoulder blades. Golden skin . . . from the sun, no doubt. Women in his time did everything in their power to preserve a milk-white complexion. Ne'er would they be caught basking in the sun, as women in this country did.

And then there was her heart-shaped mouth, which was red from his kisses . . . an observation which caused his man-pride to puff up. As if his mark on her was something to commend.

And her body . . . well, her body he could grow accustomed to . . . and already had.

Best of all . . . or worst of all, since this had to be a passing liaison . . . was her zest in the bedsport. Luta had at best endured his lovemaking. Lydia gave as good as she got.

"I was married to a woman named Luta . . . a girl, really," he started. "When I was twenty-five and she was eighteen, we had a son. A mere two weeks after the birthing, she rose from her bed and left my keep, taking the babe with her. Disappeared like the wind, she did. Only later did I discover that she'd had a lover afore our marriage . . . a merchant . . . who returned and took her off on his trading ship—willingly, I might add. Rumor has it that they all died in a violent sea storm, but—"

She put a hand on his arm. "But you haven't been able to accept the death."

He nodded. "I searched for more than a year, but nothing. Oh, I cared not what happened to the traitorous Luta, but my son . . ." His choked voice trailed off.

"You loved him very much, then, even though you'd only had him for a few weeks?"

"I loved him in the womb. I loved him as I caught his wee body coming out of the womb. I loved the way his big silver eyes stared up at me, as if he recognized me." He ignored the tears of sympathy welling in her eyes. "Several months past I got word that a woman and boy resembling Luta and Miklof had been seen in Baghdad."

"Ah, so that's why you were in Baghdad?"

"Yea, my brother Steven and I traveled there with our seamen. To no avail. It was not Luta."

She was frowning now, trying to figure out what all this had to do with her. When understanding came, she gasped. "You can't believe that Michael . . . Mike . . . and your son are one and the same."

"The evidence is there," he said, pointing to the picture in front of him on the low table.

"He is *not* your son."

"So you say."

For a brief second, she did not see the implications of his contention, but then she did. "No! You cannot have him. He's mine." She tried to stand, but he pushed her back down and held her at his side with a firm arm around her shoulders. Only when her squirming and flailing of arms and kicking of legs and spitting out foul words had died down did he seat her on the low table in front of him, betwixt his widespread knees.

Still holding her by the shoulders, he said, "I need to see the boy. Methinks I will know for a certainty if he is

Miklof. Just as there is a maternal bond, a father knows his son, too."

"That's bull. You're looking for a substitute for your lost son, and you'll see things that aren't there."

"Like you see your dead husband in me?"

"That's different. I'll tell you this, I'll never let you see Mike if there's even the remotest chance you plan to take him from me."

"Who said aught about taking him?" *Especially since I have nowhere to take him at the present time.*

"What then?"

Bloody hell! How do I know? "Mayhap we will raise him together."

That caused her mouth to drop open.

He waggled his eyebrows at her, the way Steven did when playing the fool. "Mayhap I will even pretend to be your Dave, if you are very nice to me."

Her mouth slammed shut, and her eyes flashed blue fire, but then she said, "When pigs fly."

He just laughed and stood, drawing her up beside him, then tugging her along like a troublesome puppy as he walked to the bedchamber where he had left his *den-ham* braies.

At first she balked, no doubt figuring he was up for another bout of swiving. He was, but that would have to wait. Pulling a piece of parchment out of the leather money pouch that had been in his braies pocket, he handed it to her and said, "I need you to tap this number into your telephone."

"What? Whose number is it?"

Thorfinn had become familiar with the amazing talking device known as a telephone, but was still unclear how to do it himself. On this parchment was a series of numbers Torolf had given him in case of an emergency.

"Do not worry yourself about who it is. Just do it. In fact, make us something to break our fast whilst I am talking."

She sputtered her indignation at his giving her orders. Stubborn wench!

"I have a fierce hunger . . . for food. Well, for that other, too, but first things first," he continued. "That meal you prepared for us earlier was not enough to satisfy a cat."

"You ate enough to feed a horse, and it was followed by a quart of strawberry ice cream."

"And your point?" Whilst they talked, he was already walking back toward the scullery, where he'd last seen the telephone. She muttered as he led her by hand after him, grinning to himself, enjoying the ease with which he could rouse her temper.

Lydia tapped in the numbers and began rummaging through the cold chest, searching for provender. He sat on a high stool, listening to the ringing sound from the phone pressed up to his ear. Every once in a while, he gave her an exaggerated lustsome look, just to annoy her. This whole time-travel nonsense must be causing his brain to regress back to childhood if he got his pleasures in such boyling pranks.

"Hello!" Torolf barked into the phone.

"Greetings."

"Son of a bitch! Is that you, Finn?"

"My mother was not a bitch, and well you know it."

"Where the hell are you? Are you all right?"

"Of course I am all right. I am here, spending time with my love slave."

"Oh. My. God!"

Lydia threw eye-daggers his way.

"You're going to get yourself arrested!"

"Arrested? Dost mean by the law men? Nay, that will not happen. The wench made me her love slave first."

"Oh. My. God!"

"You are repeating yourself, cousin."

"You are the dumbest arrogant brick-for-brains idiot in the world. Give me your address, and I'll come pick you up."

"Nay. Not yet. I still have much love-slaving to do yet."

Lydia muttered something a lady should not say.

"Give me your damn address," Torolf yelled into the telephone.

"Nay, I do not think that would be wise."

"Let me talk to your . . . to the woman."

"My love slave is busy."

"Doing what? Shit! You're not getting a blow job while we're talking, are you?"

He moved the phone away from his ear and asked Lydia, "What is a blow job?"

Her face went bloodred, and her eyes fixed on the region of his male parts.

He frowned, then figured it out himself. He was not a

total lackwit, despite what Torolf thought. "Nay, not just now," he said into the telephone. "But last night, for a certainty, praise the gods!"

"I am going to kill you."

"For getting a blow job? Hey, I blew her, too. Do you and your *sweet* wife not blow each other?" 'Twas hard for him to picture Hilda engaging in such acts. If it were him, he would not allow her teeth within biting distance of his manparts.

"Don't you dare ever ask Hilda that question. She would draw and quarter you."

"She could try. Really, Torolf, you need to exert some authority over your woman. She gives new meaning to the word *shrew*. Dost want to be considered a milksop like Ivan the Woman-Whipped?"

After Torolf gave him the telephone numbers for his tutor, with Thorfinn repeating them aloud so Lydia could write them down, his cousin asked, "How long do you expect to be with your . . . um, love slave?"

In the background, he could hear Hilda squawking, something about, "Love slave? That male chauvinist cousin of yours is going to land us all in jail."

Ignoring Hilda's prattle, to Torolf he said, "About two sennights . . . till I meet my son."

There was silence at the other end. Then a long sigh. "Finn, your son is dead. You've got to accept that and get on with your life."

"Mayhap he is, and mayhap he is not. I must needs be sure."

"Listen, buddy, I'm going operational tonight, and I

might not be back for a week or so. I would feel a lot better if you were back here at the apartment, or at Blue Dragon."

"I will be fine here. Do not worry. If there is a problem, I will call Ragnor or your father, whose numbers you gave me along with your own. Is Geek going with you?"

"Why?"

"Just answer me."

"No, Geek won't be traveling with us. He sprained his ankle in P.T. this morning."

"Good."

"Good? Geek being hurt in physical training is good? What kind of half-assed remark is that?"

"Enough of this prattle, Torolf. May Thor guide your weapon arm on your mission and Odin give you wise counsel for strategy. We will speak on your return." Thorfinn clicked off the talking connection before his cousin could question or chastise him more. Really, Torolf treated him like a youthling, not a grown man of thirty winters.

Next he consulted the parchment he'd given Lydia with the numbers on it. This time, with much care, he tapped in the numbers for Geek himself, and prided himself on his success.

After first gaining a pledge of secrecy from Geek as to his whereabouts, he made arrangements for the young man to come there later that afternoon, urging him to bring his lap computer, a magic invention which was helpful in his studies.

He was only half-attending when the phone rang in his hand, jolting him with surprise. Studying the different buttons, he pressed the green one and put the phone to his ear.

"Hullo!" a young voice said. "Who's this?"

"Thorfinn. Who are you?"

"Michael. Where's my mom?"

Thorfinn slapped a hand over his suddenly racing heart. There were so many things he wanted to say, but he was unable to speak over the lump in his throat.

"She is here," he choked out.

"What's she doin'?"

"Making a meal."

"Lunch?"

"Yea, we are breaking fast. Ham burglers, I think."

"Be careful she doesn't sneak some veggies in, especially onions."

He lifted his head from the phone and asked Lydia, "Are you putting onions in my ham burgler?"

She went suddenly stiff and stomped over to him. "Who are you talking to? I thought you were talking to Torolf." She grabbed the phone out of his hands.

He moved to a chair by the table, leaned back, and watched her interact with what could very well be his son.

"Who was that? Oh, nobody."

She calls me nobody, does she? We shall see about that.

"Uh-uh. A friend."

I do not know what is worse . . . that she considers me a friend, or nobody of any worth.

"Yes, I know you've never met him. He's a new friend."

Gor the Gruesome is my friend. Cnut the Courageous is my friend. You, m'lady, are not my friend.

"Will I bring him with me to Minnesota?" She turned to look at him.

He favored her with his best glower.

"Maybe." She listened for awhile then. Even from here, he could hear the boy's chatter, though not clearly enough to make out the words. He noticed one thing. Lydia's face fair glowed when she talked to her son. "Why do you want me to bring your cowboy hat? Oh, right. Itchy has a cowboy hat; so, you have to have one, too. Listen, sweetie, I've got to go. I love you bunches, honey bear." She grinned at something he said then.

She smiled whimsically at the phone as she clicked it off.

"Why are you smiling?"

"He called me honey bee."

Well, that was a lackwit thing to smile about, in his opinion, but he said naught as she went back to preparing their meal. She had to be aware of the effect the boy had on him. Was she being sensitive to his feelings, or did she just not care because he was a nobody, as she had told her son?

He watched through narrowed eyes as Lydia bustled about the scullery, banging pots and pans together, slamming metal food containers on the cabinet tops, muttering under her breath. She was clearly annoyed with him, for some reason.

He cared not a whit for that. He was enjoying himself too much. In the black garment which hugged every nook and crevice of her body, she was temptation in its purest sense. With her hair piled in a loose knot atop her head, her neck and her shoulders were bare, showing evidence of his whisker burn and sex bites. Her breasts, which provided an endless feast when they made love, tempted him constantly. They were full, full enough to fill his big hands, and hard-tipped. A woman's breasts.

Her legs were alluring, too. Extra long length with muscled thighs and calves from all her dancing, he supposed. Good for hugging his hips when the bedsport got vigorous.

What he liked most about Lydia was her zest for loveplay. She was unapologetic about her needs, and thus allowed herself to peak, repeatedly, sometimes loudly, sometimes with delicious moans or sweet keening. Other than strumpets, most women he knew endured bedsport as a marital duty.

Not that he was complaining.

Oddly, he had spent much effort in giving her pleasure, too. He could not recall it mattering much to him in the past whether his partner peaked or not. But with Lydia, her pleasure was his pleasure.

He watched now as she bent over, opening a lower door, searching for some item or other. Her buttocks were round and curved, like half moons, with enough flesh for a man to grab on to. He grinned to himself, imagining something he might try in that regard.

As if sensing his scrutiny, she glanced his way over her shoulder, then glanced again. "What? Why are you staring at me?"

Dost really want to know? He linked his hands behind his neck, his body relaxed, legs extended and partly spread. And continued to stare at her.

"No," she said.

He arched his eyebrows.

"No more sex."

Definitely more sex. "Dost think you are in a position to dictate to me, wench?"

"And stop calling me wench."

"What wouldst thou prefer? Dearling? Sweetling? Heartling?"

"Don't be ridiculous." She was standing now, backed up against the cabinets.

"Do not get any romantic notions about the sex we have both enjoyed. 'Tis no more than animal hunger, easily sated."

"What an ass! No wonder your wife left you."

"Your tongue exceeds your good sense, Lydia. You know naught of what went on betwixt my wife and me." *And, believe you me, it was not much.*

"I can guess. You probably pulled *wham-bams* in bed with her. No foreplay. No sweet words. Just stick it in and satisfy yourself. Two minutes in the sack and a day full of loneliness."

Lydia's assessment hit closer to the truth than he liked. "I satisfied *you*."

"Well, you know, it's been five years. Anything in pants could have done the trick for me."

That was a low blow. "What did you do for these long five years to find release? A passionate woman like you would not do without."

"Same as you, buster."

It took several moments for him to understand. "You pleasure yourself?"

Her face bloomed with color.

Was there ever such a woman as this? "Do you blush, m'lady?" He paused. "Frigg's feet, you do!"

"Hey, this is the twenty-first century. Women have just as much right to sexual gratification as men."

Gods bless the twenty-first century. A slow smile crept over his mouth. "Show me."

"I . . . I beg your pardon."

"Take off that garment and show me." *Before I explode with overenthusiasm.*

"I will not. Besides, lunch is ready."

"Food can wait." *'Tis food of another type I crave.*

"No."

"Do you say me nay?" *Not in this lifetime, wench.*

"N. O. No."

Dost want to wager on that? "That is a word I will not accept. You have two choices. Either I bind you to your bed, spread-eagled and naked, as I was. Or you show me how you pleasure yourself."

She gulped a few times. "I can't. Don't ask me to. Please."

"Would you do it for Dave?" He thought of something then. "*Did* you ever do it for Dave?"

The deepening flush on her cheeks was answer enough.

He was beginning to really dislike this husband of hers, even dead. "Do it!"

She closed her eyes and brushed her fingertips over her breasts, bringing the nipples into even greater prominence. Then, while one hand played with her nipples, the other skimmed over her abdomen and belly to caress the joining of her thighs.

Oh, my gods and goddesses! He had never expected her to actually do it. He had been teasing. But now that she was, every male particle in his body was standing to attention. And his manpart was standing more than all the rest.

"Take off your garment," he said in a raw voice.

Her eyes flew open, and they were filled with tears. Of panic. And shame.

In truth, he had intended to shame her, but now he found himself filled with the same emotion. He understood, without being told, that when she had done this in the past with her husband, it had been an act performed with love . . . a love given and returned. A pang of jealousy shot through him, an emotion he had never felt before.

That did not mean he would end this game anytime soon. He was not a total lackwit.

"Come here. I will help you," he said, feeling sympathy for her modesty, which he was raking through the coals . . . erotic coals, to be sure, with or without the love element.

Slowly, she walked toward him, chin high. When she stood between his widespread knees, he eased the straps off her shoulders and arms, then peeled the rest of the garment down to her feet.

"You are so beautiful . . . like a goddess. Are you sure you are not a Valkyrie?"

She smiled then, a small, tentative smile.

And an odd clenching occurred in the region of his heart.

"Are you thinking that flattery will get you everywhere?"

"I can hope." He smiled at her then.

"You have the most gorgeous smile. And a dimple."

"A dimple? I do not have a dimple. Babies have dimples, on their arses. Not full-grown men."

"Yes, you do. Right there."

He turned his head when she touched his cheek and nipped her forefinger.

She went to back up, but he held her tightly between his thighs.

"Show me now." This time he urged, not ordered. "And do not close your eyes. Your ardor gives me pleasure." *Plus, I want you to see exactly who you are with. I. Am. Not. Dave.*

Chapter 9

These games were not for children . . .

Lydia felt as if she were in the middle of some X-rated fantasy. It wasn't really her. And this definitely wasn't Dave.

So, why am I being so compliant?

Because I want to?

No, that's too simplistic.

Because this is the first time in five years I've even wanted a man.

But there have been lots of other men and other opportunities. Why this particular man?

Because no matter what he says, there is some connection to Dave here.

He wanted her to touch herself, to bring herself to orgasm while he watched. Okay, she could do that, but she would be damned if she would do it alone.

Before he could blink those silver Dave-eyes at her, she lifted one leg, then the other, over his thighs, still covered with jogging pants, so that she now straddled his lap. Then she put her hands on his shoulders. His arms that had been raised and linked lazily behind his neck fell to his sides, and he inhaled sharply.

Yeah, you should gasp, buddy. Now it's my show.

It was always good to catch a guy off guard; that's what all the women's magazines in her studio lobby proclaimed. Who knew all that "How to Turn on Your Man" nonsense would come in handy one day? *When I lose my mind with a Dave clone.*

She had never been promiscuous growing up on a Minnesota farm. In fact, Dave had been her one and only lover. But he'd taught her to be uninhibited. To enjoy sex. Somehow, in her extended grief, she'd forgotten that.

But it was all coming back. With a vengeance.

With a soft laugh, she shimmied her bottom up closer to his crotch, then moved her breasts from side to side across his chest hairs. She couldn't stop the full-body shiver that overtook her at the delicious contact. So, she did it again.

And, hot damn, he shivered, too.

Finn's fingers grasped her waist, and he showed her how to move her lower half against him, the way he liked. His lips were parted now and his breathing heavier, his eyelids half-mast.

It didn't take much to turn him on.

Or her, for that matter.

She knew if she touched herself, down there, she

would be damp already. But no touching yet, she warned herself. She wanted to extend this loveplay as long as possible.

Using her breasts to caress his chest again, she asked in a sultry voice she didn't even know she had, "Do you like that?" *Good heavens! Where am I getting the nerve?*

"Is it not obvious?" He bucked his hips up against her, just once, to show how aroused he was.

Yep, he likes it. Leaning in even more, she pressed her mouth against his lightly, then used her tongue to wet his lips, before kissing him in earnest. "Open for me, baby," she urged against his lips. *Mama's got a present for you.*

He smiled back against *her* lips, in response. "Gladly," he husked out.

Then, she kissed him. Open-mouthed. Alternately hard and soft. With her lips. With her nipping teeth. With her tongue sliding in and out of his mouth.

"I ne'er had much taste for kisses afore," he told her, kissing her back. "But you are giving me a new appreciation for this foresport."

"I love kissing. I love kissing *you*."

She could feel his heart beating *thud-thud-thud* against her breasts, and his hands, which had been at her waist, were now holding her buttocks, directing her in a slow rhythm against his erection.

"Wait," she said, shimmying back a bit on his lap and reaching for his wallet on the table. Taking out a condom, she ripped it open with her teeth, tugged down the elastic waistband of his pants, releasing a very impressive

"Howdy!" you-know-what, and had him sheathed before he could mutter, "Bloody hell!" Which he did. It was one of his favorite expressions.

"Now, watch." She lifted her own breasts. She caressed them with her palms. She flicked the nipples with her thumbs. When her hands lifted her hair off her neck—it had come loose from its claw barrette—her breasts presented themselves to him, higher and more forward. A provocative, deliberate pose, which had him smiling in appreciation and probably a bit of shock. *Hey, I'm shocked, too.* With her arms still raised, she began to undulate her hips. Advance, retreat. Advance, retreat. Just brushing the tip of him.

He gritted his teeth, and his hands left her butt to fist at his sides. Yep, he was definitely shocked now . . . and appreciative.

Was there anything more pleasing to a woman than to watch her man try to control his raging libido under her seduction?

Not that he was *her* man.

Or was he?

Actually, she was having trouble fighting her own approaching climax, but she didn't want to come 'til he was inside her.

With a long, drawn-out growl, he took the decision out of her hands, so to speak. Arching his hips off the chair, he entered her, to the hilt. He stretched her; she clenched him. Eyes closed, jaw tense, unmoving, he attempted to slow down his arousal.

"Do you still want to watch, honey?" she purred at him.

His eyes shot open.

And while he watched, she put a fingertip to that place where their two bodies were joined. Immediately, her inner muscles began to spasm around him, and he grew even larger inside her. As her eyes drifted shut, long-unused folds began to move in accommodating his growing size.

"Open your eyes, you saucy witch," he ordered with a chuckle. Then he took over the loveplay. He was a master at the game, no doubt about it.

But when the game was over, and she'd come another two times, and he'd roared out his climax, and they were both panting, it was debatable who the winner was.

He wasn't THAT kind of a Viking . . .

Thorfinn was lying beside Lydia on the bed after another bout of lovemaking.

Truly, he had engaged in more sex this past day or so than he had the past year. At first, he had been plagued with a faint worry . . . very faint . . . that she would wear him down to a nub. Instead, he seemed to get bigger with each bout.

Amazing!

And exhilarating!

He could not wait to tell Steven. He did not need those magic elixirs Steven had purchased in Baghdad. Instead he just needed to swive 'til he was woolly-witted.

Of course, he might not ever have the opportunity to tell Steven, and that fact saddened him greatly.

She interrupted his reverie as she raised herself on one elbow to stare down at him. "I have to go to work to-morrow."

"Work? What kind of work?"

"I own an aerobics dance studio."

"*Arrow-backs?*"

"Everybody knows what aerobics are." She frowned at him, waiting for him to explain.

How can I explain the unexplainable? "Not me."

"It's a type of exercise. People come to my studio to get in shape, or keep in shape."

"Do they pay you for this service?"

"Of course."

There is no "of course." "If you leave, I might never see you again . . . or my son."

"You don't trust me?"

Does the tinder trust the flame? "Hah! You would no doubt run like the wind if you knew who I really am."

"Oh, God! Are you a criminal? An escaped convict?" Her body stiffened and she sat up, tugging the bed linen to cover her nudity.

Now she goes modest on me. I do not think so. He yanked the linen back off and flicked it over to the floor on the other side. "Nay, I am not a law-breaker. Leastways, no law I am aware of." He exhaled loudly, then confessed, "I must needs confess . . . I am a Viking."

She paused for a further explanation which was not forthcoming. "A Viking. That's all?"

"'Tis enough."

"Hey, sweetie, I'm from Minnesota. Vikings abound

there. But I don't recall your name ever being on the roster. What years did you play?"

"Play what?"

"Football."

"The game where grown men run around kicking balls and tackling each other to the ground?" *Why does every conversation in this country feel as if I am wading through mud?*

"Yes," she replied, hesitantly.

She thinks I am a lackwit footballer. "You truly must consider me a lackwit. I am not *that* kind of Viking. I am a real Viking from the Norselands."

"Okay, so you're from Norway and . . . ?"

"Eleventh-century Norselands."

Her jaw dropped. Then she laughed. "When I asked if you were an escaped convict, I should have also asked if you're an escaped mental patient."

Nay, that is what they called my uncle Jorund. "I know it sounds demented. I thought so, too, when it first happened. I still do."

"When what happened?"

"The time travel."

"Oh, good grief!" She burst out laughing again. "This is a joke, right?"

I wish 'twere so. "You may as well know the entire story so you can laugh some more." He sat up next to her and wrapped his arms around his raised knees. "I was attacked by six men in Baghdad. I had just lopped off this one villain's head when . . ."

"Oh, no! You lopped off someone's head?"

"They were trying to kill me. What did you expect me to do? Ask them to dance?"

"What did you use?"

What do you think? A butter paddle? "A sword, of course. Why do you look so horrified? Did your precious Dave never kill anyone?"

"I'm sure he did, but he never talked about it."

"I never talk about it, either. It is naught to boast of."

"Even so, it doesn't sound so bad if you use a gun. A bullet is, well, cleaner."

"Are you serious? There is naught clean about death, no matter how it comes about. And guns are no more civilized, either, afore you make that claim. Besides that, in the eleventh century, guns were not available."

"I don't know."

Well, I do. "Dead is dead, dearling. Back to what I was saying about my being attacked in Baghdad. Just when I thought all was lost, my cousin Torolf and his band of barmy SEALs rescued me, put me on a flying bird, and brought me here. Now I must adjust to not only a new country, but a new time."

Her eyes went wider and wider as he spoke. "What did you do when you were . . . um, back there? To support yourself, I mean."

He thought about telling her he had been a warrior, but most Vikings were warriors at one time or another. It went without saying. "For the past few years, I have run my estate, Norstead, whilst my brother Steven is at Amberstead. We are from Norsemandy, now known as Normandy, but we went to the Norselands, now known as

Norway, to help . . . on a mission, and stayed." That story of the battle against the evil Steinolf he would save for another day.

"Estates?"

Based on his recent studies, he knew that estates meant something different here. She was probably picturing some grand mansion with picturesque grounds. "It sounds better than it really is," he said with a laugh. "A wooden castle. A *small* wooden castle, in the Frankish style. A sizeable *hird* of soldiers or housecarls. A dozen or more house servants. A weaving house. Smithy. Brew house. Stables. Fields. Cotters' huts. That kind of thing."

"And you managed it all?"

He nodded.

"My goodness! Why would you come here if you had all that?"

"Dost have dust in your ears, m'lady. I told you, I had no choice."

"The 'being drawn' business again?"

At first he did not understand what she meant, but then he did. He had told her about being "being drawn" through time to this country. He nodded again, then added, "I have been engaged in tutoring these past three months so that I can fit in here, assuming that I do not get thrust back to the past. Now, do you understand?"

"Hardly. I can't believe I'm involved with a thousand-year-old man. Amazing!" She smiled as she said the latter.

"Dost think it is funny?"

"You must admit it's a far-fetched idea."

"More like brain-tetched." But then he homed in on something else she had said. "*Are* we involved?"

"Having sex a half-dozen times in twenty-four hours? Yeah, I think that qualifies as involvement."

He could not help but grin. He was a Viking man. Virility was a trait much to be admired.

"As for the time travel, you're pulling my leg, right?"

He frowned. "Nay, I am not pulling your leg, though I will if you want me to."

"What? Oh, you!" She smacked him on the arm. "*Pulling your leg* is an expression. It means that you're teasing."

"I came here from the eleventh century, Lydia, and that is a fact."

She seemed to be pondering what he had said. Then, instead of looking at him with shock, or revulsion, or disbelief, she started to stare at him in the oddest way, as if he had given her some marvelous gift. "So that's why you talk so funny?"

"I do not talk funny."

She smiled and patted his hand. "Dave sent you."

All my earnest explanations, and we are back to step one. "Dave again," he muttered, putting his face on his upraised knees with a groan.

"It's a miracle. Thank you, God. Thank you, thank you, thank you."

Raising his head, he looked at her adoring expression and rolled his eyes.

Still, whilst Thorfinn didn't believe a bit of the miracle

blathering, a small part of him wondered if this woman . . . and her child . . . were the reason for this journey through time. There was only one way to find out.

"We will go to Minnesota."

Sweet captivity . . . uh, captivation . . .

"You captivate me," he told her later as she prepared to go to the grocery mart whilst Geek came here to tutor him. She had promised him that she would return.

"How do I captivate you?"

"I cannot get enough of you. I have always enjoyed bedsport. I am a Viking, after all. But with you, it is different. In truth, I have never had sex with a woman who shared my . . . um, enthusiasm."

"And it's even better when two people are in love."

Oh, please! Bring on the skalds. "Well, I do not know about that. I just know that I have need of you in the most compelling manner. No sooner do I tup than I want you again. Mayhap you have bewitched me."

"Or maybe it's a miracle."

He scoffed at that notion. "A sex miracle?"

"What? You only believe in miracles when they surround your supposed time travel?"

I wonder how soon we can have sex again. "Do your food shopping, sweetling. I will rest after Geek leaves." He gave her a parting kiss. "There is something unusual I am thinking about trying later. Unless you will think it too . . . perverted."

That shut her mouth, good and quick.

Now, he would have to think of something special.
Aaaahhhh.

Nude jogging? Now there's an idea . . .

"Do you believe in miracles?" he asked Geek later as they sat before his lap computer on the scullery table, drinking beer and studying history. That Abe Lincoln was quite a fellow!

Geek cocked his head at Thorfinn. "I tend to look for scientific explanations for most things. Why do you ask? Oh, you mean the time travel."

"That and other things."

"I don't know what happened with you and the rest of Max's family that brought you here. Or why I went back in time with Max and the other guys that one time. We all have our own explanations, but mostly we try not to think about it, or we pretend it was a big joke that will be revealed to us eventually. Or, yeah, a miracle, I suppose. Myself, I expect someday there will be an explanation, that scientists will find that time travel really can work. But not anytime soon."

"You know whose keep this is, do you not?"

Geek nodded. "Lydia Denton. Dave Denton's widow."

"She thinks I am a miracle, sent by her dead husband to console her."

At first, Geek looked surprised. Then he chuckled. "Been doin' a lot of consoling, have you?"

"That I have." He could not help but grin.

"Where is she, by the way?"

"The food mart. And mayhap a stop at her dancing establishment."

"Oh, that's right. She owns that aerobics club in Coronado."

"Yea, she does. And truly, Geek, I cannot fathom a country where people pay someone to make them sweat and work their muscles 'til they nigh scream in pain. My men go to the exercise fields to practice their fighting skills, not to have a winsome thigh or shapely buttock." Thorfinn tapped the computer then. "Dost think any of this is going to help get me in SEALs?"

"It can't hurt. And believe me, Torolf made it through BUD/S on a lot less knowledge than you've gained the past couple months. Besides, getting in is mostly a physical thing, and you seem to be in pretty good condition. Have you been jogging?"

He groaned. "I hate running. 'Tis such a useless exercise, lest someone is chasing you."

"Well, you gotta do a lot of jogging in SEALs. A whole lot."

"I will run this evening on the beach."

"How about your water skills? You'll have to survive the drown-proofing rotation."

"My father always said I was leather-lunged. I do not think that will be a problem."

"I agree. Your problem is that you're older than the average SEAL trainee. It's only the past year or so with the shortage of special forces and the rising terror threat that they've been more lenient on taking older guys."

"I am not yet in my dotage. I can do as well as any twenty-year-old."

"Maybe."

"Besides, the age on my identification papers says twenty-five. How old are *you*?"

"Twenty-eight, but I've been a SEAL for six years."

"Really?"

"It's my baby face. Fools people all the time."

"And works to your advantage, no doubt."

"No doubt." Geek waggled his eyebrows for emphasis. "More important, buddy, you have an ego the size of Baltimore."

"*Ball-to-more?*"

"My hometown."

"As for ego, seems to me all you SEALs have overblown opinions of yourselves." *As do Vikings.*

"You could be right. Still, while you're in training, there are a lot of bullshit orders that you have to obey, without question. And, frankly, there are a few asshole instructors that're gonna make your life hell."

"Dost think there are no asshole Vikings?"

Geek chuckled. "I would imagine there are more than a few."

A short time later, Geek left, promising to return on the morrow when they would be discussing: one, table manners—apparently, polite men used forks and did not belch at the table; two, his swear words—*Holy Thor!* and *Freyja's Tits!* were not modern enough; three, clothing— in particular, boxers or briefs, though he thought a codpiece would do as well; and four, weapons—what kind of soldier carried no sword?

He had spent more time with Geek than he'd expected, and still Lydia was not home.

But he had agreed to trust in her.

After Geek left, Finn took a metal container of mead . . . rather, beer . . . out of the ice box and went outside. His patience and trust were rewarded shortly.

"Finn," she said, sticking her head out the glass door. "I'm back. Did you miss me?"

"For a certainty. I have a treat for you."

"I've had enough of your treats, mister," she said, but there was mirth in her voice. "Any more sex and they'll be putting your dick in the *Guinness Book of World Records*."

Thorfinn had no idea what she meant, but he suspected it was a compliment. "Not that kind of treat," he said, tweaking her on the chin.

She arched her eyebrows with skepticism.

"I am going to let you chase me on the beach," he informed her with a bright smile . . . well, bright for him. "And you will not even have to be naked."

Chapter 10

'Twas the season for gift-giving . . .

"Are you sure it's not five miles yet?" Finn asked her as he dropped down to the blanket next to her, even though he was hardly panting.

"No, it's only three miles. Get your butt in gear, buddy," Lydia told him with a grin. For some reason, he'd set a goal of five miles of jogging for himself, but she'd never heard such a physically fit man complain about exercise so much. When he'd done a series of sit-ups and push-ups earlier, you would have thought he'd been plucking out his fingernails.

"It is insanity, that is what it is. Grown men running for no reason at all, just to develop muscles. I can grow more muscles by engaging in swordplay exercise. Or riding a destrier over a Saxon field. Or wrestling with one of my *hirdsmen*."

Lydia just let him prattle on, admiring him as he stood above her, wearing nothing but nylon shorts and athletic shoes. Other than Dave, he was the most attractive man she'd ever met, and she couldn't exactly say why.

His long hair was pulled back off his face, which was hard-planed and mostly somber. Well over six feet tall, he was broad-shouldered and by no means lean . . . not in terms of fat . . . no, he did not have much body fat, but he was big-boned, and, well, just big all over. He had a man's body, with all its various scars. She'd have to ask about those later. And a man's face, too, which showed his age with brackets about his eyes and mouth.

"Dost like what you see, wench?" he asked, giving her a rascally wink, which was unusual for him. Thus far, he had not been playful by nature.

"Too much," she admitted.

He put up a halting hand. "Do not say I remind you of Dave again or I may heave the contents of my roiling stomach."

Truthfully, she was still confused, but even the remotest possibility that Dave had sent him, or that God had sent him to make up for Dave, had her willing to accept him as he was. Even his stupid Viking time-travel story.

"Let's go for a swim," she suggested, standing and tugging the long T-shirt off and over her head. "Then I'll run with you."

He just stood, staring at her.

"What?"

"In that garment"—he waved a hand to indicate her one-piece maillot bathing suit, nothing scandalous— "there are other things I would rather do with you."

"Don't you think we need to give it a rest?"

"It? Dost mean my manpart? Believe you me, *it* needs no rest."

Still, he followed her out in the shallow water, then dived into an oncoming wave after her. Once on the other side, however, he proved that he did, indeed, need no rest, and he gave new meaning to the term "a dirty swim."

Later, he showed her the famous Viking S-Spot on her body, which resulted in a number of unending, spectacular multiple orgasms. Once sated, or rather depleted . . . both of them . . . Lydia stared up at Finn, too stunned to speak.

"We Vikings are a generous people," he told her with one of his rare, dimple-flashing smiles. "We like to give gifts."

"Some gift! I have none to give you in return."

"Well, I do not know about that."

That night, she did a dance demonstration for him in her basement. With the pole as a stripper prop and Aretha Franklin belting out "A Natural Woman."

Afterward, with both of them splatted out on the carpet, naked, and the mirrors all fogged up, he said, "Are you sure you are not Viking?"

She was pretty sure that was his way of saying he liked her gift.

**The lackwit maiden thought he was the answer to
her prayers . . .**

In the middle of the night, Thorfinn awakened to find
himself alone in bed.

Quickly, he pulled on his *den-ham* braies and stomped
out into the solar, where he stopped dead in his tracks.

The room was dark, but dim light filtered through the
windows from a half-moon outside. Wearing a silk robe,
Lydia was on her knees, hands folded in front of her
breasts.

"Dear God," she prayed. "Yeah, I know. Long time no
see." She sighed, then continued, "Ever since Dave's
death, I lost my belief in you and everything holy, but this
Finn . . . God above, did you send him to me? Did Dave
ask you to send him? It feels like a healing since Finn's
arrival, and I can't help but think . . ."

He realized then that she was weeping. Conflicted, he
leaned against the wall, not sure whether to interrupt her
and proclaim the idiocy of any god having an interest in
him, never mind sending him on a blessed mission, or
whether to just back up and pretend he had never missed
her in the bed. He did neither. He stayed and continued to
listen.

"Please, God, let Finn be the answer to my prayers.
Let him stay and be a family with me and Mike. Let him
be Dave, but if not Dave, let there be love in my life
again. Just not another military man. I cannot face the
fear with every mission."

Uh-oh! Thorfinn realized in that moment that she did

not know he had been a warrior, or that he planned to become a SEAL. Somehow, deliberately at first, but later, without planning, he had failed to inform her of those crucial facts. *And why do women always have to confuse lust or liking for that love pap?*

"If you do these things for me, I promise to be a better person. To go to church. To have Mike baptized. All the things I've neglected these past five years."

Lydia put her face in her hands and began to sob.

He could stand by and watch her pain no more. Without warning, he walked over, picked her up in his arms, and carried her outside, where he sank down into the cushioned glider. Using his feet to propel the gliding motion, he rocked them forward and backward, over and over, her on his lap, his arms wrapped around her, his lips in her flower-scented hair.

Several times, she tried to speak.

"Did you hear everything I—"

"I didn't mean for you—"

"You must think I'm cra—"

But each time he soothed her, "*Shhh!*" and kissed her gently into silence. He did recall her prayers, though. All she wanted was love.

Thorfinn had never been in love, and would not know how to be. He was, in fact, repelled by the notion.

But family . . . she wanted a family for her and her son.

Thorfinn's heart ached at the possibility. A family! Was it possible at this late date?

There had to be a trade-off. What would it be? The gods . . . even the One-God . . . gave naught without exacting some payment; leastways, that had always been his experience. What would he need to give up? His heart? His need for vengeance? His return to the past? His very freedom?

Thorfinn felt as if he were knee-deep in quicksand, and he was not sure he wanted to be saved.

Hair today, gone today . . .

It was probably the biggest mistake of her life . . . taking Finn with her to her dance studio. It was an indication of his trust in her, so she felt the need to reciprocate.

Still, she'd made sure that Torolf and Hilda were gone when she went over to their apartment to pick up clean clothes for her Viking. And she'd double-checked her class rosters for the morning to ensure there would be none of the Magnusson clan around.

Despite her misgivings, she was having fun. Finn was a regular chatterbox today. Worse than Mike with his "Why? Why? Why?" questions.

"Why do women wear garments that expose their legs and bosoms if they are not harlots?"

"Why are all these people being led on leashes by their dogs?"

"Why do you need so many food marts in this country?"

"Why are there no forests?"

"Why do you moan when I touch the back of your knees?"

"Why do women here wear breast harnesses? Do their men not like jiggling flesh?"

"Why are some condoms called ticklers?"

"Why does that Scotsman need so many eating establishments?" He was referring to McDonald's, of course.

"Why have I seen not one horse whilst in this country?"

"Why do you rouge your lips when their natural rosy hue is so enticing?"

They arrived at her studio early, and she showed him around before any of her employees or customers would arrive. He seemed impressed, showing an interest in everything she said. "Do you earn a great amount of coin for these services?"

"Enough to support me and Mike. Although I'd never be able to afford a house on the beach, even a modest one like I have, if David hadn't inherited some money from a great-aunt. The house passed to me on his death. Plus, I used the insurance money to buy the studio."

He nodded, though she wasn't sure if he understood everything she'd told him. There was something weird about Finn, but she wasn't ready to accept that he might have actually time-traveled. For now, she chose to put him in the miracle category.

Leading him back to the lobby, she introduced him to her manager, Lisa Malone, who was clearly interested in the handsome man and what his relationship to the owner might be. Lydia ignored Lisa's raised eyebrows and told Finn, "I need to teach two classes. Why don't you wait for me here, or maybe you'd like to walk down by the water?"

He nodded.

She hesitated then, not sure if she should give him a

kiss or not. If it were Dave, she certainly would have. *What the hell!* she said to herself, walked up, stood on tiptoe, and gave him a fleeting kiss. "See you," she said.

Glancing back over her shoulder, Finn stood in the same place, rather stunned. She wondered what he was thinking.

Thorfinn was thinking that the quicksand was getting deeper and more enticing. That he could be aroused by the mere touch of her lips was a sure indicator of his declining control. And, really, he needed to regain control of his life.

So, he made his own choice. He did not sit. Nor did he walk to the water, where an early morning haze would soon be melted away by the hot California sun. Instead, he went outside and headed in the other direction, away from the town center.

Coronado was a peninsula only a mile wide from the Pacific Ocean side to the San Diego Bay on the other. The North Island Naval Air Station occupied the whole entire north half of Coronado, and the Naval Amphibious Base, where the Navy SEALs trained, was on the south side. Then there were the town center and residential areas, where he was now.

Under the warm sun, its beaches were a great attraction to swimmers, bodysurfers, sand sculptors, and whale watchers, and wasn't it a wonder that people here had the time or inclination to stand about doing such frivolous things? SEAL trainees could be seen jogging along the shores, chanting out songs.

Coronado was beautiful, and as different from the cold,

mountainous terrain of his country and its thousands of
fjords as night from day. Not that there was no beauty in
the Norselands. Just a different kind of beauty.

As he walked the tree-lined roads he noticed all the
keeps around him. Well, not keeps. Houses, they called
them here, no matter the size. None of them had much
land with them, no more than some of the cotters' huts at
Norstead, and not a bailey or drawbridge in sight. With
good reason. The population of the world, according to
Geek, had gone from 55 million to 6.5 billion in the past
one thousand years, even with the birthing control de-
vices. No room for everyone to have even one hide of
property.

There was a similarity, Thorfinn noted. What many
people did not realize was that Vikings were not vicious
rapers and plunderers, as the monk historians portrayed
them—leastways, not all of them—but just men wanting
to find homes for their families. The rocky terrain of the
Norselands had little tillable land and could not provide
for them all.

Despite all the fine prattle in this country about equal-
ity, Thorfinn had learned that there were classes of society here, too. He and his brother Steven straddled the
lines between karls, or wealthly landowners, and the higher
jarls, which could be anything from all-kings to chief-
tains, comparable to English earls. Below these two classes
were the cotters and then thralls.

Whereas in America wealth seemed to be the primary
divider among the classes. There were no kings. Nor were
there slaves, not anymore. And for a certainty, there were

vast estates here for the very wealthy, including Torolf's father, who owned a vineyard named Blue Dragon with his wife, Angela.

One glaring difference, it occurred to him, was that this was a peaceful place, whereas Norsemen were always fighting, if not with the Saxons or the Franks, then with each other. Even with huge gray military warships visible in the distance, even in the midst of a war with another country, people in America could walk about without fear of death. Children played freely, for the most part. There was the terrorist threat, but mostly it seemed far removed.

If he was stuck in this country, would he live in a house like these? Would Miklof be with him? Or other children? And what about Lydia?

Really, his life was in such flux. He did not even know what he could do for a living here. A military job, that was for certain, though Lydia might pray to the contrary. Fighting was all he knew. Of course, he knew how to run a large estate, as well, but what market was there here for a man to direct the activities of his cotters and housecarls?

In truth, he had no place in the world, and that scared him mightily.

Straightening, he resolved, *I will make my own place.*

On that resolution, he walked back to Lydia's Silver Strand Studio. She was still teaching a class. He watched through a window in the door for a while as she and the other women, and two men, jumped and pranced about to the music. No pole dancing here, although Lydia did look fine in a red, skin-hugging garment, similar to the black one he had taken great joy in removing yesterday.

He decided to leave Lydia to her dancing and walk outside some more. This time he walked toward the town center, where the Hotel del Coronado could be seen. Torolf and Hilda had taken him for dinner there last month, and even they had to admit it resembled a white fairy-tale castle with its red-tiled roof. He passed taverns where people ate and drank at outside tables, chatting merrily, many of them wearing what he had come to recognize as Navy uniforms.

Hilda had told him on that dining trip that there were more than seventy eateries in Coronado.

He had countered with, "Such excess! Just like you having twenty pairs of shoes. Torolf needs to rein you in, wench."

To which Hilda had raised her middle finger at him. It had not been a compliment, if Torolf's laughter had been any indication.

Along the way, several women gave him appraising glances, and he sensed they would welcome his advances. Curiously, he had no desire in that direction. In truth, Lydia more than satisfied all those needs. Which could be dangerous, to be so reliant on one woman, but that was something he would worry over later.

There were glass-fronted clothes marts he passed, where bright clothing was displayed. Still other marts sold nothing but *sherts*, emblazoned with Coronado or Navy SEAL words. And there was the bank where Torolf had taken him to open an account, after selling several of the gold and silver coins he had carried with him. He still wore his gold armbands, which were portable wealth if he ever needed it, according to Torolf. A church, a school, food stalls, a toy mart. Who knew there were marts that sold naught but playthings for children? Noticing a set of miniature chain mail, gauntlets, and a wooden sword, he went in and purchased it for Lydia's son, who hopefully was *his* son.

"Is this enough?" he asked the young man who placed his purchases in a parchment bag.

"Dude!" the young man exclaimed. "That's three hundred dollars. The Sir Lancelot outfit costs only sixty."

His confusion over money got the same reaction when he went into a medicinal mart to purchase condoms . . . five boxes. Apparently, hundred-dollar bills, of which he had many, were of considerable value. Also, it must be unusual for a man to buy five dozen condoms at once. Sweet Valkyries! A man had to be prepared, did he not?

He shrugged at the white-jacketed man and pocketed the remaining money. What a strange country, to use parchment for money!

He was better prepared when he came upon a jewelry mart, where he handed the merchant two hundred-dollar parchments for a hunk of amber that had caught his eye in the window. It would serve no purpose, this polished stone the size of a fist, except that the specks of dirt in the center resembled a star, and for some reason he'd thought of Lydia. A gift, he supposed, which was new for him. Oh, Vikings loved gift-giving, but he could not recall ever giving Luta a gift. Mayhap that had been his problem . . . or one of them.

In another trader's stall, he purchased a Minnesota Vikings *shert*, which he thought might generate a smile from Lydia. He wore it now as he continued his walk and shook his head at his fancifulness in caring whether the wench was pleased at his appearance or not.

Just then, he noticed a place with a red-and-white striped pole in front. Inside, men were sitting in chairs, having their hair trimmed. Hesitating for only a second, he went in and waited his turn. His hair seemed to mark him as different in this country, especially this military base. If he was resolved to find his place here, cutting it off would be a first step. Besides, he was not a vain man. It was only hair.

"What'll it be, buddy?" the barber asked once he was in the chair.

Thorfinn glanced over to the next chair. "Like him," he ordered.

"A high and tight," the barber concluded.

A woman walked up to him and said, "Hi! My name is Sally Enders. Would you like a manicure and pedicure while you're having your hair cut?"

He must have looked unsure, because she quickly added, "Never had your nails done before?"

Slowly, he shook his head.

"C'mon, give it a try. Half price."

And so he underwent the amazing process of having his fingernails and toenails clipped, sanded, and buffed, with the cuticles "cleaned up," ending with wonderful hand and foot massages. It had actually been a nice experience, though he could not imagine his hands or feet staying this clean after doing a warrior's work. Nor could he imagine ever telling his fellow Vikings that he had pampered himself so.

While she worked on him, Sally talked. And talked. And talked. He soon learned without ever asking—only an occasional grunt was required—that she was betrothed to a seaman who was deployed to the Arab lands. Devon, her fiancé, was great. He made love like nobody's business. In fact, she told him in a whisper, "He gives good oral sex."

Frowning, he asked, which was probably a mistake, "Is that like a blow job?"

She laughed and punched him playfully in the arm. "You kidder! No, a woman gives a blow job."

"Oh," was all he said, recalling his phone conversation with Torolf and realizing yet another of the mistakes he had made.

She also told him about her two-year-old daughter from a previous marriage, her interfering mother-by-marriage, the high cost of gasoline for her German bug, a sale at Victoria's Secret, some stud named George Clooney, and how important it was to floss. When Thorfinn exited the shop, his head buzzing from all of Sally's blather including a tearful good-bye over his giving her a hundred-dollar bill in thanks, he held two beaded war braids in his palm. The air felt surprisingly good on the back of his neck, and his body felt lighter. The barber, who had listened to Sally's chatter without remark, except for rolling his eyes occasionally, had clipped his hair very short on the sides and left an inch or so on top, which he told Thorfinn to care for with the gel he sold him.

He liked his new haircut.

He wondered idly what Lydia would think.

Chapter 11

She saw dead people . . .

Lydia thought she was losing her mind.

Finn was gone, and she was in as much pain as she had been the first time she'd lost Dave. Which was insanity because Finn wasn't Dave. She knew he wasn't. So why was she running around like a chicken with its head cut off?

When she'd finished with her classes, she consulted with her manager over instructors to replace her for the rest of the day. In fact, she planned to take off the rest of the week. She had plenty of backup help, so a minivacation was no big deal to arrange.

When she went out to the lobby, she found Finn gone. That didn't surprise her. But then she'd gone outside to see if he'd walked down to the water or around the neighborhood. No one had seen him. And the first inkling of alarm set in.

Two hours had passed since the end of her classes. She stood in the parking lot leaning against her car. He was gone, she just knew he was. As quickly and amazingly as he had entered her life, Finn had disappeared. The grief staggered her with pain.

But then, through the haze of her tears, she saw something.

Ambling toward her as if he had all the time in the world was . . . Dave.

"Oh, my God!" she moaned, two hands pressed against her heart. "Oh, my God! Oh, my God! Oh, my God!" Her words were as much prayers of thanks as exclamations of shock.

His long legs were encased in jeans. He wore a Minnesota Vikings T-shirt. And his dark hair was cut in its usual high and tight. A small smile tugged at his lips as he got closer, causing the dimple to emerge.

Dimple!

Dave didn't have a dimple.

Blinking away the tears, she saw now that it was not Dave after all, but Finn with a haircut. The disappointment was palpable. The pain was excruciating.

Running up to him, she began to pound him on the chest. "How could you? How could you?"

"What in bloody hell . . . ?" He dropped his bags to the ground and picked her up bodily by the waist, feet dangling off the ground. Being held tightly against him didn't stop her; she pounded at his shoulders and head, sobbing the whole time. Somehow he managed to get her arms within his embrace so that now she was held tightly against him, feet still dangling. Against her ear, he was attempting to soothe her with shushing sounds and words of comfort, "*Shhhh*, sweetling. Do not fret. *Shhhh.*"

When her sobs finally subsided to sniffles, he set her feet back on the ground and practically dragged her to the car. Once inside, he turned to her, waiting for an explanation of what must seem bizarre behavior.

"I thought you were gone."

"I did not realize how much time had passed. And you were that angry over my being late?"

She shook her head, dabbing at her eyes with a tissue. "I was upset . . . worried . . . that you were gone, but when I saw you . . ." She stopped herself and glared at him. "You got a haircut," she accused him.

"And you are angry because you do not like my haircut?" He was incredulous, and he deserved to be.

"No! Why would you get a military haircut? Oh, never mind. It doesn't matter. It's just that at first . . . oh, hell, from a distance, you looked just like—"

He put a hand over her mouth, and he was the angry one now. "Do not dare say one more time that I looked like Saint Dave."

"Dave was no saint."

"What a wonder! The way you worship his memory I thought for a certainty that he was. And just so you know,

I am beyond sick of being compared to your dead husband."

His surly attitude annoyed her, but first she needed to continue her explanation. "At first, I thought you were Dave, but then when I saw that you weren't, that you had just gotten a haircut, I was devastated all over again."

"And that is supposed to make me feel better?" He appeared to be gritting his teeth.

"I'm sorry."

"Let us depart." He didn't even look at her.

As she pulled out of the parking lot and headed toward home, she said, "I need to stop at the grocery store on the way home."

He didn't respond.

"Be in a mood, then. See if I care."

"*Mood* is a mild description of the emotions battering my already beleaguered brain. I was almost happy this morning, happier than I have been in years. I had resolved to try to fit into this country, to make a new beginning for myself."

"Oh, I see. Your haircut was the first step toward fitting in," Lydia concluded, though why it had to be a high and tight was beyond her. It didn't have to be that short. But she'd better watch how much she criticized; so, all she said was, "And I cut you off at the knees for the effort. I really am sorry."

He waved a hand dismissively. "'Tis past time I concentrated on the most important thing. Finding Miklof. When will you be going to Minnesota to get your son?"

Lydia stiffened, but managed to curb her first instinct denying him access. "On the twenty-seventh. As I told you before, there's going to be a ceremony the next day honoring . . ." She stopped midsentence. Any mention of Dave could set him off again.

He was deep in thought before he added, "I will go with you."

"No! Oh, no, no, no! That would not be a good idea."

"You cannot keep me away from the child forever."

"I know that, but I need time."

"Time will alter nothing. Either your son is Miklof or he is not."

"And what if he's not? What will you do then?"

"I will do as I have always done. Nay, that is not true. I had already decided back in Baghdad to give up my search. If your Mike is not Miklof, I will give up my search and get on with my life, such as it will be."

She wanted to ask where she would be in his life, in that case, but feared what he would say in his present mood. "And if you decide they're the same, then what?"

"I will not be separated from Miklof again. Beyond that, I am not sure."

"Can't you wait 'til I bring Mike back here?"

He shook his head. "I have waited five years. That is enough."

She pulled into the parking lot of Albertsons, shut off the ignition, and looked at him. Maybe she could turn this rotten-egg day into a yummy quiche. "I like your haircut."

"*Pfff!* Too little, too late, m'lady."

She hoped not.

A land of plenty, and plenty, and plenty . . .

Thorfinn had been in a food mart before with Hilda when Torolf had been off doing SEAL work, but she had rushed him through the aisles, telling him he "dawdled" too much. Hah! The more she had nagged, the more he had dawdled, but in the process of attempting to annoy the wench he had had no opportunity to really study the place.

Now he was taking his time, and it was a paradise. For this alone he could stay in the future.

In the produce department, he touched with reverence the various fruits, some of which he had never heard of before, smelled their delicious scents, and marveled at the colors. Apples, lemons, limes, oranges, bananas, peaches, pears, plums, apricots, watermelons, cantaloupes, blueberries, blackberries, raspberries. He put some of each in the cart, even though Lydia kept chastising him that it was too much. Finally, he went back to the entrance, got his own cart, and told her, "Begone!"

Lydia did as he ordered but kept coming back to check on him, rolling her eyes. He was still angry with her for her continual Dave-comparisons. So, mostly, he ignored her.

He was not ignored, though. Not by Lydia, and not by the women who eyed him, or even came up, offering to help. He knew what they were really offering and rebuffed them by saying, "I thank you for your offer, but my woman gives me all the *help* I need."

Lydia overheard and hissed at him, "I am not your woman."

"How do you know I was talking about you?"

"Oh," she said, going off again, red-faced this time.

She followed him for awhile, and he noted dozens of different kinds of bread. Loaves. Sliced. Rolls of various shapes. White bread, rye, pumpernickel—*whatever that was!* Bread with raisins, dates, nuts, seeds, and bananas— a fruit new to him, for a certainty, and didn't it have a suggestive shape! "In my land, women wake before dawn to begin making the unleavened manchet bread for the day. First, they grind the wheat with a mortar and pestle, mix the dough, then bake the circles of bread, leaving a hole in the center so the loaves can be stored on a short pole in the scullery, rather like pizza. A daily, arduous process. But here, for the love of Frigg, women have only to walk in and purchase their supply. What an easy life women have!"

"Hah! Next, you'll be talking about how you had to walk five miles in the snow to get to school, after chopping wood and milking the cows."

Thorfinn's head jerked to the side. He had not realized he'd spoken aloud, but, really, this woman could be irksome, except for those times when she was . . . well, not irksome. Usually, that was when nakedness was involved. Or kissing. He had developed a new appreciation for kissing. Who knew there were so many kinds? But, really, he was a man of great pride, and she had no cause to make mock of his ignorance. "Nay, I am practically a high jarl, and that is servants' work. As for school, we have none. The monk scholar came to tutor me and my brothers, whilst my sisters learned a woman's role in running a large household."

Her jaw dropped, as it often did when he talked of his land. He got some small satisfaction in that. "Wo-woman's *role*?" she sputtered.

"Yea, that is what I said, and do not think to call me a male pig, either."

"*Male pig*?"

"Must you repeat everything I say?"

"Male pig? I don't understand. Do you mean a boar?"

"Nay, I do not mean boar. I mean what I say. *Male pig*. That is what Madrene and Hilda call me betimes . . . well, truth to tell, all the time."

She thought a moment, then laughed. "You mean *male chauvinist pig*?"

"Ah, her thick head thins," he mused into the air above his head.

She made a low growling sound.

Tossing two loaves in his cart, rye and date nut, he left her behind and went to the meat section, which was next to the milk and egg section. Dozens of cuts of beef, pork, and chicken, not to mention fish of numerous species, were displayed in windowed cases, or wrapped in a clear film so they could be seen. And none of it was rancid. He pondered this bounty of offerings. Then, puzzled, he went through the door behind the display cases.

"Hey! You can't come back here," said a burly man in a blood-spattered white apron.

"I just wanted to compliment your hunters who brought in all this meat. And, holy Thor, where are the cows that provide the milk? Or the laying chickens?"

The man's jaw dropped with each of his questions.

"Dost have any boar flanks? I have not had a good boar steak for ages, since Uggi Big-Arms brought down that massive broken-tusked boar in the Rus lands."

Before the gaping man could reply, Lydia shot through the doorway, grabbed him by the arm, and yanked him back into the store, saying over his shoulder, "Sorry. My friend is a little confused."

More like a lot confused. He shrugged off her hand-hold. "You do not need to apologize for me."

"If you have any questions, ask me."

When are we going to have sex again? "I am not speaking to you." A foolish statement to make when he had just spoken to her, but he could not care.

"Well, then, I guess you're not interested in the surprise I was going to buy for you." Her eyes twinkled with devilment.

Does it involve sex? He arched his brows in question. No words.

She held out a small bottle.

Reading the label, he said slowly, "Ting-ling Mass-age Oil." *Yes!*

"That's okay. I can take it back."

He grabbed it from her hands and tossed it in his own cart. Then he smiled at her, no longer angry . . . leastways, as long as she did not mention her dead husband again.

She pushed her cart up beside his, leaned up, and kissed him on the cheek. "Does that mean we get to have make-up sex?"

"As long as it involves tingling."

They were dancing fools . . .

Lydia was back at work while Finn went off to practice driving with Geek, after which he would take his California driver's exam. Oddly, she felt bereft without her constant companion. She was missing a man she had only known for a few days.

"Okay, ladies, this is our first day of pole dancing. Are you ready?"

"Yes!" the dozen women in the room yelled, including Kirstin and Alison Magnusson and Madrene MacLean.

If she'd bought more portable poles, Lydia could have filled the class with twenty more women. As it was, she had two more classes today, all filled to capacity. In fact, she'd been invited to demonstrate her program at a half-dozen private parties for women, even Tupperware ones, for goodness' sake, following a feature article about her in a local weekly newspaper. Women expected to come out of these classes as sultry vixens, even the shy ones.

"I know most of you are here because of the naughty factor," she teased.

They all laughed, even while they warmed up with

knee extensions and waist bends, following her lead. None of them disagreed.

"If you let loose, you can have fun with your sexual partner or just gain a little self-confidence about your body. The main reason I'm offering the pole-dancing workout, though, is to help you tone your bodies."

She did a brief demonstration for the class first, dancing to "Private Dancer," which she flicked on her CD player. As she danced and even pretended to make love with the pole, she narrated the various moves: the swing walk, leg hook, pole bend and slide, corkscrew, firefly, climb and spin, body inversion, pivot, and freeform arch. In the end, she showed them the "helicopter," warning them that this was an advanced move that required upside-down spinning in a crunch position with legs and toes forming a vee with the pole.

"Wow!" Kirstin Magnusson said. "I think I'm way out of my league here."

"You? I can scarce lift my leg that high, let alone do it in midair," Madrene added.

"Now, now, I told you that was an advanced move for much later. Today, we're going to learn the basic fireman, where you grip the pole, swing up as high as you can go, then spin downward like a . . . fireman. Watch carefully and save the vamping for later, please."

By the end of the hour, they were able to perform the move, clumsily on some parts and with curses from others. But they were all feeling good about the class as they walked out laughing and talking.

"Kirstin," Lydia said, "do you have a minute? My next class doesn't start for an hour."

Kirstin stopped, telling her family members to go ahead, that she would catch up. After they left, Kirstin arched her brows at her.

"I wanted to ask you about . . . someone," Lydia started hesitantly.

"I knew it! I knew there was something different about you."

Kirstin slid down to the floor and grabbed for a towel to dab at the perspiration on her face and neck, the whole time smiling.

"Different how?"

"Well, my guess would be that you are gettin' some, honey. Either that or you're pregnant. You glow, girl."

"No, I'm not pregnant, but I do want to ask you about your cousin Finn."

Kirstin's eyes went wide, and her jaw dropped for a moment. "You've been getting it on with Finn, the world's biggest male chauvinist?"

An apt description. "The very one." She sank down next to Kirstin.

"The family has been worried about him since he disappeared several days ago."

"Four days."

"Oh, my God! He's been with you."

She nodded.

"So what's the problem?"

"Well, he tells the most outlandish story."

"Uh-oh!"

The fine hairs stood out on the back of Lydia's neck. "I know you'll think this is crazy, but he claims to have time-traveled from the eleventh century. Ha, ha, ha."

Kirstin was not laughing in return.

The fine hairs were practically doing the hula now. "What?"

"It's true."

The blood drained from Lydia's head. If she hadn't been already sitting, she might just have fainted. "It can't be true."

"I come from a rather strange family."

I already know that. "There is strange, and then there is *strange.*"

"Really strange, honey." Kirstin's eyes darted to someplace over Lydia's right shoulder, then she made a beckoning motion with her fingertips before calling out, "Come join us. You need to hear this, too."

Madrene and Alison, now in street clothes, headed over and quickly sank down to the rug and sat cross-legged in front of them.

"Lydia is asking me about the time travelling," Kirstin said, raising her eyebrows meaningfully at the other ladies and shocking the spit out of Lydia.

How could her friend betray a confidence like that? "Kirstin!"

She patted Lydia's hand. "It's okay."

"How do you know about . . . it?" Alison asked, her face turning almost as red as her hair.

"Thorfinn," Kirstin answered in a *ta-da* fashion before

Lydia could speak. "He and our pole-dancer queen have a thing going on."

"Kirstin!" she chastised again.

"Surely, you are too intelligent to fall for that arrogant toad," Madrene remarked. "The insufferable man told Ian that if he ever wants to get rid of me, my breasts are so big they could float a longship."

"Hilda is the one who really has a personality conflict with him," Kirstin said. "He keeps telling Torolf how shrewish she is and that it's his job as a Viking man to tame her."

"I would like to see him try," Madrene said with a huff. "Oh, my gods and goddesses, you are the love slave."

"What?" Kirstin and Alison squealed.

"Torolf told me that Thorfinn was living with his love slave. Bloody hell! I just remembered something. Thorfinn said some woman made him her love slave first."

Lydia could feel her face heat with mortification. "It was just a joke," she lied.

No one believed her.

In fact, Kirstin gave her a high five. "Way to go, sister!"

"He *is* good looking," Alison conceded. "There are a lot of women who wouldn't mind him putting his boots under their beds."

They all turned to Lydia then.

"Has he?" Alison asked.

Oh, yeah! Like a time or two . . . or twenty. She didn't have to answer; her face said it all.

Alison smacked herself upside the head. "Well, of course he has, if they were playing love slave," she mused aloud.

"Maybe it's not too late." This from Madrene, who turned to her. "You haven't fallen in love with the lout, have you?"

"I don't know. Maybe. You people are being too hard on him, though. Yeah, he's a bit overbearing, but he's not all bad. He has a vulnerable side, too."

Four sets of eyebrows shot up with disbelief.

"He thinks my son Mike is his son Miklof, and no one can deny he misses his lost baby tremendously."

"That is true. That is true." Madrene had a soft heart, despite her usually shrewish nature.

"Back to the original issue . . . the reason Kirstin called you over. I was telling her about Finn's outrageous idea about time-traveling."

There was an ominous silence.

Then Madrene put a hand on her knee. "'Tis true. I come from that time period, too, as do Hilda and Kirstin."

Lydia turned to stare at her friend.

Kirstin just shrugged. "I was only fourteen when my family came here."

"Ragnor didn't come here 'til after Madrene, just a few years ago," Alison added.

"And you believe in time travel, Alison?"

She fully expected Alison, who was a physician, to scoff at the idea. Instead, she shrugged and said, "There's no other explanation."

The ladies spent the next fifteen minutes explaining things that really could not be explained. In the end, Kirstin summed it up. "If you can't accept the science of it—and who can?—then call it a miracle."

A miracle. Lydia could believe in that. Especially if Finn's appearance was somehow tied to Dave.

Madrene and Alison left with promises to get together that weekend for some gathering at Blue Dragon Vineyard, where things would be more clear. Kirstin stood next to Lydia as her next class began to shuffle in.

"There's one thing I don't understand, Lydia," Kirstin said, picking up her towel and carryall. "I thought you vowed never to be involved with a military man again."

Lydia's brow furrowed. "I did, and nothing's changed."

"But Thorfinn . . ." She let her words trail off. "You don't know, do you?"

"Know what?"

"Thorfinn was a famous warrior in our time, and he plans to try out for SEALs. If that's not military, nothing is."

As Kirstin elaborated, a film was being torn off Lydia's eyes, and she was seeing clearly for the first time in days.

Lydia felt like such a fool.

Chapter 12

Oooh, boy, was he in trouble! . . .

Thorfinn could not recall the last time he had had such a wonderful day.

Everything had gone well, starting with Lydia waking him up just past dawn by licking the backs of his knees. More licking went on after that, by both of them.

"Amazing what a good lick can do for a man's outlook on a new day!" he'd told Lydia once he had been sated and able to catch his breath.

"A woman's, too," she'd agreed. *The saucy wench!*

"Now get up and prepare me a meal. I must needs break my fast, lest I lose my stamina," he'd teased, and he hardly ever teased.

"Uh, you ever heard of women's lib, Finn? How about you prepare me a meal?"

And he had. For the first time ever, he'd made a meal for himself and his lady. And, surprise!—he enjoyed doing so more than he ever could have imagined.

Then Geek had taken him out to some country road to practice driving his car. And Geek hadn't even yelled at him, or hidden his head in his hands, like Torolf was wont to do. Then they'd gone to the driver testing center, where a policing man checked his driving abilities. And he'd passed, praise the gods! Although the officer was not amused about his seeming jest concerning horseless carriages. Now he could drive whenever he wanted, and mayhap even buy his own vehicle.

He was whistling as he entered the number on the security pad on Lydia's door. That was when he was hit in the chest with one of her cloth running shoes.

"Ooomph," he said, then ducked as the matching shoe hit the closed door just over his head. "Lydia! What is amiss?" When he'd left this morning, she kissed him farewell, but now it did not appear there would be any kisses on his horizon anytime soon.

"You jerk! You obnoxious arrogant lying worm!" She had an orange from the fruit bowl in hand now. When she lobbed it at him, he caught it in his right hand. The apple landed in his left hand. With no hands remaining, he rushed forward, dropping the fruit, and tackled her to the floor. "Desist! Dost hear me? Leave off with this nonsense."

"You liar! You liar! You liar!" she was screeching as he knelt, straddling her hips, both of her hands held to the floor above her head. Even as she berated him, tears streamed down her face, and, if her red eyes were any indication, she had been doing much weeping afore his return.

"Lydia! What happened? Oh, good gods, it is not Miklof, is it?"

That caught her attention. "No, it is not Mike. It's you."

"But I am safe."

"Not for long." She attempted to raise her knees and no doubt hit him in some vulnerable spot.

He tightened his grip on her hips with his knees and half-sat on her thighs.

"You bastard! You horse's ass! You son of a bitch! You slimy loser!" On and on she hurled expletives at him, some very creative, some downright insulting. Finally, she wound down with a hiccough, then whispered, "Damn you."

"I am going to release you now, Lydia, so you can explain what this is about. If you start railing at me again, I give you fair warning: you will be across my knees, your bare, blistered arse facing northward."

"You wouldn't dare."

"Dost dare to dare a Viking?"

"Let me up. I'm calm now."

He arched his eyebrows, unconvinced. Still, he rose in one fluid motion, then took her hand, raising her to her feet. Immediately, she pulled her hand, away, as if his touch were repugnant. Then she went to the kitchen and grabbed some paper handkerchiefs, dabbing at her eyes and blowing her nose.

He watched her the whole time, hands folded over his chest, waiting.

"You were a soldier," she accused him. "And you plan on joining the teams."

Whew! I thought it was something grave and life-threatening. "That is so."

"'That is so,'" she mimicked in an offensive, mock-masculine tone. "You lied to me, you rat."

He shook his head. "I did not lie. I never lie."

"Are you trying to say that you told me you planned to join the military . . . the SEALs? Oops, my ears must have been plugged that day."

He felt his face heat. "At first, I did not tell you, deliberately, because I am new in this country, and I was warned not to give out too much information about myself. Especially not about the time travel or SEALs. Later, after I overheard your prayers, mentioning how you could not be involved with another military man, I decided not to volunteer the information, but I did not realize it mattered this much to you." *Even I find that hard to believe.*

"A lie of omission."

"That does not signify." He gritted his teeth. "I value honesty above all else. If you had asked, specifically, I would have told you."

"Oh, that's just great. Try to lay the blame on me."

"Why must there be blame in this? Is there shame in being a warrior?"

"No, of course not. Dave was military to the bone."

He threw his hands out in disgust. "Can we have a single conversation that does not involve your dead husband?"

Her shoulders slumped, and she sank down into one of the fabric chairs in her solar. "You have to understand, every time Dave went on a mission, and there were dozens and dozens of them, I died a little. The roller-coaster ride of fear, elation, fear, elation, over and over, took its toll. And it took a toll on Dave, too. Toward the end, I could see that all the killing . . . and, yes, I know it was a noble cause . . . was eating away at his soul."

He nodded, understanding her emotions. Still . . . the willful woman gainsaid him at every turn. One moment nigh attacking him with lust and the next nigh attacking him with fruit.

"I can't love another man in the military. I just can't."

He was about to ask her when love became an issue with them, but bit his tongue. In truth, the prospect of her loving him held an odd appeal. As for him loving her . . . any woman, for that matter . . . that prospect was enough to curdle his blood. "What would you have me do?"

"I don't know. You said you ran an estate or something. Can't you do that here?"

Now she wants to dictate my life. He inhaled deeply and exhaled. "I am a warrior, Lydia. A far-famed one, truth to tell. It is who I am, and I do not apologize for ridding the world of tyrants and villains. Even if I had other choices, it is what I want to do."

"Even if it means the end of us?"

He bristled. "Is that an ultimatum?"

"It's the way it has to be." She was weeping again.

Well, he would not be swayed by tears. This issue was too important. He stared her down, expecting her to fold, to admit she had been hasty in her words. To have make-up sex, that wonderful modern invention, which was not all that modern, except they did not give it a name in his day.

She did not budge.

Now *he* was angry. Thorfinn's pride was great. He could not allow a woman to rule his life.

"So be it," he snarled, heading toward the door, where he stopped momentarily, adding, "But heed me well, Lydia, we are not through, not by a Viking longshot. I will see my son. Either I go to Minnesota with you, or I go myself. In the meantime, fare thee well. I have enjoyed swiving you."

And he left.

Lydia stared at the closed door in shock.

What had she expected? That he would apologize and promise to go work at Wal-Mart, or do construction work, or anything other than fighting? To give her flowery declarations of love, instead of crude mentions of sex? Was she a fool to have drawn a line in the sand?

Despite her second-guessings, she did not regret her anger at Finn for not telling her of his military aspirations. Nor could she conceive of bending on this issue, ever.

But, oh, his leaving felt like losing her beloved all over again. How would she survive?

When vengeance turns bloody . . .

Jamal watched the Hartley farm—Mill Pond Farm, it was called—through binoculars from his perch on a nearby hillside.

The parents-by-marriage of the Navy SEAL came and went, along with Denton's little boy. A happy, healthy boy about the same age his own Baasim would be today, Jamal realized with an aching heart.

Intelligence ran in Jamal's family; his brother was not the only one with an advanced IQ and education. In fact, Jamal had graduated from Oxford and had been a researcher at Baghdad University at the time of the explosion.

He had not worked since then, relying only on meager funds he had saved or been given by sympathetic friends. His mission consumed him. But this celebration to honor his wife and son's murderer would finally put his savage anger to rest. Maybe he could get his old job back. Maybe he could even find another woman to marry and give him other children. He was still a young man.

Jamal was patient. He waited, unmoving for a long time, 'til dusk finally rose from the horizon. Only then did he lift his rifle to his shoulder and aim. *Bang, bang, bang, bang, bang.* One cow for each year of his suffering.

It was a small price for those below to pay. But it was just a forewarning.

More was to come. And soon.

The pig meets the shrew . . .

Thorfinn was so consumed with fury that he walked for two hours afore he realized he was in the neighborhood of Madrene and Ian MacLean, who also lived on the beach in San Diego. His ill humor would do best without company, but he needed someone to drive him back to Torolf's apartment in Coronado.

"Greetings!" he grumbled to Madrene when she answered his knock on the door.

"Thorfinn!" a surprised Madrene greeted him.

He pushed her aside and stomped into her house.

"Well, look what the cat drug in. Not that our sweet Samantha would put her teeth to your tough skin. What are you doing here?" This was not an unusual "welcome" from Madrene, who had shrewishness down to an art form. Everyone said so.

Just for emphasis, the fat cat in question sidled up to him, hissed, then waddled away. Off to deposit a large amount of hair on the furniture, no doubt, or piss on the carpet.

Madrene just grinned at him and led the way into the solar. Leastways, he thought she meant for him to follow.

She wore very short braies that exposed her long legs and a tight *shert* that outlined her voluptuous breasts. In truth, her bosom was the first thing people, especially men, noticed about Madrene. The second was her waspish nature, which almost, but not quite, wiped out the allure of her udders.

"Welcome to you, too, cousin," he drawled, hoping to embarrass her over her rudeness. Every good Viking knew that hospitality was important . . . every good Viking, except Madrene, apparently.

"Hello to you, my dearling cousin."

"Your sarcasm is not appealing, Madrene."

"Dost think I care, you loathsome lout? How did you get here?"

"I want you to drive me to Torolf's keep. I walked from the home of Lydia Denton. Dost know her?"

She nodded, a look of shock on her face, whether at the fact he knew Lydia or that he had walked was unclear.

"That's more than five miles," said her husband, Ian, a Navy SEAL commander, walking toward him and into the solar, where he and Madrene stood. Ian had come through an open doorway in the hallway, which must lead to the lower level, where music could be heard. "What're you doing with Lydia Denton?"

"She's his love slave," Madrene answered for him with a smirk.

Ian's head jerked toward his wife. So did Thorfinn's.

She added, "But he was *her* love slave first." Then more smirking.

"It appears my love slave has a flapping tongue," Thorfinn observed. He sank down onto a low sofa and clicked on the television set. It seemed everyone in America had one of these picture boxes, just as Torolf did. Immediately, music blared forth, and young people were dancing or flailing their arms and legs about.

"Shhhh!" Madrene shushed him, running over and turning the television off. "My children are napping."

"Has anyone ever told you that you are a harridan?"

"Has anyone ever told you that you are lackwitted?" she shot back.

Only then did he notice that Ian was *shert*less and barefooted, just now buttoning his *den-ham* braies. And

Madrene, well, there were whisker burns on her cheek and neck, and her nipples . . . surely, they were not always so distended. In that moment he realized he had interrupted them in bedsport.

He waved a hand dismissively at them both. "Resume your bedplay. I will wait here 'til you are finished."

Ian laughed. "You think we're going to engage in sex while you sit down here twiddling your thumbs?"

"And why not? 'Tis not as if I will be standing over you, watching. Lest you make a lot of noise, I might not be imagining exactly what you are doing." He flashed Madrene a deliberately lascivious glance. "*Are* you noisesome in the bed furs, Madrene?"

"Male chauvinist pig!"

"Irksome witch!"

"Now wait a minute." Ian glowered at him. "There's no need to pick on my wife."

Thorfinn exhaled with a *whoosh* and leaned back, hands folded behind his head. "Just go and finish what you started. Later, by your will, I would appreciate a ride back to Torolf's. I got my driving license today, but—"

"Thorfinn on the road? Spare us, oh, Lord!" Madrene interjected.

He glared at her and continued, "But I have not yet purchased a jape."

"A jape?" Ian asked.

"He means a *Jeep*," Madrene translated for him.

"That is what I said. I wish to buy a jape like Torolf's, but only if I pass my SEAL test, and only if I stay in this country." He realized his slip instantly. He had been warned not to discuss the time travel with just anyone.

Ian shook his head and looked to his wife. "Another one?"

She nodded.

It was Ian then who said, "Spare us, oh, Lord!"

"First of all, neither Torolf nor Hilda are at home," Madrene told him. "Torolf is still on a mission, and Hilda decided to delay her return from her women's shelter in the north. No doubt to avoid your delightful company."

Thorfinn shrugged, deciding his best path was to ignore Madrene's vocal jabs. "I can stay there myself. I would not be good company anyway—"

"Like you ever are!" Madrene remarked.

"Can you not control your wife, Ian? Truly, a biddable wife is a blessing."

"Like your wife was biddable? Is that why she left you?"

"Madrene!" Ian rebuked her.

He could tell Madrene regretted her words, but stubborn wench that she was, she just lifted her chin. Her eyes softened, though, and she said, "Did you and Lydia have a fight?"

"Not precisely. Apparently, someone"—he gave her a pointed look—"told her that I had been a warrior and would be joining the military here. She refuses to be with another military man, after losing her husband."

"Oh, Thorfinn, I *am* sorry." She sat down next to him and put a comforting hand on his knee.

The idea of Madrene soothing him was so appalling that he moved to the other side of the sofa, putting distance betwixt them.

"Do you love her?"

"Whaaat?"

"Well, you would not be upset if you were not smitten."

"We had sex without stop like lustsome rabbits, that is all," he told her, though he did not believe that any more than she did. *I am bloody hell smitten, all right. Besotted. Besmitten. Bewitched. I must be barmy.*

Ian grinned. "Like rabbits, huh?"

Madrene smacked his arm. "I hesitate to suggest this . . . I must be losing my mind, but why not come to Blue Dragon with me?" Madrene offered. "I'm going tomorrow, and Ian will be coming on the weekend. They're having a harvest festival. It would take your mind off your broken heart."

Thorfinn considered her offer, which was generous considering their grating reaction to each other, not that he was suffering a broken heart, even if he did feel a constriction in his chest at the prospect of not seeing Lydia again. *Good gods, Big-Mouth Madrene will be telling everyone of my broken heart, as if I were a youthling in the first blush of sex.* "It is kind of you, Madrene, but I really must needs practice those half-brained exercises in order to take my PST test next week." *See, I can be polite, even with a shrew.*

"If you want, you could take the test on Friday and go up with me on Saturday," Ian suggested. "They're giving make-up tests for those recruits who couldn't make it last week."

Madrene gave a visible sigh of relief, no doubt at the prospect of being spared his company.

I am relieved, too. Hours confined in a car with her and three bratlings would be torture.

"That is, if you think you're ready," Ian added.

"I am as ready as I will ever be." *And if it means forgoing Madrene's company, I will for damn sure be ready.*

"You can stay here tonight and go in with Ian in the morning. Mayhap he will let you practice drills with his SEALs," Madrene said, getting up. "Dinner will be ready in about an hour."

"In the meantime, go finish what you started, you two," he said, lying down on the sofa, putting a small pillow under his head. He took great pleasure in Madrene's eyes staring daggers at his shoes. "Really. I understand."

"Do you?" Ian asked with a laugh. "Actually, Madrene was demonstrating one of the dance lessons that Lydia gave this week at her studio." He waggled his eyebrows at him. "Pole dancing."

"Ah," Thorfinn said. "A great invention, that, especially when . . ." He paused. *Should I?*

"Especially when . . . ?" Ian prompted.

Why not? "Man to man, Ian, I must tell you, it is best viewed when the dancer is, um, nude."

Madrene gasped and would no doubt like to make another remark to him about his crudity. *Or smack the smirk off my face.*

Ian, on the other hand, gave him a considering look. "You are a man after my own heart." Then he turned to his wife. And winked.

Later Thorfinn walked down to the basement with Ian, who wanted to show him his weight-lifting corner.

"Thor's teeth! What is this?" he asked on viewing the dozens of candles arranged around the darkened room with scarves floating from one of the support poles.

"Aromatherapy."

"Are the flameless lights broken? The electricity, I mean."

"Nope. This is for atmosphere."

"It smells like a bloody flower garden."

"It's supposed to be romantic."

Thorfinn gazed at Ian in wonder. He was a supposedly intelligent man. "Surely, all Madrene would have to do is take her clothes off to get your sap running. Bloody hell, a certain look would do it, I would think."

"Ah, but the idea is to have her be along for the ride."

"I do not understand."

Ian laughed at him. "You don't need to understand. It's fun, dammit."

"Fun and sex. Ah." Thorfinn did understand then.

He wondered if he would ever have the chance to have this kind of fun again . . . with Lydia.

Oh, my stars! . . .

Lydia was miserable.

For the first few hours she was righteous in her indignation. In fact, she went down to the basement storage room and pulled out some boxes she hadn't opened for four and a half years.

The first box contained all the things she was saving for Mike when he was older. The flag that had adorned Dave's casket. His uniform and Budweiser, the nickname given to the SEAL trident pin. The Purple Heart and framed proclamation. A baseball mitt, tennis racket, hockey stick, and high school football cleats. Yearbooks. Sports trophies. She'd even saved his duffel bag containing a toiletry kit, complete with toothpaste and toothbrush, razor and shaving foam, deodorant, comb, aspirin, and Gold Bond powder for chafing in the desert. Finally, there was a red-ribbon-tied bundle of letters . . . letters they had written to each other over a ten-year period, from way back when she'd still been in high school. She held them to her chest, then put them back, knowing she wasn't strong enough to read them yet. Maybe she never would be.

Next she pulled out the box of star memorabilia. Some people collected pig trinkets or geese, cows, angels, or snowmen; she had a fascination with stars. In fact, the box contained several strings of star lights for a Christmas tree, along with dozens of kinds of star ornaments she'd gathered over the years, mementoes from trips, coming-home presents. Star picture frames, a star lamp base, star wind chimes and sun catchers. She could account for the provenance of every one of them, and most were connected to Dave. There was even a star pendant and dangly silver star earrings.

Her pain was palpable as she put the boxes back in the closet. How could she possibly sustain this kind of grief again? How could she love another military man? The answer was that she couldn't.

But then she went back upstairs and wondered how she could face the loneliness. Maybe she had been too harsh with Finn. After all, it wasn't his fault he was military. Maybe she could have an affair?

But, no, she was not the affair type. Love would have to be involved.

Is it already?

Oh, my God! Is it already too late?

Do I love him?

The question was answered later that night when she was cleaning the bedroom, trying to keep herself busy so that she would not have to think. And mourn.

Under the bed, she found several bags which Finn must have stuffed there. She assumed they were his purchases from the day he'd disappeared for several hours in Coronado, the day he'd gotten the infamous haircut.

In one bag there were five boxes of condoms . . . sixty total. She shook her head at his overconfidence.

The next bag held a miniature Sir Lancelot costume. She smiled, knowing that Finn must have bought it for Mike, even if Mike wasn't his son. Which he wasn't, of course.

Finally, she opened the last bag from a Coronado jewelry store. A gift for her?

She gasped when she saw the contents. It was a piece of amber, and in the center was a tiny star. She sobbed openly before setting it on the bedside table.

It had to be a sign.

Chapter 13

Running with the wolves . . . I mean, seals . . .

By late Friday morning, Lydia was frantic.

She had called Torolf's place repeatedly 'til she'd had to admit that Finn had not gone back there. She'd called Kirstin to see if she knew where Finn was. She didn't. Kirstin called Hilda up at Hog Heaven, and even Hilda didn't have a clue, her response having been, "We should be so lucky that the lackwit is lost!"

"He'll show up somewhere, honey," Kirstin had assured her.

But Lydia wanted to talk to him now, and she feared the longer they were apart, the harder it would be to heal the rift. If indeed he wanted to get back together with her. Not that they'd had any kind of understanding before.

Really, she just needed to talk with him.

And maybe kiss him silly.

Then she got some more bad news.

Her cordless phone rang about noon.

"Finn? Is that you? Thank God!"

"Uh, honey. It's me. Your dad."

"Oh." Her disappointment felt like a lead weight on her shoulders. Then her daughter-antenna went up. Her dad hardly ever called her. It was always her mother who called, occasionally passing the phone to her dad for a quick hello. "What is it, Dad? What's wrong? Is it Mike?"

"Now, honey, it's nothing like that. I just wanted you to know, before you hear it somewhere else. We had a little trouble here last night. A few cows were killed."

"Killed?"

"Shot through the head."

"Who would do a thing like that?"

"Maybe it was just a hunter with a vision problem."

She laughed. "You don't really think that, do you?"

"Nope. Not when it was five cows."

"*Five?* What's going on, Dad?"

"It might be one of those animal-rights cuckoo birds, or some teenager wantin' to show off his shootin'."

"Maybe I should come get Mike."

"Now, there's no need to do that. The police have been here, and we're keeping close tabs on the little one. Plus, he'll be going over to the Dentons' soon to stay there for a week."

"If you're sure."

"I am. If I think he needs to go home, I won't hesitate, little girl."

Little girl? Thirty years old, and he still calls me little girl. "Okay, I'll see you next week. Love you."

"Love you, too, honey."

No sooner did she click off than the phone rang again. She knew enough this time not to assume it was Finn. And it wasn't. It was Kirstin. Still, she was disappointed.

"Lydia, I know where Finn is. He's been staying with Ian and Madrene, and he's over at the base this morning taking his PST exam."

"So soon? I thought that wasn't coming up for another week or two."

"Apparently, Ian got him in sooner. Finn was anxious to take the test, and . . ." She seemed to stop herself.

"And what?"

". . . get out of here. I'm sorry, Lydia."

So that was that. He was trying for the teams, definitely. And what exactly did "get out of here" mean?

Her heavy heart gained a few more pounds.

"Want to go over and watch?" Visitors often went to Coronado just to see the SEAL trainees in action. The spectators couldn't get too close, but then they didn't need to. Or necessarily want to. Unless they were her.

Two hours later, with a little pull from Kirstin's brother-in-law, Commander MacLean, they were in. Lydia was laughing at something Geek said to her out in the hall of the Special Forces Center. Lydia had her nose pressed to the window in the commander's office, which overlooked the grinder where SEALs and potential SEALs were put through their paces.

Lydia was surprised at her lack of distress on viewing this familiar place again . . . the compound itself, with the blacktopped grinder and the O-Course, the obstacle course best known to SEALs as the Oh-my-God course. Dave used to say it looked like an adult playground, one designed by the Marquis de Sade, maybe. And he was right.

The rope-climbing wall known as the Cargo Net. The Spider Wall. The Slide for Life. Tire Sequence. Parallel bars. The Dirty Name . . . a log-climbing torture device. The Weaver. The Tower. And, of course, the hated IBSs, or inflatable boats, small, that had to be carried everywhere. All to provide rotations during BUD/S training that would build upper-body strength, stamina, and the will to survive. And, actually, they weren't just for trainees. SEALs themselves had to continually maintain their physical condition by working out there alongside the swabbies. In fact, there were a half dozen SEALs there now.

"Do you see Finn?" Kirstin asked, coming into the room.

"Oh, he's not there," Geek said, following after her. Geek had been one of the youngest men to ever join the SEALs, in addition to being the smartest. With his baby face, he'd always given the impression of being such an innocent, but somehow over the years, without anyone noticing, he'd turned into quite a hunk. He still had a kidlike expression on his face, but it was belied by the twinkle in his dancing eyes.

"Where is he?" she asked.

"Oh, Ian and some of the guys gave him a good practice workout this morning, but the PST test didn't start 'til thirteen-hundred," Geek told them. "Finn did the five-hundred-yard swim in ten minutes, thirty seconds . . . one minute under the minimum, and he was okay on the forty-two push-ups and fifty sit-ups in two minutes, each, but he struggled with the six pull-ups that immediately followed. Right now, the gang is doing a one-and-a-half-mile run in boondockers." He checked his wristwatch. "They should be coming in any minute now."

At that moment a guy walked by, then came back with a double take. "Hey, y'all." It was Justin LeBlanc . . . Cage. Like Geek, he wore shorts, a T-shirt with the Navy SEAL emblem, and the heavy boondocker boots. Walking into the room, he slapped Geek on the back, almost knocking him over. "You were supposed to be spotting me, dipwad." Then he turned sweetly to Kirstin and said, "Darlin', you look hot, as usual."

Kirstin rolled her eyes at what everyone knew as the Cajun's usual pickup line.

Then he gave Lydia a big hug. "I haven't seen you in ages, sweetheart. You are a sight for sore eyes." Still holding her, he leaned back and pretended to give her a lascivious once-over. "Talk about!"

Cage had been a teammate and good friend to Dave. She hadn't seen him much the past few years, but suddenly, she wondered why she'd avoided him. "You're not looking bad yourself, hot stuff," she replied, hugging him in return.

"Whatcha all doin' here?" Cage asked. With an arm looped over Lydia's shoulders, he looked out the window to see what they were all looking at.

"We're waiting for new guys to come in from their run. The ones taking the PST," Geek explained.

"I heard there are only fifteen left," Cage reported. "They started with thirty."

"Is . . . is Finn . . . I mean, Thorfinn . . . still in?" Lydia asked.

Cage looked down at her with surprise. "Ah, so that's how it is, darlin'?" He squeezed her shoulder.

She thought about protesting, but just then the runners were approaching from the beach. Staggering would be a better description. Finn wasn't at the head of the line, but he wasn't at the tail end, either. He looked beaten down and pushed to his limits, but still standing—rather, running.

One by one the guys sank to their knees, panting with exhaustion. They were covered with sweat and sand. Probably the result of "sugar cookies," a SEAL brand of torture that involved running, taking a quick dip in the ocean, rolling in the sand, running, then repeating the process over and over. Two of the guys rushed to the side and threw up.

For some reason, Lydia felt inordinately proud of Finn. A strange country. A strange time, if he was to be believed. And still he'd managed to survive.

"Did he pass?" she asked.

"This part, probably," Cage answered.

"Well, he'll pass the verbal test next week if it kills *me*," Geek added.

"Assuming he gets through each of these hurdles, when will the next BUD/S class start?"

"Not 'til the fall," Geek said. "They have a new WEALS class to launch first." WEALS was the female version of SEALs that had been started a year or two ago.

"That means you might have a few weeks of hanky panky with lover boy down there," Cage told her with a grin.

She gave him a playful slap on the arm, then hugged him spontaneously for no reason other than renewed friendship and possibly the hope he'd given her that things might resume with Finn.

Unfortunately, it was at just that moment that Ian alerted Finn to the fact that they were up here. And when he glanced their way, it seemed that she was in Cage's embrace.

He glared at her with disdain. "Faithless wench!"

Then he turned his back and walked away.

Men are all the same, really . . .

Thorfinn sat in the Wet and Wild once again.

It was early, so there were no musicians and blaring music. Nor crowds of men and women looking for partners in bedsport. Mostly, it was men and women stopping on their way home from a day's work.

This time he was having dinner with Ian, his housemate for another evening since Madrene had left with the children for her father's winery at Blue Dragon. He would go there with Ian late tomorrow. *I must truly be losing my senses to willingly place myself in the midst of that Magnusson clan.*

With them were Geek and Luke Avenil, known as Slick, another SEAL. A dark and brooding man—just as Thorfinn himself had ofttimes been described—Slick was older than the rest. More than thirty-five, he would guess.

Torolf was still off on a mission with yet more SEALs, named JAM, Sly, F.U., and Scary Larry. *And I thought Vikings had odd names!* Torolf hoped to return afore his father's harvest feast this weekend.

He could have stayed at Torolf's apartment, alone, but Ian convinced him it would be more convenient to stay with him. He intended to have him "work out" in the morning. Thorfinn did not want to know what "work out" meant. He had a fair clue it involved sweat and pain. In truth, there was not a bone or muscle in his body that did not hurt, but there was satisfaction in having passed the PST.

"Here's the deal," Geek said after wiping the red sauce from the hot wings off his mouth. The best thing about the hot wings, Thorfinn had discovered, was that so much good beer had to be consumed to cool off the tongue. He had also discovered a taste for ice-cold beer, whereas in his country and time, beer, or mead, was lukewarm at best. "We'll study together twelve hours a day for the next week . . . after you get back from Blue Dragon on Sunday night, that is. Then you can take the verbal test next Friday."

"I'll see if there's any way you can be given the test

orally," Ian added. "Since English is your second language, they might waive the written test. They've done it for some foreign military personnel in the past."

"Where's Cage?" Slick asked. "I thought he was supposed to meet us here."

Thorfinn's ears went on alert at the question he had restrained himself from asking.

"He has a date." Geek rolled his eyes. "I saw him at the commissary buying a pigload of condoms."

Well, that is just wonderful. Cage and my woman!

Well, not my woman anymore

If she ever was.

Aaarrgh!

And, really, Cage is military, too. Why him and not me? Does she think he is a milksop who polishes weapons and ne'er uses them?

Bloody hell! I am not going to pine after a woman. She doesn't want me? Fine! I will find another woman.

Or better yet, I will give up women.

Hah!

Even I know enough not to bite off my cock to spite my stubborn head. Ouch!

"So what do you think?" Geek asked him.

"What?" Thorfinn had been only half attending and worried that he had spoken his pitiful thoughts aloud.

"I asked if that schedule for studying would work for you."

Whew! THAT question. "Yea, it would, except I will be going to Minnesota next weekend."

"Minnesota!" the three others exclaimed.

Ian half turned all the way around in his chair to stare at him. "This is the first I've heard of it."

"What? You think just because you grant me hospitality that you own my life?"

"Has anyone ever told you that you're an asshole?" Ian countered.

"Plenty of times since I have entered this godforsaken country," he responded, as if it were a compliment.

"You know, there are a hell of a lot of Scandinavians in Minnesota. Mostly farmers, I think," Slick pointed out. "You planning on moving there?"

"Did I not just take a test to become a SEAL? Nay, I am not planning on moving to Minnesota. And do not, any of you, make a jest about my playing idiot football, just because I am a Viking going to Minnesota."

They all grinned at his vehemence.

"Uh-oh! Isn't Lydia from Minnesota?" Geek remarked.

"She is." He tried to sound nonchalant, but his face must have shown something.

"I thought you two were broken up," Ian said.

"Broken . . . I did not break anything." *But I would like to break something. Like a Cajun head.*

"He means that you and Lydia are no longer involved romantically," Geek interpreted.

"*Romantically?* We were never involved romantically, not like Ian and Madrene, for Thor's sake. With smelly candles and scarves and pole dancing in the dark. We just swived 'til our eyeballs rolled back in our heads."

Now all eyes rested on the commander, whose red face matched his thinning reddish-brown hair.

"Uh, how do you *swive*?" Slick wanted to know, but by the twitching of his lips Thorfinn assumed he already knew; so, he did not answer.

But then Geek said, "Finn and Lydia were playing the love-slave game."

Slick choked on his beer, and Ian's face turned so red he best be careful he did not burst the bulging vein in his forehead.

"'Twas not a game, lackwit," Thorfinn said to Geek. "But, 'tis true, Lydia and I are no longer together. Even so, she promised to take me to see her son, who is visiting his two grandsires in Minnesota."

"Why would—?" Geek started to ask, but stopped at Thorfinn's glower.

"How come no woman ever wants to play love slave with me?" Slick wanted to know.

"A lot of women would if they knew about that McMansion of yours in Malibu," Geek answered Slick. Then he added, "So how's the situation with your ex-wife? I hear you were in court again last week."

"Hopefully, it's finally over. Five frickin' years she's been dragging me through the court system, trying to get more and more money, as if she didn't about bleed me dry the first time around. What she really wanted, and thank God the Superior Court of California didn't give it to her, was the Malibu house I inherited from my great-aunt, Lucy. And, no, it's not a mansion, thank you very much. Just a prime real estate location."

Slick explained to him then how he was divorced from a coin-hungry wife these many years, but she kept trying to get more and more from him.

"I knew women like that back in my country, but when they get too irksome, we just slice off their blathering tongues. That quiets them good and proper." When he noticed the shock on everyone's faces, he added, "You lackwits! I was jesting. Viking women are bothersome, too. The best remedy is to not wed at all."

"I disagree," Ian said.

But he was the only one.

"With the right woman, marriage can be the best thing life has to offer," Ian persisted.

Still, no one agreed with him.

"Hey, Geek, wanna catch a flick later?" Slick asked. "That old Bruce Willis movie is playing at the Bijou."

"Uh, I don't think so. I have a date. Sort of. Julie is meeting me here . . ." He checked his watch. "Any minute now."

"Would that be Julie of the cock-wax-job invention?" Slick wanted to know, a rare smile blooming on his usually grim face.

"It's a penile glove, ferchrissake!" Geek exclaimed, then he explained to Thorfinn. "Women in this country have hand waxes all the time in beauty spas. Men, too. People put their hands in warm wax to get a massage kind of thing. When they put their hands in the warm wax, then take it out, it shrinks as it dries and hardens, but not real hard . . . more like a tight, form-fitting rubber glove. But the neat thing is when they pull it off, slowly, starting at the wrist, it's a really sensual sensation."

Ian and Slick were snickering.

Thorfinn just gaped at the half-brain fool. "Surely, men are not putting their penises in such a concoction?" Thorfinn was incredulous, but really men through the ages did just about anything if it brought their precious manparts pleasure.

"Oh, yeah! I helped my friend Julie set up a website when she first invented it, www.penileglove.com. These guys here are just jealous because Julie is now a millionaire, and I made a bundle investing early on."

After a long silence, Thorfinn remarked, "My brother Steven would love this sex glove. He's as half-brained as the rest of you." Then he asked, "What is a bundle?"

Everyone laughed, not at all offended, and Geek explained, "A bundle is a lot of money."

"How much?"

"Never mind."

"Anyhow," Ian said, swiping tears of mirth from his eyes, "has good ol' Julie come up with any new inventions lately?"

"Actually, yes. We're working on the new website tonight."

"And it's called?" Slick prompted.

"Tentatively, www.niplicks.com. And that's all I'm gonna say on the subject."

More silence as everyone let what Geek had said sink in and draw vivid mind pictures. Then there was a communal smile.

Before anyone could ask more questions, Geek glanced across the room, then stood.

The woman who approached was of medium height, compared to Geek's long, lean frame. She was striking, with short spiked purple and blonde hair. Her curvaceous body, adorned in leather braies and a leather vest, would do a harem houri proud. Not that he had ever seen one wearing braies.

"Hey, lover!" the vixen said, raising herself on tiptoes to kiss the grinning Geek.

And Geek—the slyboots who gave the impression of only being interested in books and computers, of being ignorant about the ways of men and their baser urges— kissed her back, with vigor, and surely a bit of tongue. And, yes, that was his hand on her buttock.

'Twould seem they had all underestimated the supposedly shy Geek. 'Twould seem they had all just been given a lesson in making quick misjudgments about people.

If only that were true in his case! But, alas and alack, he'd seen the proof of *his* vixen's perfidy with his own eyes.

Chapter 14

**She's gonna wash that man right outta her heart,
or die trying . . .**

On Saturday night, Lydia was on her hands and knees scrubbing the kitchen floor when she sat back on her knees, slapped the wet rag into the bucket, and exclaimed, "This is ridiculous!"

She had vacuumed and dusted every inch of her small home, including the closets. She'd rearranged the kitchen shelves, wiped off the window blinds, scoured the bathroom tiles, and baked three dozen chocolate-chip cookies to take for Mike this week. As if her mother didn't bake on a daily basis!

All this to keep herself busy so she wouldn't think about you-know-what. Or rather you-know-who. Okay, you-know-what *and* you-know-who.

The rat fink's look of disdain when he'd looked up at her from the grinder yesterday would be imprinted on her mind forever. What had she ever done to merit such scorn? Yeah, she'd said she couldn't be involved with a military man again. Maybe he'd taken it personally. Of course he had. But it wasn't. Really.

If he'd appeared the least bit hurt, maybe she could understand. Or forgive. But he'd looked at her like she was a piece of crap.

So, Lydia followed her usual pattern when something happened to her, aside from the fanatical cleaning. First, she was shocked. Then, hurt. Then, angry. And finally she shifted into determination. She would be damned if she would let him make her feel so bad. After all, she hardly knew him.

But . . . and this was a big BUT . . . she still had to get through a trip to Minnesota and back with him, not to mention two full days at her parents' farm. She'd purchased the airline tickets yesterday and expected he would reimburse her for his half.

Okay, she had six days to straighten herself out. Six days to stop thinking about him in a sexual way. Six days to not fall in love with him.

All thoughts of sex or love or stubborn jerks flew out the window when the phone rang, and her dad announced, "Someone burned down the Denton barn last night."

And he's just now telling me? "Dad! What's going on? First, your cows. Now, the Denton barn. What do the police think? Is Mike safe? Are you all in danger? Should I bring Mike home? Maybe you and Mom and the Dentons should come stay here with me."

"Now, slow down, honey. First of all, the farmers in the area are on the alert, and we have surveillance teams working round the clock. We're safe. The police found some grubby motel room down the highway where some foreign guy had been staying. In the waste can there was a crumbled copy of the local newspaper with the article about Dave's memorial."

"Terrorists? Oh, my God!"

"The FBI has been called in."

"The FBI! Oh, my God!"

"Hold on, now. It's not a terrorist group. They think it's just some anti-American wacko."

"Maybe they should cancel the memorial service."

"The town council held an emergency meeting tonight, and they decided they damn well weren't going to cave in. So, the service is on, but there'll be more police than regular folks, I imagine."

"I'm coming as soon as possible."

"Will you take Mike back right away, or stay for the service?"

"I don't know. I'll see what the situation is when I get there."

"Honey, don't worry."

How could she not worry?

When she clicked off, Lydia realized that she was shaking, too distraught to cry. She wasn't sure why, but the first call she made was to find Finn. She tried Ian's number, where Finn was staying. No answer.

Next she called the airline and changed the reservations. For both of them, although she assumed she would be traveling alone since she couldn't reach Finn. The earliest flight she could get was six A.M. the next morning.

She was in her bedroom packing when she heard a crash in the living room. It sounded like glass breaking. Rushing out, she saw that her sliding glass door to the deck was broken, and a newspaper-covered brick lay amongst the shattered glass on the carpet.

This was too much of a coincidence. The incidents in Minnesota. The brick through her window.

Quickly, she got Dave's pistol out of the locked drawer in the kitchen. She had no idea if it was loaded, but she felt secure just having it in her hand. Next, she put on rubber gloves and peeled the newspaper off, spreading it on the counter. It was the article in the Coronado newspaper about Dave's memorial service and her aerobics studio. There were three names circled with black marker. Dave's. Mike's. Hers. And red drip marks stained the newsprint. Blood, she assumed.

With a whimper, she grabbed the cordless phone and ran to the bathroom, locked the door, then called 911. After that, she began calling everyone she knew. Kirstin, Ian, Geek, getting only voice mail. Finally, Cage answered, thank God, after six rings, his voice sounding husky. Had he been asleep? At nine P.M.? But then she heard a female voice in the background and knew he'd been in bed, all right, but not asleep. That couldn't concern her.

"Cage, this is Lydia. *Help!*"

Even wine didn't help . . .

Thorfinn sat in a low wooden armchair on the deck behind the house at Blue Dragon, sipping fine wine from a
fragile-stemmed glass, in the midst of Magnus Ericsson's
two hundred closest friends and kin. And had never felt
more alone in all his life.

They had all come to celebrate a grand harvest of
new grapes which would go into the fine wines for which
this vineyard was known. Laughter and music came
from the vast lawns to the side of the house, where he
would be forced to return soon, lest he appear an un-
grateful guest.

Kirstin had been giving him black looks ever since he
arrived last night with Ian. Madrene and Hilda gave him
black looks, too, but that was the usual pattern with them.
Kirstin's attitude was new. If he were not so tired and dis-
illusioned, he might trouble himself to ask her what was
amiss. Then again, probably not.

Someone approached, carrying an empty glass in one
hand and a wine bottle in the other. It was Magnus, the father to this unruly clan of Vikings, who had settled here in
the Sonoma Valley. More than fifty, he was still a formi-
dable Norseman. There were threads of gray in his long,
light brown hair, but his big body was well-honed from
hard work, and his face was mostly unlined. Fourteen
children in all this man had bred over a lifetime, and
Thorfinn had not even one. Well, mayhap he had one, but
that remained to be seen, and was something he could not
dwell on now.

"Magnus," he said, indicating the chair next to him.

Sinking down with a long sigh, Magnus leaned over and refilled Thorfinn's glass, then filled his own, setting the bottle on the wood floor.

"Is my sister Katla in good health?"

Katla was Thorfinn's mother and the youngest sister of Magnus, and of Geirolf and Jorund Ericsson, both of whom were here today with their families, all of whom had presumably bloody well time-traveled.

"Last I heard, Mother fared well."

"She was only fourteen when she wed her Norman groom, you know?"

He nodded.

"'Tis odd that in this country fourteen is still considered a child. But when I look at my little Marie, who is approaching seventeen, I am astonished to think anyone would think her old enough to marry and have children."

"Different times and places," he commented, a bit slowly, the wine beginning to affect his senses.

"And, you, Thorfinn, how fare you?"

He shrugged. "Not so well, I fear."

"'Tis hard to adjust at first. Give yourself time. May the gods bless me, I am still adjusting, and I have been here more than seventeen years."

"Was that supposed to make me feel better?"

The two men smiled at each other.

"Madrene tells me you are smitten with a woman."

"Madrene has a big mouth."

"That she does. Some say I left the Norselands to

escape my oldest daughter's nagging, but do not tell her I said so."

Thorfinn laughed, then grew serious again. "Lydia . . . she's talking about Lydia Denton. She was married to a Navy SEAL."

"Bloody hell! Is every man in the world a SEAL?"

"'Twould seem so. Leastways, Dave Denton died in service to his country, and she says she cannot be involved with another military man." He took a long sip of wine, emptying his glass, and set it aside. He'd already had too much to drink.

"Is that all?"

"'Tis enough. Fighting is all I know. And do not tell me I could become a grape grower, or farmer, or any other bloody thing. 'Tis bad enough I feel like a lackwit over the simplest things in this country."

"Believe me when I tell you that you will adjust. Unless . . . do you want to go back, Thorfinn?"

"I do not know. For a certainty, I would not want to leave anytime soon. There is more involved here, Magnus. You know that my wife Luta left me five years ago and took my son Miklof with her."

Magnus nodded, though his brow was furrowed with confusion.

"It's very possible that Lydia's son Michael is my son Miklof."

"How could that be?"

"I do not know. At first, Lydia thought I was her husband, Dave, come back from the grave, all because we share the same gray eyes."

"Your eyes *are* an unusual color."

"What difference does ... Leastways, she seems to have given up that notion. Now she thinks her dead husband sent me to her."

"And the child?"

"He has my eyes."

Magnus downed his wine in one big swallow. "Whew! I thought I had heard some amazing things, but your story beats them all. Could it be true?"

"I am hoping that when I see the boy in person next week—he is visiting his grandsires in Minnesota—I will know."

"What a tangle you are in, Thorfinn! Not just your feelings for this woman, and, nay, do not deny you have feelings for her. It is on your face, clear as a Norseland sky on a summer day. But also there is the issue of her not wanting a military man. Then, finally, the boy. I would not want to be in your boots."

Just then, Torolf rushed up to them, still dressed in his camouflage outfit. He must have just arrived back from his mission across the ocean.

"Thank the gods you're here, Finn. Come quickly. We've gotta catch a plane for Minnesota."

Thorfinn stood abruptly, all his senses on alert.

"Lydia and her son are in danger."

Old MacHartley had a farm, E-I-E-I-O ...

Lydia was still settling in at her parents' house at Mill Pond Farm, after hugging Mike 'til he protested he couldn't breathe and went off to help his grandmother feed the chickens. Lydia was now drinking her third cup of strong black coffee, which she needed to keep her awake following a sleepless night at Cage's apartment.

You'd never know that danger lurked as her dad and Lanny Brown, his full-time farmhand, went about their regular work, accompanied by a fascinated Cage, who'd never been on a working farm before. Her mother was busy, too, notwithstanding the lurking danger. Once she was done with the chickens, her mother would come in to can the three gallons of tomatoes, which were bubbling behind Lydia on the gas stove.

Well, what could she expect? They milked one hundred and fifty Holsteins here, with three hundred cattle total, half of them "replacements" ranging in age from just born to two years old and ready to give birth and join the milking herd. There were twice-daily chores on a farm, day in and day out, including milking, feeding, cleaning the barn and milking parlor, as well as seasonal chores, such as mowing, raking, baling hay, planting corn, and combining to make silage. Not to mention all the inputting of data onto a computer that was required on a modern farm—not that Mill Pond was all that modern.

As an indication of the silent menace, Cage wore a pistol under his jacket. And she'd noticed his eyes were always on the alert, scanning the perimeter, even when he was talking to one of them.

Mike, oblivious to the danger, loved it here, especially with all the fat, healthy cats that thrived on the milk they were given. She'd loved it, too . . . up to a certain age. If he'd asked her once, he'd asked a hundred times if they could bring a cat back to California with them. One of these days, she might agree. Or else get him a dog. In fact, a guard dog might be a good idea, in light of the brick incident.

Her cell phone hadn't rung since she'd been here, and Lydia realized that she'd forgotten to charge the battery. No sooner did she plug it in than it rang.

"Hello."

"Lydia? Is that you?"

"Finn. Finally!"

"Where are you?"

"At my parents' farm."

"Stay inside and lock the doors."

"It's okay. Cage is here with me."

It sounded as if he was swearing under his breath in some foreign language.

"I tried to call you last night."

"You did?" He was no longer swearing.

"I couldn't get anyone to come to the house. Except Cage."

"He was not there already?"

"No, why would he be?"

"Why, indeed?"

"Huh?"

"Tell me what happened."

She told him, but then she started to sob. Why she'd been able to hold herself together without tears so far, but break down now, she had no idea.

"Oh, sweetling, do not cry. I will be there soon."

That caused the tears to dry up real quick. "You will?"

"I am calling on Torolf's phone from up in the sky."

"You're on an airplane?"

"Yea, I am. See the sacrifice I am willing to make for you? In any case, we will be there soon."

"*We?*"

"Believe me, you do not want to know."

A Norse version of the Motley Crew . . .

Thorfinn was in another flying bird surrounded by the most lackwitted *hird* of soldiers a chieftain ever had. A private jet-plane was all they had been able to hire, and even then, they could not leave 'til the next morning.

Air-plane, jet-plane, whatever they called them, Thorfinn found riding in them a fist-clenching, heart-thumping, not-to-be-favored experience. What was wrong with a good old horse and cart? Or even an automobile?

But time was of the essence.

When Torolf had explained the danger that Lydia and her family were in, and that it somehow tied in with her ex-husband because he had been a Navy SEAL, every SEAL not on a mission who had ever worked with Dave Denton demanded to come along. That meant Geek, JAM, Sly, Slick, F.U., and several others whose names Thorfinn did not know. All of them carried deadly weapons.

"All for one and one for all," Ian—Commander MacLean—had told him last night before he reluctantly headed back to the base.

On the remote chance that Mike might actually be his

son, and therefore family, the Ericsson men said they were coming along, too, as was their right as elder warriors: Magnus, Jorund, and Geirolf, the three of whom carried their broadswords and battle-axes, which—*believe you me*—had been hard to explain to the policing folks at the airport.

"There is naught mightier than the sword," Magnus had asserted.

While Uncle Magnus was a vintner, Uncle Jorund ran an athletics school in *Tax-us* for crippled people, crippled in mind, as well as body. When Thorfinn asked if he ever taught pole dancing, his uncle's jaw dropped nigh to his chest. Then there was Uncle Rolf, who had built and managed Rosestead, a reproduction Viking village in far-off Maine, complete with longships, longhouses, and craftsmen. Thorfinn would like to see that. Many of their wares were marketed on the Internet . . . a place that he did not quite understand involving computers, he had learned from Geek and the bad-breath Blade.

Never let it be said that Vikings did not know how to adapt to the times.

Then Magnus's six other sons had jumped on board: Storvald, Njal, Jogeir, Hamr, and Kolbein, who had all seen more than twenty winters, and Ragnor, who was over thirty, same as Torolf. Ragnor worked with computers; a strange job for a Viking, if you asked him, which nobody did. But no more unusual than a Viking merchant on the Internet superhighway, he supposed.

"Young blood is needed to get the job done," Jogeir had declared.

Hamr was a football player, nicknamed The Hammer. Not with the Minnesota Vikings, but the San Diego Chargers. Traitorous, it was, in Thorfinn's opinion. If a man was going to engage in bloodsport for a living, it may as well be with fellow Vikings and involve a bit of pillaging. Kolbein, who was studying to be a priest—*imagine that, a Viking priest!*—came, no doubt, to give last rites to the villain, once dead. Jogeir, who had been lame as a child but was no longer, due to some medical operation, was an Olympic runner who shared his father's love of farming and would return to Blue Dragon one day. Njal, ever the mischievous one as a child and still was if the twinkle in his eyes was any indication, was a high-up officer in the Navy. Storvald, the eldest son, next to Ragnor and Torolf, was a sword-maker at Uncle Jorund's Viking village.

What a motley group they all were!

The villain terrorizing Lydia and her family was going to take one look at them and either piss his braies or run for the hills. With them in wild pursuit. He could scarce wait.

A woman in a dark blue jacket and a short garment known as a skirt was pushing a cart down the aisle. When she got to Thorfinn and Torolf, who was seated on his left, she asked, "Would you like a beverage?"

"Yea, I would like a beer," he said.

"Beer?" Torolf snickered. "It's only ten A.M."

"So? 'Tis better than that black sludge you drink." Turning back to the woman, who was tapping her high-heeled shoe with impatience, he inquired, "Dost have beer?"

"Yes," she said huffily, and left her cart to go up front, where she got a metal container of beer and handed it to him, along with one of those throw-away cups. What he wouldn't give for a good old horn of mead! That was the way to drink beer. Then she gave Torolf his coffee and both of them a tiny bag of nuts.

"What in bloody hell is this?" he asked Torolf, who was already tearing apart the bag and munching on the nuts.

"Breakfast."

"You jest."

"Just eat the damn things."

A short time later, he told Torolf, who had his eyes closed, attempting to sleep, "Cage is in Minnesota with Lydia."

Torolf cracked open just one eye. "So?"

"Dost think he is tupping her?"

"Oh, good gods! I hope you don't intend to ask her that."

"Why not?"

"You are an idiot. Because it's tantamount to asking if he's fucking her."

"And that is wrong . . . why?"

"You don't drop the F-bomb around women, unless you can absolutely help it."

Thorfinn just shook his head at this impossible-to-understand country.

"So, I take it Lydia isn't your love slave anymore."

He shook his head. "She does not want a military man."

"You mean it was getting that serious already? Holy crap! You move fast. Pickup sex to wedding bells in a nanosecond. You must be something in the sack."

"The sack?"

"Bed furs."

"Oh, well, of course I know my way around the bed furs, but that is neither here nor there. And I was not speaking of marriage."

"Oh, yes, you were. You just don't know it."

"Explain yourself, lackwit."

"When Lydia told you that she didn't want a military man, she meant for the long haul. If it was just sex, what difference would it make?"

He frowned. "I have no intention of wedding again."

"Did you tell Lydia that?"

"I do not recall. I must have. Well, mayhap not. Whether I said the words or not, she must have known."

"You are dumber than dirt."

"Your insults are not appreciated."

"Listen, Finn, are you in love with Lydia?"

"No! But I do get this squeezing sensation in my chest when I see her. And I do miss her, but that is probably just the incredible sex I am missing. And I sure as sin felt jealousy for the first time over her and Cage."

"Okay, buddy, how do you know she's involved with Cage?"

"I saw them embracing. That same night, Cage went out on a date. And now they are in Minnesota together."

"I admit that looks bad, but don't rush to judgment."

"So, you think there's a chance he is not swiving her?"

"Hell, no! But if it makes you feel better, you can be dumbass hopeful. And, by the way, around women you should say *making love*, not swiving or tupping. And never, ever ask a woman to give you a blow job or to eat her. You say flowery things, like, 'I want to taste you, baby.' And you refer to it as 'the most intimate kiss.'"

"Why?"

"Why? Why? Why? You're worse than a child."

"I would feel stupid asking a woman to give me a 'most intimate kiss.' What's wrong with saying, 'Blow me'? Short and descriptive. It's not like saying, 'Take me in your mouth and suck me dry.'"

Torolf rolled his eyes. "It's too crude."

"Sex *is* crude."

"Women prefer to romanticize sex."

"Does Hilda romanticize sex?"

"Of course, and, frankly, Finn, so do I when it comes to my wife. I *make love* to her." He grinned at him, then added, "And on occasion I swive and tup her, too. You would not believe what Hilda can do in front of a full-length mirror to turn me on. *Whoo-boy!*"

"*Pfff!* Now you are a self-proclaimed master in the art of loveplay?"

Instead of answering, Torolf made much fuss over pushing his chair back, folding his arms over his chest, and closing his eyes. A deliberate attempt to shut him up, no doubt. Well, he could fix that.

"Does Hilda ever pole dance for you . . . naked?"

To his great satisfaction, Torolf's eyes shot open, and he turned very slowly to gaze at him.

He was bloody hell not thinking of Thorfinn as a child now.

Chapter 15

"Let's rumble," sayeth the Vikings . . .

There was a famous Anglo-Saxon saying that Lydia had read in a history book one time. "Oh, Lord, from the fury of the Northmen, please protect us."

How true!

She set about doing the lunch dishes, while her dad, Mike, the hired hand Lanny, and his son Itchy were out in the barn, mucking manure. Her mother was gathering eggs, and Cage was over at the Denton farm. Lydia heard the sound of a car pulling into the lane, and her heart skipped a beat when she realized it was probably Finn.

She opened the front door and went out on the porch, then plopped down with shock onto the top step at what she saw. It wasn't just Finn. More than a dozen men emerged from the limousine and two rental SUVs. Navy

SEALs, some of whom she recognized, and honest-to-God Vikings, if their attire was any indication. All of them were bickering about one thing or another, as would be expected when grown men were confined in small spaces for too long.

"Where's my AK-47?" Sly grumbled. "If my weapon is back at that frickin' rinky-dink airport, I'm gonna kill someone."

"Holy shit, F.U.!" Geek exclaimed. "Why did you bring a grenade launcher? We're hunting for one tango, not a herd of buffalo."

F.U. said his name back at Geek.

"I have my broadaxe, but where's my battle-axe? Do you have it, Rolf?" One Viking man was speaking to another Viking man; they were both older men, dressed in belted tunics over slim pants with cross-gartered ankle boots. Their hair, threaded with gray, was long, with thin braids on either side of their faces, like Finn had worn the night she'd first met him.

Her eyes shot to Finn then. He stood in the background, just staring at her. She walked up to him and whispered in an undertone, "Who are all these people?"

"Your private *hird* of soldiers," he said with a shrug. Taking her by the forearm, he led her over to the three older "Vikings," who were still arguing over swords. "Lydia, these are my uncles: Rolf, Jorund, and Magnus." And to the uncles, he said, "This is Lydia Denton."

"Greetings," the three replied.

"The rest are my cousins . . . Magnus's sons. You can meet them later." Said sons were carting boxes up to the

porch. Some clearly holding wines from Blue Dragon
Vineyard. Another containing something called *Gammelost*. Fresh grapes . . . purple, green, red, and blue.

She nodded to the young men, who nodded back, a
few with more than casual interest, which caused Finn to
glare at them, and them to just grin back at him.

Then the third of the older Vikings, Magnus, who she
recalled ran some winery in Sonoma Valley, sighed, "This
is a wonderful farmstead. Do you have cows?"

Her eyebrows arched. "Three hundred of them."

"I noted vast ploughlands, as well."

"Four hundred acres."

He clapped a hand over his burly chest as if she'd
just announced that there was a pot of gold in the back
pasture.

"He is a farmer at heart," Jorund explained with a grin.

"Has manure in his veins," Rolf added, also grinning.

Magnus shoved the two of them so hard they almost
fell over, then walked away with a long sigh, presumably
off to find a cow.

Geek walked up then and told her, "Half of us are going over to the Denton place, half will secure the perimeter here. The cavalry has arrived, baby."

She gave a little wave to Sly and F.U., two other SEALs
she did not recognize, Ragnor, three more of Magnus's
sons, and the two uncles, who crawled back into the two
SUVs and took off, following the limo, which was presumably returning to the airport.

"What's going on?" she asked Thorfinn then.

"The SEALs are here because of Dave Denton, and they will stay 'til the miscreant is caught and 'til the honoring ritual is over."

"And you?"

He gulped several times as if searching for the right words. "I am here for you."

She launched herself at him, then burst out crying. His neck was wet from her tears, but he just held her tight, running a soothing hand over her back, shoulders to waist, over and over, crooning, "You are safe now. No one can hurt you."

When she finally calmed down, he stared at her and asked the question she had been dreading.

"Where is he?"

She didn't need to ask who he meant.

Mike.

"Come," she said, holding out a hand to link fingers with him. "I'll take you to him."

Now it all made sense . . .

He was about to meet the boy, who might very well be his own son, and he was more elated and frightened than he had ever been before.

They circled the side of the house, then walked toward the large barn surrounded by hides and hides of pasture. He could hear cows mooing, and he could smell the usual barnyard smells. Magnus was leaning against a railed fence watching some of the young calves chewing their cuds in the sunshine. A man about the same age, with short white hair, leaned on the fence next to him, talking, farmer to farmer, he supposed.

An older, gray-haired woman came out of a chicken coop and began to walk toward them, curiosity in her eyes. At the same time, the man talking to Magnus turned. They both appeared stunned.

"PopPop! I cleaned up all the cow poop. Now, can I—" Out of the open barn door, a boyling came skipping, his talk halting abruptly as he noticed Thorfinn approaching. He had black, rumpled hair, was missing two front baby teeth, and had scabs on his bare knees. He wore a tiny *shert* that read, GOT MILK!

Blood drained from Thorfinn's head, passing in waves down to his toes. His knees felt like butter. He put a fist to his mouth to suppress a groan.

Screeching to a halt just before them, the boyling craned his head to the side, staring up at him.

It was as if time stood still as everyone watched him and the child face each other, but only he and Lydia understood the significance of the moment. Lydia gave a little whimper beside him.

"Who are you?" the boyling demanded.

"Thorfinn Haraldsson," he said in a croaky voice, a war of emotions rending him nigh speechless. He released Lydia's grip on his hand and hunkered down to put himself at eye level.

"You're big."

"Yea, I am," he said, smiling.

"Your eyes are the same as mine."

He nodded.

"Wanna see the kittens in the barn?"

What he really wanted was to pull the child into his embrace and never let him go. Instead, he said, "I would like to see your kittens, above all else."

With tears in his eyes, he took the boy's tiny hand in his big one, and walked off with him, alone.

Five years of pain and grief were over. No matter what the future held for him, this was a moment of perfect happiness.

It was his son, Miklof. He did not care what anyone else said. He did not care what some modern *dean-aye* test proved.

Without a doubt, Mike was his lost boy, Miklof.

"Thank you," he whispered, not sure if it was God, or the gods, or Lydia he was thanking. It did not matter.

This was why he had traveled through time.

Daddy knows best . . .

"Who is he?" her father asked as she entered the barn that evening for the second milking of the day.

"Magnus? He sure knows a lot about farming, doesn't he?"

"No, not Magnus. You know who I'm talking about, girl. Your young man."

"He's not my young—" She halted at the disbelieving look in her father's all-knowing eyes. "Thorfinn Haraldsson. He's from . . . uh, Norway. He wants to be a Navy SEAL."

Her father nodded at that. "For a second there, when you two were walking across the yard, I could have sworn he was Dave. Must have been the sun blinding me."

She nodded, choked for words. That had been the reaction of everyone who'd met him so far today. Her mother, Lanny, even Itchy. She shuddered to think how Dave's parents would react when they met him tomorrow.

One thing was for certain. She would never, ever forget the image of Finn's face on seeing Mike for the first time. Oh, that every father had such pure love for his child!

"Mikey certainly took to him right off the bat."

With good reason. "Yes, he did, but then Mike is a friendly boy."

He made a scoffing sound. "Not that friendly."

"What are you trying to say, Dad?"

"Don't know exactly. Except somethin's fishy."

"I know we're overrun with uninvited strangers, but don't you want all these strong men here to help protect us and the Dentons? I for one would be a little leery of only having the four-man Farmdale police department protecting us."

Already, the eight men staying here—some of whom would be sleeping in the house and some in the barn— had set up patrols around the clock. The house and farm certainly seemed to be secure now. Tomorrow everyone was meeting at the Dentons' with the FBI, whose noses were a bit out of joint at the SEAL invasion.

"I'm not dumb enough to turn away good help."

You have no idea how good, Pop. "That's that, then."

"One more thing, honey. Are you in love with the guy?"

I'm afraid so. "Maybe."

Surprisingly, her father wasn't surprised. He just nodded his head approvingly.

He thinks there's going to be a wedding. He's probably hoping we'll come back here to farm. I can't let him set himself up for disappointment. "There's no future for us, though. Finn's military, and you know I can't go through that pain again."

"Honey, that's nonsense. Let me ask you this. If Dave were to suddenly come back, if his death were all a mistake, would you push him aside, just because he was military?"

"That's different."

Isn't it?

Lydia was so confused.

They did more than milk cows in that barn . . .

Thorfinn was so confused.

He nodded to Lydia's father, the hired man Lanny, and his son as they left the barn and walked up to the farmstead house. Dinner would soon be ready now that the nighttime milking was done. Lydia was still in the barn, and that was the direction he was headed. This was the first chance he'd had to find Lydia alone.

"Lydia."

She jumped from where she was standing before a sink washing her hands. *Who ever heard of running water in a barn?* Bloody hell, they did not have running water in homes where he came from, even royal estates.

But that was neither here nor there. He had more important things to accomplish here. To seduce Lydia. After his talk with Torolf on the airplane, he was not sure he had a flair for finer skills. *Mayhap I should just say, "Come here, Lydia. Let us reconcile with a good tupping."*

No, no, no! Behave yourself, Thorfinn. She needs to be calmed, like a skittish mare afore the mounting. Oh, bloody hell. I hope I do not blurt that aloud.

She dried her hands as he came closer, her eyes troubled and scared. Why? She had no need to be frightened of him.

Remember the mare, he told himself. *Nice and easy.* "He is my son, Lydia. You know that," he said in as gentle a voice as he could manage.

She turned. "I don't know what I know at this point."

He patted his chest, over his heart. "I know it here."

"Maybe it's just what you want to believe. We can have DNA tests done."

He waved a hand dismissively. "You can do all the testing in the world. I know what I know."

"What are you going to do about it?"

Now that I have Miklof, I will never be separated from him again. "I am not certain, but you will be involved in whatever that final decision is." *As long as it fits with my plans.*

"Thank you," she said, tears brimming in her eyes.

Oh, gods, now come the tears. That is usually my cue to leave, but I cannot bear my Lydia crying. Whoa! When did I start thinking of her as MY Lydia? "Do not weep. This is a joyous occasion." He moved closer.

She backed up a bit.

Skittish, for sure. "I have not seen Cage today." Another step closer.

"He's over at the Dentons'." She took another step backward and hit the barn wall. A nearby cow mooed its disapproval.

He stretched an arm out and pulled at the clip holding her hair back into a queue. Her black hair spilled over his hand like threads of silk. Leaning forward, he sniffed, relishing the flowery scent.

"Did Cage sleep here yestereve?" *I will kill him if he did.*

She frowned, whether at his question or the fact he was pressing against her, clearly aroused. "Why would Cage sleep here?"

Mayhap Cage will be spared . . . for now. "Why indeed?" he murmured, running the backs of his fingers over her chest, watching with satisfaction as her nipples beaded. *Her sap is rising just as mine is,* he realized, but he recalled Torolf's words of caution earlier today and was careful in choosing his next words. "Have you *made love* with Cage?" *Holy Thor! My tongue has a life of its own. I did not intend to say that.*

"Good heavens, no!"

Praise the gods and pass the mead! He smiled then, and without asking, "May I, please?" as Torolf the lackwit would no doubt advise, he had her *shert* off and over her head and her *den-ham* braies undone and down at her ankles. Only then did he allow himself to look at her. "Sweet Frigg! What is this?"

"Victoria's Secret."

"Whose secret?"

"Never mind. I bought it this morning at the mall when I knew you were coming."

She wore a flesh-colored scrap of lacy material over her breasts, which seemed to be higher and squished together. Her matching undergarment barely covered her dark fleece, and left her arse cheeks almost totally uncovered. Slipping his fingers under the lace, far enough that his fingertips touched her pouting nipples, he said in a raw voice, "I like it." *Now that is an understatement if I ever heard one.*

"I'm glad," she whispered.

Cupping her bare buttocks in his hands, he lifted her 'til her woman's channel rode his erection. Then he leaned down to kiss her, murmuring against her mouth, "I have missed you, wench." *More than you can possibly imagine.*

She could not answer because he was plundering her mouth with his lips and tongue and teeth, his hunger like a wild wave through his body. But she moaned, low in her throat, and he took that to mean she had missed him, too.

"Let me take off your shirt," she said, while he moved to her ears, feasting with his wet tongue and hot breath. "I need to feel your skin against mine."

Ah! A woman with her own mind! And a like mind at that. How did I get so lucky? He held her up, still with his hands under her buttocks, but leaned back a bit so she could remove his shirt and the scrap of lace off her breasts. Then she brushed her breasts back and forth across his chest hairs. They both groaned then.

"Lydia," he husked out. *What was it my cousin said about not being crude?* "Wouldst like to have me inside you, or wouldst like me to first give you . . . um, the most intimate kiss?"

"*What?* Where did you ever hear that term? Have you been reading romance novels?" She was laughing so hard her breasts were bouncing.

"I am going to kill Torolf," he muttered. *Enough with the asking! I will do things my way.* Her legs still clutched his hips with her ankles crossed behind his back. "Do not move," he said, tearing at the sides of the scrap of silk and lace covering her woman's place. It fluttered to the floor. "I am sorry. I will buy you another."

"Don't be sorry." Her voice was erotically low and sensual.

While he was still leaning back, he reached down and undid his braies, releasing himself.

She was trying to move her hips so he would enter her.

Was there e'er a prettier sight than a woman in the throes of enthusiasm? But she would not be controlling this loveplay. Not this time. He took her hips in hand. "I must needs get a condom."

"No need. I am on the pill."

Now she tells me! He thrust into her so long and hard that her body moved up the wall a few inches. "Did I hurt you?"

Her laughter came out on a gasp. "It hurt so good." As

if to prove her words, her inner muscles convulsed around him.

Has a woman's channel ever felt this good? He could scarce keep himself from peaking, too, but that would be too soon. "Open your eyes, sweetling. I want to see your bliss."

Her blue eyes were half-lidded and glazed with continuing arousal.

"Keep your eyes open," he insisted and began to play with her breasts, watching her reaction the whole time. Massaging them up and around in circles, the hard nipples pressed against his palms. By the time he fluttered his middle fingers against the tips, she had peaked again, and was whimpering. "Please, please, please."

"Please what?" *As if I do not know!*

"Please move, dammit."

Who knew that a woman ordering me about could be so sweet? He reached between them and parted her folds more, so that when he began the short, hard strokes, he kept hitting that special nub of woman pleasure. Her keening accompanied the spasms, which were unending, milking him closer and closer to completion.

But then she put a palm against his chest. "Now *you* open *your* eyes. I want to see your climax, too."

That is a new idea. Can I manage to control my enthusiasm and keep my eyes open at the same time? Bloody hell, I can try. He began to thrust with a hard rhythm into her channel, nigh slamming her into the wall each time. Then he arched his back, and howled his release, pressing himself into her, surely as far as her womb.

Lightheaded and more sated than he'd ever been in his life, he sank to his knees on the floor, and she straddled his lap, his half-hard cock still inside her. They were both panting. Perspiration dotted her upper lip. He was equally affected.

She rested her face against his neck for a moment, then sat up. "Have I told you how much I missed you?"

He could barely breathe, let alone talk. But finally he gasped out, "Yea, you did. And showed me, too."

"No. I don't think I did." She smiled at him then, a saucy temptress smile. Rocking forward and backward, the minx caused his cock to rise to attention. Again.

"You are right, dearling. I am not nearly convinced yet."

I hope my eyes are not crossing at the sheer pleasure-pain.

The terrible trouble draws closer . . .

Jamal watched the Hartley farm from his hiding place on the hill. He was still rolling up his prayer rug, having completed his evening prayers.

All the men who had arrived at Mill Pond Farm and Green Meadows Farm did not trouble him. The most important thing was that Denton's wife had arrived. With her and the boy here, everything was now in place. What he had planned would take them all by surprise. If there were others who got killed or injured, so be it. Just collateral damage, as the Americans were quick to say of bombings in his country.

Aware that Denton's wife had been in the barn, alone, with a man, he was not surprised. She was a whore. If he hadn't known it before, he did after reading the newspaper article about her teaching wanton dances to women. What good was a woman like that to the world? Just another loose-moraled bitch to tempt men to sin.

The boy was another matter. Killing a child was not an easy thing to do, but he had no choice. An eye for an eye. A child for a child.

When his noble duty was completed, he would make a trip to Mecca in atonement. Allah would forgive.

Only a few more days.

Chapter 16

A regular melting pot in a farm kitchen . . .

There were eleven people seated at the kitchen table, and another three posted outside who would eat later. Lydia's mother was in her glory.

Her father and mother kept glancing at Finn. They were suspicious of his silver eyes and the instant affinity he had with Mike; they had told her so.

They were also suspicious of what she and Finn had been doing in the barn, as well. Lydia hadn't realized why 'til she'd gone to her old bedroom and seen in the mirror that her lips were kiss-swollen, her neck whisker-burned, and her T-shirt all wrinkled. Not to mention her eyes, glistening with postcoital satisfaction. Then there was Finn, who looked like a man who had just had the time of his life and was happy that everyone knew it. The louse! The lovable louse, that is.

Also at the table were Geek, JAM, Torolf, Magnus, and one of his other sons. And a babbling Mike, who had attached himself to Finn's side like a burr, one he welcomed. Slick and two more of Magnus's sons were outside. If the situation weren't so serious, it would seem like a joyous occasion. While he talked with Mike on his one side, Finn clasped Lydia's hand under the table on his other side, occasionally, almost distractedly, using his thumb to caress her wrist, which kept her in a constant state of arousal, probably obvious in her flushed face.

Her mother had made her famous pot roast with dark gravy, potatoes, carrots, corn on the cob, homemade bread and butter, salad, and a red-velvet chocolate cake with whipped cream icing, which had won her a blue ribbon at the county fair three years in a row when Lydia had been in high school. Everything was made in quadruple amounts to what she usually prepared. Pitchers of cold milk, equally cold beer, and ice water were consumed in vast quantities.

Before they ate, her father said grace, which everyone respected, but she could tell it was not a common occurrence. Not with the Vikings, nor the SEALs.

But Magnus soon rid her of that notion. "My mother was a Christian who also insisted on grace afore meals. I lost the habit for many years, but started again when I married my wife, Angela, who was raised in the Catholic faith."

"Obviously, I am not unaccustomed to prayer," said JAM, who had once studied for the priesthood.

"Well, here on the farm, we keep with traditional values," her father said. His remark seemed to be directed at Finn. Was he hinting that he didn't want him sleeping with his daughter? Too late for that!

Out of the blue, Mike told Finn, "I saw a cow making a baby today." He spoke with a slight lisp because of his missing front teeth. The second teeth were already peeping through the gums.

Finn choked on a mouthful of beef and quickly washed it down with water.

"Mike!" Lydia's father cautioned.

"The breeder guy came and stuck his arm all the way up Lubelle's butt, then he put a long straw in. There was *sea-man* in the straw. Betcha doan know what *sea-man* is."

"Mike, honey, this really isn't appropriate conversation for—"

"That ol' Lubelle was mooin' and mooin' and mooin'. I was scared 'cause it sounded like she was screamin', but PopPop said she was jist tellin' the breeder what a stud he was."

"Dad!" Lydia glared at her red-faced father.

"Travis Hartley! How could you?" Her mother walked over and smacked him with a dish towel. "What a thing to show a little boy!"

"I'm not little," Mike protested. Then, turning to Finn again, he said, "Maybe we can go see the breeder makin' babies again tomorrow. PopPop sez Vanessa is horny 'n oughtta be in heat by now. That means a cow is hot ta trot."

"Let me guess. PopPop told you that, too." Lydia was shaking her head at her father. But she couldn't really blame him. Life tended to be earthy on a farm, by necessity. She'd seen many a cow serviced by a bull in her day, then inseminated by artificial breeders as the herd grew and modern technology took over.

Meanwhile everyone at the table was laughing now, including her mother. Her adorable son, with his milk mustache and two missing front teeth, was beaming at his audience.

"I do not understand. What is wrong with the usual way of breeding? A strong bull. A willing cow." This from Magnus, who supposedly had had a huge farm in the old country. "All this science when the old ways work just as well."

"Too dangerous now," her father explained. "Bulls can be mean sons a bitches . . . I mean, they are a danger to other animals and people, too. Besides, there are more accurate results with artificial insemination."

"When I first came to this country, I would have considered a farm like yours sheer paradise . . . Valhalla, to us Vikings," Magnus told her father. "To this day, I yearn to return to farming, even with the fancy new methods."

"Not to worry, father," Jogeir said, patting Magnus's shoulder. "I will be the farmer in our family."

"Then who will take over the vineyard when I am gone?"

"Maybe Marie." Torolf grinned at his scowling father.

"Marie is only seventeen years old," he scoffed.

"She won't be seventeen forever."

"I would think growing grapes has a lot in common with farming," Lydia's father interjected.

"It does. My sons still do not understand that I can take soil in hand and tell if it is good for growing by smell and taste. There is no modern test better than the human tongue. Fertile soil has its own taste."

Her father nodded.

"Yuck! Do they eat dirt?" Mike wanted to know.

"Betimes." Magnus reached across the table and ruffled Mike's hair. He looked warmly at Mike, then Finn, and Lydia knew he saw the resemblance, as her father and mother did, too.

"How about you, Finn?" her father asked. "Do you have any taste for farming?"

"Daaaaad!" She was embarrassed that her father was so overtly thinking that if Lydia married Finn they might ultimately take over Mill Pond Farm, as Dave had never been inclined to do. Finn would probably get the same reaction from Dave's parents tomorrow.

"What?" Her father played the innocent. "I was just asking."

"Nay, I will not be a farmer. I hope to become a SEAL."

And that was that.

Lydia tried to pull her hand from his, but he held on to her, tightly.

"What do you do with all your manure?" Magnus asked her father.

The question stunned everyone.

Except Mike.

"Manure is cow poop," Mike announced in case anyone didn't know.

Magnus's sons just grinned, knowing their father's obsession with anything agrarian, even cow poop.

"We spread it on the fields. And Mary likes it for her rose bushes and vegetable garden. We have tomatoes big as saucers, and her roses win ribbons at the fair every year." Her father smiled at her mother, the love apparent between the two of them, even after all these years. That's what she had thought she would have one day. If it hadn't been for the military . . .

She snuck a glance at Finn and saw him watching her parents, too.

"Are you a Viking, too?" Mike asked Finn. He must have picked up that word from Magnus's conversation.

"That I am." Finn ruffled the boy's hair, a loving gesture that no one missed.

"I have a book called *The Viking Who Cried.* Wanna read it with me?"

"Well, I do not know if that is a good name for a story about a fierce Viking man."

Mike giggled. "It's not about a Viking man. It's about a Viking boy who ran away on a longship, and then he misses his mommy. That's why he was cryin'."

"Oh, well, then, it sounds like a fine story."

"Why don't I take Mikey up for his bath while you people talk about . . . other things," her mother offered. "I can do the dishes when I come back down."

"Thanks, Mom, but I can handle the dishes."

"I don't wanna take a bath. I ain't dirty."

Everyone laughed at that. Aside from his hands and arms, which he'd been forced to wash before eating,

Mike had smudges of dirt on his nose, different stains on his T-shirt and jeans, some of which might very well be manure, and his hair was going every which way, with a few sprigs of hay mixed in.

"You can come back down after your bath, honey," Lydia told him. "Since it's a special night, you get to pick three books tonight."

When Mike trudged off behind her mother, grumbling, Finn turned to her. "He is a fine boy. You have done well with him."

She wanted to say thank you, but all she could do was nod.

After that, she and Jogeir took the plates off the table and began to run a first load in the dishwasher, which did not meet with Finn's approval, she could tell, but there was nothing he could do about it. Jogeir was a good-looking man of about twenty-five who resembled his father not just in stature but also in love of farming, apparently.

When Torolf came over to help, Finn jumped up to help, too.

Finn said the oddest thing to Torolf while they were jostling each other in front of the sink. "By the by, cousin, your love advice stinks."

Torolf burst out laughing. "You didn't! Oh, God, don't tell me you actually said *that*?"

Finn shoved Torolf, who almost fell over.

"Wait 'til I tell Hilda what you said about her doing intimate things in front of a mirror."

"Don't you dare!" Torolf gave Finn a good shove then, too. Soon they were on the floor wrestling.

While Torolf and Finn behaved like children, Geek took over coffee-dispensing duties, and JAM washed the pots and pans. When everything was relatively cleared up, Lydia sat down at the table with them.

"The FBI wants to meet with us tomorrow morning," Sly said. "At first we planned to gather at Green Meadows Farm, but there's too many damn people here now. So, they suggested the conference room at City Hall. They'll let us in on what they know so far, which isn't much."

Lydia had talked to Julie and Herb Denton this morning to tell them that she had arrived and everything was calm at the moment. Although normally Mike would be going to their farm, starting tomorrow, for a week's stay, they decided to hold off 'til the danger had passed. When she dropped by there the next day, it would be the first she'd seen them since Christmas.

"Well, we've already got a few leads," Geek said, surprising them all. "We figure there must be a connection between Lydia, Mike, Dave, the SEALs, and the memorial service. Who would have a grudge that encompasses all of those?"

"Could it be connected to SEAL missions in general?" Sly asked.

Finn shook his head. "Nay. If that were the case, others would be targeted, too. It has to be one particular mission that has sparked rage in this villain." Finn might not be a modern soldier . . . yet, but he had the right mind for it.

"Okay, can you have Commander MacLean pull up data on every mission Dave was on?" Sly asked Geek.

"He's in the process of doing that right now. We should get the faxes any minute," Geek replied as they all walked to the living room. "But the lead I mentioned . . . the Fibbies got an anonymous call a few weeks ago, which they traced to an Arab doctor in Michigan. He warned about something his brother was planning. It was kind of garbled, but it might have something to do with that last bloody mission of Dave's . . . the one where the . . . um, explosives . . . I mean . . ." Geek's eyes darted to Lydia, uncomfortable at the reminder of Dave's gory death. No one ever spoke of it, but she suspected there were only body parts in Dave's coffin at Arlington. Dave had once told her about a phenomenon called "pink mist," which occurred in an explosion involving people. It had needed no explanation. "They're interviewing him as we speak."

Everyone was uncomfortable then at the reminder of Lydia's dead husband and the SEALs' dead buddy.

The living room looked like a NASA launch headquarters with computers, monitors, TVs, faxes, and a state-of-the-art ear mike system that connected all the SEALs. And probably the FBI and police, after tomorrow.

"Another thing," JAM said. "Tomorrow a dozen or more of us will spread out and search the wooded areas around both farms."

"Good idea," Finn said.

"Are we safe?" Lydia asked.

"Yes. As long as we're careful." This from JAM.

"Hah!" Finn said. "Anyone who attempts to harm Mike . . . or Lydia will have to do so over my dead body. I protect those under my shield."

Her father frowned. Whether at Finn's strange language or his vehemence in protecting Lydia and Mike, she wasn't sure. One thing was certain. Her father would be grilling her once he got her alone.

"So, Mr. Hartley, it would be best if you and Mrs. Hartley went about your business, as usual. With covert protection," Geek advised. "The rest of us will get to work in your living room and try to come up with a plan."

Her father nodded, then looked at Lydia. "Why don't you come out to the barn with me, honey? We'll check on the cows ready to calve tomorrow."

"Oh, can I come help?" Magnus asked, as if it would be a privilege.

"I suppose," her father said, clearly disappointed that he wasn't going to get her alone . . . yet. He left through the back door, accompanied by Magnus carrying a huge broadsword, which caused her dad's eyes to about bug out.

Finn then tugged on her arm and pulled her into the hallway. "Do you want me to speak with your father?" He was tracing a forefinger along her jawline as he spoke.

"About what?" Even as she was alarmed, she leaned into his hand, relishing the soft caress.

"My intentions."

"*What?* Don't you dare. I don't even know what your intentions are. And none of that matters anyhow, if your intentions don't jive with mine."

He just smiled and hunkered down a bit, kissing her softly.

"I mean it, Finn. You and I have unfinished business. Don't be jumping the gun here."

"The only jumping I will be doing is into your bed furs, sweetling."

"That's another thing. Yikes! Stop that."

"Stop what?"

"Touching me *there*."

"So, what was the other thing?"

"We can't sleep together in my parents' house."

He frowned. "Why not?"

"Because they wouldn't approve."

"Did you and Saint Dave not share a bed here?"

"Of course we did, but we were married."

"Ah."

"What does that mean?"

"You are withdrawing your favors to gain a marriage proposal."

"I am not!"

"I think I care for you, Lydia, but marriage . . . I vowed never to wed again. Besides, my time will be consumed soon with SEAL training."

"You *think* you care for me? That's big of you."

"Sarcasm ill suits you, Lydia. I will speak to your father, and all will be well."

"If you do, I'll never speak to you again." At the contemplative expression on his face, she added, "And I won't have sex with you, either."

"You did in the barn."

"That was a lapse in judgment."

"Spectacular *good* judgment, if you ask me."

"Just out of curiosity, since marriage is out of the question, what exactly would you be telling my father?"

"That we are going to live together and raise Mike, as good as wed without the ceremony."

"Without marriage?"

He nodded slowly.

"Oh, that'll go over great."

"Assuming I am accepted into the teams, my BUD/S training would not start 'til September, then last for many months. I intend to spend every minute of that time getting to know my son. That means living in the same keep. With or without you."

Finn's insistence that Mike was his biological son continued to distress her. She could see his wanting to be close to Mike because he reminded him of his own son. She was even able to concede the time-travel stuff as one of those God-made miracle thingees. But Mike could not be Finn's actual son. He just couldn't be.

Unless . . .

Unless he is Dave inside that Viking body.

Which he is not.

Of course not.

But if there could be the miracle of time travel, why not the miracle of reincarnation?

And then he dares to say he thinks he cares for me. Not love. Just caring. And then only a maybe. And based on that flimsy offering he expects me to open my home . . . and my legs . . . to him. We shall see about that.

"You have no rights, Finn."

"I have every right. Dare to defy me on this, and you

will find how strong-willed a Viking can be. And that is what I will tell your father. I will be living with his daughter henceforth."

"You have a thicker skull than I thought if you think any red-blooded American dad would agree to that, without marriage."

"Marriage, again!" He snorted his disgust. "I will not be coerced."

"Neither will I be, big boy."

A squeal of laughter came from upstairs, and she realized that Mike must have finished his bath. He always protested taking a bath, but it practically took a bulldozer to get him out. "I need to go read to Mike and put him to bed." She turned stiffly for the stairs.

"I will come with you. But do not think this conversation is over." Under his breath he added something that sounded like, "Nor is the bedsport."

Pulling on a father's heartstrings . . .

"Come and sit with us while Mommy reads us a story." Mike patted the thin strip of mattress available.

Lydia and Mike were sitting on his bed, propped against two pillows each, a pile of children's books betwixt them. He sat on a rocking chair by the window, just watching.

"I would never fit," Thorfinn said with a laugh.

"I can sit on your lap," Mike offered. "C'mon. Mommy reads real good."

So it was that Thorfinn found himself sitting on the

small bed, his shoulder and thigh rubbing against Lydia's rigid shoulder and thigh. She was angry with him, though he could not fathom why. Mike cuddled on Finn's lap, wearing a sleeping garment adorned with images of purple dragons. The boy's skin smelled of mint and of Miklof as he had been soon after his birth.

Thorfinn blinked several times, fighting the strong emotions which nigh overwhelmed him. *This is my life as it should have been.* Then, girding his loins with resolve, he added, *This is my life as it WILL be.*

Sensing his distress, Lydia squeezed his hand, then immediately dropped it, recalling that she was supposed to be angry.

Inroads, he thought.

Then she began to read, "Once upon a time, there was a grizzly bear named Pete . . ."

She read them three stories, which Thorfinn had to admit enthralled him, as well as his son. When she finished the last one, *The Viking Who Cried*, Thorfinn said, "That saga is well and good, but not entirely true. First off, Vikings do not wear horned helmets. How ridiculous! And little ones are closely guarded by their mothers. Ne'er have I heard of a boyling who went a-Viking."

"Do you know any Viking stories?" Mike craned his neck to peer up at him.

Thorfinn could not help himself. He gave the boy a hug and a quick kiss on the top of his head.

"Mayhap I can think of one. Well, this is a real story. It is about your great-grandfather's brother . . . I mean, my grandfather's brother, King Olaf."

"Your grandfather was a king?" Mike's eyes were wide with wonder.

"Nay, my grandfather's brother. In any case, Olaf and my grandfather Eric developed a most wonderful talent, which has been passed on to every male in our family." He proceeded to tell him how they could catch a spear aimed at them by an enemy and, by a deft flick of the fingers, turn it and lob it back at the villain. "It would be comparable to modern soldiers turning bombs or bullets off their targets and sending them back to the enemy, all in a split second. Like this . . ." He picked up a pencil from the bedside table, twirling it in his fingers and tossing it at the opposite wall.

"Wow!" Mike exclaimed.

"My mother is going to kill you if you put pencil marks on her wallpaper."

He chucked her chin playfully.

She did not return his smile.

Mayhap those inroads are rockier than I anticipated.

"Can you show me how?" Mike wanted to know.

Thorfinn nodded. "On the morrow."

"But we doan have no spears here." Mike pulled a long face, a ploy of children through the ages.

"We will use broom and rake handles."

"I don't know . . ." Lydia started to say.

"Shhh," he said, putting a forefinger to her lips. "It will be safe. Besides, it is a sight to behold watching my three uncles at the game."

Lydia tried to nip at his finger, but he quickly removed it.

"Okay, kiddo." Lydia rumpled Mike's hair, picked up the book, then slid off the bed, standing. "Time for bed."

"One more book, please."

She shook her head. "That's what you said last time. Besides, tomorrow's going to be a long day. You'll be seeing Grandma and Grandpa Denton."

He smiled. "Betcha they give me a present."

"I have a gift for you back at your home," Thorfinn told him.

"Goody. What is it?"

"A surprise."

As Lydia tucked Mike in, she said to Thorfinn, "I saw your gift for Mike. I also saw the amber. Did you buy that for . . . someone?"

He grinned. "Yea. Someone."

"It has a star in the center, did you know that?"

He frowned. "Yea. How does that signify?"

"I used to collect anything with stars. Star tree ornaments. Star wind chimes. Star canisters and pot holders. And every time Dave went on a mission, he would bring me a gift back. Always with stars on it somewhere." She paused. "Was there any special reason why you bought that amber?"

His first reaction was to rail at yet another reminder of her dead husband. But then he began to wonder if there might actually be some connection. A far-fetched idea, that, but worth noting. So he just nodded. "I saw it in a merchant's display, and it drew me." He shrugged.

Mike said his prayers, blessing everyone in the whole bloody world, Thorfinn included. But not to get a big head, he had to note that Mike also blessed the cows and chickens.

Lydia turned off the light, leaving on only a dim "night light," and bent over the bed to kiss Mike, giving Thorfinn a nice view of her curved arse in tight *den-ham* braies. "Sweet dreams, pumpkin."

"You, too, Mommy."

About to straighten up, Lydia noticed the direction of his stare and snorted her disgust.

Then Mike opened his arms to Thorfinn.

It was Thorfinn then who bent over the bed, and he did not mind at all if she ogled his arse. He brushed his lips across the boy's smooth cheek, unprepared for Mike's grabbing him about the neck and pulling him closer. Into his ear, he whispered, "I said a secret prayer t'night."

"What was that, little one?"

"I prayed fer you ta be my dad."

Chapter 17

And then she saw stars . . .

It was with much trepidation that Lydia drove up the lane to Green Meadows Farm with Finn, Magnus, and Mike. Torolf, Geek, Slick, and Sly went on to town, where everyone would meet up at noon with the FBI and local law enforcement. She and Dave's parents would also be meeting with town officials this afternoon to discuss their role in the memorial service on Saturday. JAM had stayed behind with three of Magnus's sons to protect her parents and their property.

Magnus was already *oooh*ing and *aaah*ing over the farm, just as he had back at Mill Pond Farm, but it was Finn she was most concerned about. She was still irritated with him that he would assume she would be willing to live with him without love or commitment. But what worried her now was what Dave's parents' reaction to him would be.

Mike was the first one out of the vehicle, and he ran up to give big hugs to Grandma and Grandpa, immediately followed by, "Where's my present?" The scamp rushed inside the house to search.

Lydia hugged Julie and Herb warmly, too. They'd always seemed like second parents to her. Then she introduced Magnus, saying, "Magnus has farming in his blood. You won't mind if he wanders around, will you?"

"No problem," Herb said. "We've got so many men protecting us here, you'll probably be tripping over them."

"Mayhap we can rebuild your barn whilst we're here," Magnus offered blithely, as if that were a little thing.

But any response by a gaping Herb was halted when he heard his wife gasp. Then he gasped, too, as Finn came from the other side of the vehicle, where he had been gathering some supplies Lydia's mother had sent over, including one of her red velvet cakes. She must have gotten up at dawn to make it.

Finn had been bent over picking up the boxes, and when he stood, they saw his eyes. It was understandable why the first thing out of Julie's lips was, "Dave! Oh, my God! It's Dave."

Finn rolled his eyes, muttered, "Dave again," then walked over and placed the box on the porch before turning to them, hand outstretched. "Greetings! My name is Thorfinn Haraldsson."

"But . . ." Julie was frowning with confusion.

"Who the hell are you?" Herb asked, but not unkindly.

"I told you. I am—"

"No, that's not what I mean." Herb, who was the same height as Finn but wire thin, grabbed the Viking and gave him a big bear hug, not letting go.

Finn cast Lydia a pleading look over Herb's shoulder, not knowing what to do without offending the older man.

"Julie, come give . . . um, this big boy here a welcome," Herb said to his wife in some pointed way.

Lydia understood. It was code, something they always said every time Dave had come home. "Our *big boy* is home now, honey. All is good."

Well, all was not good. And she couldn't let this go on.

"Herb, Julie, I need to talk to you."

Reluctantly, Julie let go of Finn. Tears of joy were streaming down her face.

Just then, Cage came around the side of the house. He was one of the guys assigned to protect the Dentons.

"Hey, darlin'," he said, coming up and giving Lydia a brotherly peck on the cheek.

Hearing a low growl, he let his arm remain around her shoulders and turned to Finn, grinning. "Hey, Haraldsson! How's it goin'?"

"Remove. Thy. Arm," Finn said.

Herb and Julie watched the interchange with puzzled eyes.

Lydia stepped between the one grinning and the other glowering man. "Cage, would you mind going inside to entertain Mike for a little while. Finn and I have something to discuss with Herb and Julie."

Going up onto the porch, which wrapped around three

sides of the old Victorian farmhouse, Herb and Julie sat on two rockers, while she sat beside Finn on the swing. He tried to hold her hand, but she shrugged him off. He was being a horse's ass, in more ways than one.

"Let me start from the beginning," she said.

But was interrupted by the wild barking of a dog. A huge furry mass, as big as a small horse, came barreling around the corner of the house, up the steps, then launched itself at Finn. With front paws on his chest, he was barking and licking his face at the same time.

It was Whiskey, their aged German Shepherd. Dave's dog before he left home.

Everyone was stunned at the implication.

Once Finn had petted the dog and settled him at his feet like a rug that would not budge, Lydia started again, "I know how it must look, but Finn is not Dave. No, don't interrupt 'til I finish. There's a secret that I know Finn and his family would rather I not divulge, but you have to be told so that you can understand." She glanced to Finn for his permission.

He hesitated, then nodded.

They listened to her, but their eyes were on Finn, who, despite all odds, seemed like Dave to them.

"He is *not* Dave," she repeated for emphasis. Then she proceeded to tell them the whole story, minus the sex. It took her more than fifteen minutes, even without interruptions. Herb and Julie were too stunned and disbelieving at her incredible story to voice any questions . . . yet.

"Time travel? Are you crazy, Lydia?" her father-in-law asked.

"Sometimes I think so."

"And all these other people . . . Magnus, his family . . . they all believe this crap?"

"Not only believe it, they have experienced it." Finn spoke up for the first time.

"It's impossible," her mother-in-law said, but there was hesitancy in her voice.

"Do you really think there's such a thing as time travel?" Herb continued to prod her.

"Well . . ." She wet her lips, dry after talking so much. "I can only say what Finn and the others say. It must be a miracle. Not some phenomenon that can be explained by science, but something God deigned to happen."

"Finn, what do you think?"

He shrugged. "Strange things happen in this world, things that we cannot understand. We can only live with the consequences."

"And you're going to be a SEAL?" Julie was blinking away another bout of tears.

Lydia hated piling this on them when they already had enough on their plates with the barn burning and a terrorist lurking out there, somewhere.

"Hopefully," Finn answered.

"Are you sure you wouldn't like to be a farmer?" Herb asked.

And Lydia knew that the Dentons, like her parents, wished, beyond reasoning, that Finn would be the lost son come home to run the family farm.

"Nay," Finn said, but then chuckled. "Who can predict? Stranger things have happened."

Oh, great! Give them hope.

"Though I cannot imagine myself milking a cow."

Everyone laughed then, deciding to put aside all these heavy thoughts. "Come inside for a light lunch before you go into town," Julie coaxed.

"Light? Hah! She's been workin' since dawn to prepare a feast for you all," Herb teased.

"Oh, you!" Julie said, but then she seemed to notice something about Finn and did a double take. Addressing Lydia now, she remarked, "It's all well and good to say this man has nothing to do with Dave, honey, but have you noticed what's etched on that one arm ring?"

No, she hadn't.

Peering close, she saw . . .

Stars.

She slapped a hand over her rapidly beating heart.

And she could swear she heard a laughing voice in her head say, "Babe."

The memorial service would be memorable . . .

Jamal breathed a sigh of relief, just barely missing a security guard as he gained entry into the city's maintenance warehouse just after midnight on Thursday night.

No one would recognize him from a distance as a person of Arab descent, or even as a man, dressed as a restaurant worker coming home from a night shift. He wore a blond wig, blue contact lenses, theatrical makeup, a waitress uniform, and orthopedic white shoes. Thank Allah for the Internet. The hardest part had been shaving his legs, and double shaving his face. On the way here, he'd passed two men on the other side of the street, who he assumed were undercover agents. The town was swarming with them . . . FBI, police, those damn Navy SEALs.

Quickly, using a flashlight, he found the statue of his enemy, under a sheet cover. He would like nothing better than to blow it to pieces right now, but his plan called for much more. He wanted it to explode when Lydia Denton and her son were sitting on the platform in front of it during the ceremony.

He propped the flashlight so it shone steadily on the brass plate, which read:

LIEUTENANT DAVID DENTON

U.S. NAVY SEAL

PROUD WARRIOR

PROUD SON OF FARMDALE, MINNESOTA

1973–2003

His upper lip curled back over his teeth with disgust as he quickly set out his tools. Screwdriver to undo the plate. Chisel and mini-hacksaw to dig a hole under the plate big enough to hold the time-release bomb he carried in his giant purse. It was not a huge bomb. Unlike the evil Denton, he cared about collateral damage. A radius of twenty feet would do nicely.

To his surprise, it only took him an hour to complete the job and replace the plate and sheet covering.

Then he left for his new hiding place. He would not return to the hillsides near the two farms. Too risky now.

Instead he would go to the home on the outskirts of town, which he had commandeered at knifepoint, the two elderly residents tied to their kitchen chairs with duct tape.

Only a day and a half more.

Then he could get on with his life.

When life seems to be all lemons . . .

"So that's it," Emory Davis, FBI agent, said to the roomful of police, Homeland Security operatives, SEALs, and family members Friday morning, after everyone had spoken.

"To sum it up: We now know the person we're looking for is Jamal Udeen, thanks to the intel from his brother. He is looking for revenge on the Denton family . . . in particular Lydia Denton and her son."

Lydia shivered in her folding seat between her mother and father, even though she'd known this since last night. Thorfinn was standing against the far wall with his cousin Torolf and the SEALs. He nodded to acknowledge her glance, his face grim with fury. Over and over, he kept telling her that he would protect her and Mike, but she didn't see how he could keep such a promise.

"He's been camping at two hillside sites overlooking the Denton and Hartley farms. He was efficient in cleaning up after himself, but not clean enough, thanks to a few bloodhounds.

"Jamal is armed and highly dangerous. You all have pictures, but keep in mind he will no doubt be in disguise. Although we don't know his specific plan, we suspect it involves the memorial service tomorrow.

"Only those carrying invitations will be allowed within two blocks of the town square. In addition, this is a small town where everybody knows everybody; so, we have volunteers patrolling *all* the streets with walkie-talkies, ordered to report *anyone* they don't recognize. Even out-of-town newshounds who might have smelled a story. They'd better have invitations with photo IDs, or they won't be allowed in. State troopers are handling the permit situation.

"They found Jamal's computer at the dump, hacked to a pulp. Still, we have our electronics geeks at work trying to see if they can get any clues as to what he's up to.

"In the meantime, everyone go on as usual, but be very, very careful. That's all. Good day!"

What a mess! Lydia thought they should have cancelled the event. Dave wouldn't have cared. But his parents and the authorities convinced her to carry on. Once you gave in to a terrorist, it would snowball. Besides, they needed to nab this guy ASAP.

Once outside, Thorfinn gave her a one-armed hug to his side, leading her to the SUV rental. "Enough of all this gloominess. Come, let us go spend time with our son."

She should have corrected him then.

But she didn't.

One more, for the road . . .

Thorfinn was disgusted. Every suggestion he made to occupy their time, and take their minds off the villain, got a blunt "No!" from those in charge of this mission, mean-

ing the fibbies, the local law men, and JAM, who was the
SEAL leader here.

JAM was usually the one delivering the communal re-
fusals.

"Lydia, Mike, and I would like to ride some horses
over to a waterfall."

"No!"

"How about the old mill and pond? That's not so far."

"No!"

"Can we drive into Farmdale and watch a *move-he*?"
He had seen several whilst staying with Torolf and Hilda,
who had phoned him several times to give him advice on
how to behave around Lydia and her son. He'd cut Hilda
off last time mid-tirade.

"A new Disney movie is playing," Lydia had added.

"No!"

"Mr. Hartley wants to show us how his new hay mower
works in the south pasture."

"No!"

"Can we go over to the Denton farm and help rebuild
the barn?"

"No!"

"I want to go out in the barn and play with Lydia." She
had been standing nearby when he'd asked that one, thus
curbing any crudity he might have considered using.

"No!"

"Can I twiddle my thumbs?"

"Very funny."

"Mike and I are going to go watch cows get babies
with a hand up their arses."

There was a resounding silence, then, "No!"

So, in the end, Thorfinn set up acceptable entertainment for them all in the clearing between the farmhouse and the barn. He invited the three uncles, plus Torolf and Ragnor, to Mill Pond Farm, after which they gathered every wooden handle or short pole they could find, much to the consternation of Lydia's parents. Broom, mop, rake, shovel, tomato stake, bamboo fishing rod. He also invited the Hartleys to come over to get away from the stress. They were going to show these fibbies and overweight local law men, not to mention a few full-of-themselves SEALs, how Vikings played.

And, truth to tell, he wanted to impress his son.

With interchanging guards all around the farm, thus began the "games," so to speak.

The three women prepared an outdoor feast of hot dogs, which were not really made of dog meat, and catsup, which was not really cats' blood, and various other foods and sweets. So much chicken that he would not be surprised to see the raven flag of death flurrying over the hen house. Boiled and pickled-red eggs. And deviled eggs; he shuddered to think what they might be. Again, those poor chickens!

Delicious slabs of beef, called steaks, were cooked to juice-dripping perfection over an open fire. Especially appreciated by all the men. Everyone knew that animal blood, like boar, in small doses gave a man vigor, except for pig blood, which just gave a man running bowels, in his experience.

Various breads, but not a manchet round in sight. Not

that he was missing that tasteless staple of the Viking and Saxon table. And homemade churned butter, which had a much stronger taste than the store-bought kind.

Even the *Gammelost*, or old cheese, that Magnus had brought was on display, though much avoided, he noticed. With good cause. 'Twas said some Viking warriors went berserk after eating that horrid stinksome cheese. Magnus insisted that it reminded him of the Norselands. He did not eat it, either.

He especially liked Mistress Hartley's berry pies and, of course, Mike's favorite, chocolate-chip cookies, which his very own Lydia had baked afore coming here. Mistress Denton had brought fresh strawberries from her garden, which were served with cream from this farm's very own milk.

Magnus and Jogeir were in farm heaven, or, rather farm Valhalla . . . if there was such a place.

If the Dentons were not hovering about him, wheedling information from him, which they sadly hoped would prove he was their dead son inside this big Viking body, then the dog Whiskey trailed him with adoration. It was enough to put a Norseman off his mead.

But he would not let that spoil his day. He was here with his son. And Lydia. Life was good, as it had not been for him in many, many years.

He got up from where he had been sitting on a blanket with Lydia and Mike. "Well, Miklof, are you ready to see the Viking spear trick I told you about?"

"Yeah, yeah, yeah," his son said, jumping up and down, his shoes flickering lights with each bounce. In truth, the boy rarely sat still for more than a moment. "Why do you call me Meatloaf?"

Lydia shot him a glance of alarm.

Ignoring her caution, he said, with a smile, "Not meatloaf. Mick-loff. Miklof is just another form of Michael, or Mike. I had . . ." He coughed to clear his suddenly tight throat. "I *have* a son named Miklof."

"You do?" The boy's eyes went wide with wonder. "Where is he? Can I play with him?"

"This conversation is getting out of hand," Lydia interjected. "Mike, go in the house and tell Grandma and Nana to come out and watch a certain Viking show off."

Mike giggled and ran off.

Thorfinn glowered at her. "I do not show off."

She grinned. "We'll see."

Soon, Thorfinn was in his element. They had two "teams." He, Jorund, and Rolf on one side. Torolf, Ragnor, and Magnus on the other. With laughter and jeers, they lobbed the makeshift spears at each other, fielding the "attacks" and turning them back on the assailants. More than a few Saxons and Franks had met their deaths due to this particular talent. His uncle Jorund, though more than fifty, was the best of all; even today in the Norselands the old ones spoke sagas about his renowned prowess on the battlefield. Today he ran a business much like Lydia's, but he taught only folks crippled in mind and body how to exercise their muscles. In the end, to much cheering, Thorfinn's team was declared the winner . . . due mostly to Jorund.

Sinking down to the blanket next to Lydia, he said,

"Art thou impressed, sweetling?" He nuzzled her neck. To-day, she was wearing a blue-flowered white dress, which could only be described as a short, knee-high *gunna*, or gown, but the arms and shoulders were exposed to the sun. *I wonder if she is wearing any smallclothes.* Also exposed were her crimson-painted toes in skimpy barely-there white leather shoes. *It looks like her toes are bleeding.*

She pushed him away with a laugh and replied, "Very."

"Dost want to sneak inside and do a bit of sw . . . making love?" *See, I can be suave.*

She laughed again. "I said I was impressed. Not that impressed."

"Liar," he said, but he laughed, too. *I am laughing on the outside, but not on the inside. If I laugh on the inside, my you-know-what hurts.*

Taking her hand in his, he turned back to watch the next bout of "talent." In the process of turning, he noticed Mistress Hartley watching him. She must have seen him kissing Lydia's neck because she looked first at him, then Lydia, then back to him . . . and smiled.

No doubt she and her husband were back to the business of him being Dave and them wanting him to run their farm. Which was not going to happen. Bloody hell! 'Twas past time for everyone to let Dave rest in peace.

One of the Hartleys' farmworkers was demonstrating how to lasso a steer with a long, looped rope, except that the steer was actually a wooden post. He was very talented, and soon had others wanting to be taught that particular skill.

"I cannot see what circumstance would require a SEAL to lasso," he commented as Sly failed with his third attempt.

"Well, they might need to lasso a tango," Lydia replied. "You know, making do with the weapons or materials at hand."

"Or one of the webfoot warriors might need to lasso a shark. Ha, ha, ha," Thorfinn added. *That is not even funny. What a clodpole I have become!*

"That's not as funny as you think," his uncle Jorund said, sinking down to the ground beside them. "Did I tell you how I traveled here to the future? On the back of a killer whale. I jest not!" At the look of incredulity on Lydia's face, he explained. He had somehow landed in a hospitium for demented people, called a mental clinic, because of his claims to have time-traveled. As a result, everyone who had come thereafter never mentioned the outrageous happenstance of how they had arrived.

Thorfinn had heard Jorund's story before, but enjoyed watching Lydia hear it. Mike was sitting on his lap now, listening intently, which Lydia must have decided was acceptable since the little boy would just think it was a tall tale. In the end, Mike sighed. "I wish I could ride a killer whale."

"Maybe we'll go to Sea World sometime," his mother promised. "Remember how you liked the orcas there?"

Next, Cage demonstrated his guitar-playing talents, singing some Cajun songs. The music was lively and the lyrics fun. Begrudgingly, he had to admit that the SEAL had talents, even if he did enjoy annoying him with his attentions to Lydia.

Everyone was subdued that evening after dinner. He came downstairs after listening to Lydia read five books to his son, and kissing him good-night himself. Still a new, heart-tugging experience for him. He'd given Lydia a kiss, too, before she had a chance to duck his embrace. Mike had thought it hilariously funny that he would want to kiss his mother.

Now, with Mike, Lydia, her mother, and her father asleep, the men in the living room were breaking down and inspecting their weapons. He was honing his sword. Magnus was snoring on a low sofa, his broadaxe across his massive chest. Sleeping bags were scattered across the floor. No one said much. The night before a mission was much the same anywhere, at any time. Anticipation. Dread.

He, for one, would be glad when it was all over, and he could get on with his new life . . . whatever that would be.

'Twas the middle of the night when he awakened, his back aching from lying on the hard floor. By the light from the kitchen, he could see all the various bodies at rest, most on the floor, like him, except for Magnus on the sofa, and two men in reclining chairs.

He stood and made his way toward the stairs. Quiet as he was, Torolf whispered, "Is everything okay?"

"Yes," he whispered back. "I just want to check on Miklof."

Torolf chuckled.

Once upstairs, he was alarmed at first to see Lydia's

bed empty, but he found her curled up with Miklof in his sleeping bower. His heart swelled with deep emotion at the sight.

So exhausted were Lydia and Miklof, or so adept was he, that neither awakened when he picked Lydia up and carried her back to her own bed. He laid her gently on the bed and slid under the bed linens behind her. Lying on his left side, he spooned against her back, then placed one arm on the pillow over her head and the other lightly on her hip. Soon, drugged by her body warmth and floral scent, he fell asleep, too.

In the middle of the night, something awakened him. He was a light sleeper, as a warrior must always be. Listening, he heard nothing, but then he realized that the rhythm of Lydia's breathing had changed. She was awake.

And his manpart was hard and long, riding the crease of her buttocks. *Bloody hell, can you not behave this once? Oh, that is it! I am finally over-the-edge barmy . . . talking to my cock.*

And his hand was caressing her breast. *Well, no wonder you are misbehaving.*

And her nipple was engorged, its point pressing into his palm like an erotic signal. *See, it is her fault, not ours.*

"Lydia," he whispered, not wanting to awaken others in the house. They were both on their sides, still spooned together, very tightly. *Did she just wiggle her arse against me? Or was that you?* He was still talking to his manpart, for Frigg's sake!

"How did I get here? What are you doing here?"

"I was lonely."

Me, too.

That is just wonderful. IT talks back, too.

He could feel her silent laughter.

She likes me, she likes me.

Oh, shut up!

He began to caress her breasts in earnest with his one hand. Massaging. Running fingertips over them, up and down, in a washboard fashion.

Her soft gasp encouraged him to do more. *Torolf may think he knows everything about bedsport, but I know that gasping is a silent signal from females.*

He kissed her ear and used the tip of his wet tongue to stimulate her there, at the same time pinching and tweaking and fluttering her nipples.

She groaned softly and put a halting hand over his. "We can't . . . what if someone hears?"

Groaning is a signal, too. "We can. If you are quiet." *But not too quiet.*

His left hand, which had still been resting on the pillow above her head, moved down and under her so that both hands were now touching her bare breasts under her sleep *shert*. If he were not so intent on her response, he might have missed the whimper. Only then did he move his right hand down, sweeping over her abdomen, the slight swell of her belly, to her woman hair, where he soon discovered her moistness.

"You want me," he whispered against her ear.

"No kidding."

Tugging her backward, he inserted his knee betwixt

her thighs, separating her folds. Turning her head to the right, facing her shoulder, he kissed her, catching her cries as he brought her to ecstasy with a few expert strokes to her slick bud.

And he grew harder and longer, undulating several times against her crease, then stopped himself. *Not yet. Not yet.*

"Remember when I showed you the Viking S-Spot?" he mused, back to her breasts.

She nodded, unable to speak just yet, he assumed.

"Well, I saw a book with pictures at the commander's house that shows where the G-Spot is." *I wonder where I could purchase that book for myself.* "Can I practice on you, sweetling?"

A gurgle that tried to be a laugh escaped her lips. He took that for assent. *So, I add gurgle to gasp and groan.* With the heel of one hand on her nether bone, he inserted a middle finger inside her, under that bone, searching for the knot which would give her more pleasure, presumably of a different kind. She jerked when he found the spot. He began to massage her then, from inside and out. Her body began to jerk wildly with a never-ending rhythm of peaking.

Giving her no chance to recover, or change her mind, he pressed her right knee up to her chest, then he plunged into her still-convulsing channel.

"Are you trying to kill me?" she asked.

"Shhh." He remained still for a moment, wanting to calm down his enthusiasm, and make sure they hadn't awakened anyone else in the house, like her father. Then he began the age-old strokes in and out of her tight sheath, at the same time working her breasts again with his left hand. With his right, he found that she was incredibly wet and slick. Her woman dew coated his fingertips, which he used to torture her relentlessly. He wanted her to want him more than any other man . . . more even than the dead husband. He wanted this night, and this sex, to become a need to her, like thirst and hunger. He was unrelenting in his use of her. Plunging, retreating, stroking, 'til they peaked together . . . a peaking that was longer and more intense than he had ever experienced.

In the aftermath, he realized that he was the one who would want her more than any other woman. He was the one who would thirst and hunger for her. He was the one lost.

Chapter 18

A blast . . . just like the past . . .

Lydia was as nervous as a kitten at a dog show.

She and Mike, adorable in his little suit and tie, were seated on the platform, along with Dave's parents, the mayor, JAM, acting as representative for the SEALs, and various other dignitaries. Dave's life-size bronze statue was to the back of them on a high marble cube. She couldn't bear to give it more than a passing glance, so much did it look like her husband. Even when Mike craned his little neck to look behind him and asked, "Is that my daddy?" she stared straight ahead.

"Yes, it is, honey. And he was a very brave man."

"I know." He probably did. He'd been told about his father almost since birth.

In front of the platform were dozens of folding chairs to

accommodate those vetted friends, news media, and town folks. There were law enforcement people all over the place, both in uniform and not. Finn sat in the front row, wearing an old suit of Dave's that Julie had lent him. He looked different. Normal. Not that he wasn't normal.

The grim, alert expression revealed none of the passion he'd shown her last night. That shouldn't disappoint her, but it did.

"Finn is lookin' at you, Mommy."

"I know, honey. Don't stare."

She didn't know what she was going to do with this man with a past . . . from the past. She loved him. She knew that. And it had nothing to do with Dave. But today's ceremony cemented her feelings about their future together. There was none. She would not sit through another memorial service for another man. She just couldn't.

The mayor continued to drone on, followed by a state senator who used this opportunity for his own gain. Then Lieutenant Jacob Alvarez Mendozo, JAM, stepped forward.

She noticed Finn cock his head to the side, gazing at the statue behind her. Suddenly, he jumped up and hollered, "Move out of here, everyone. Move! Move! It's behind the brass plate." Rushing up to the platform, he literally picked her and Mike up, tossing them to the ground. "Run!" He did the same for Dave's parents.

"Are you crazy, Ericsson?" JAM yelled.

"Look, damn you," Finn said, pointing at the statue. "The screws holding the plaque have been tampered with."

"Mayday! Mayday!" someone shouted.

"A bomb!" someone else shrieked.

A melee broke out then as people shoved and stumbled trying to get away.

When the bomb finally exploded, tossing Dave's bronze body to smithereens . . . just as it had been in real life . . . chairs, wood, slivers of metal, and microphones flew through the air like deadly missiles. A horrified Lydia realized, slowly, that only a few people had been left within the perimeter of the blast.

And one of them was Finn.

Her keening wail filled her ears, and then she fainted.

And so it ends . . .

Jamal came out of the house to witness the explosion, happy to have at last completed his noble vengeance. He intended to slip away shortly, back to, not Michigan, but his homeland: Iraq.

However, in the settling dust, he noticed Lydia Denton and her crying son were alive and being ministered to on a bench in front of the drug store.

"Aaarrgh!" Running back into the house, he barely looked at the terrified eyes of the elderly couple still duct-taped to chairs in the kitchen. The room smelled from their soiled clothing since he'd refused to release them to use the toilet. No matter to him.

He ran toward the town center, pistol in one hand and rifle in the other. In the chaos, no one noticed him at first. So, he was able to get off two rounds before the idiot FBI and SEAL protectors rushed him. He had hit some people, but he was not sure who. Within twenty yards of the drug store, he saw Lydia Denton sit up straight and stare right at him. In her eyes, he saw not anger. Or fear. But pity.

How dared she pity him!

He shot both weapons at once before he felt a dozen bullets riddle his body.

It was over.

He fell to the ground, his lifeblood flowing out of him. Finally, peace enveloped him.

A stitch in time . . .

Lydia and Mike sat in the waiting room of Doc Fallon's clinic later that afternoon.

She had wanted Mike to go home with everyone else after they learned that Finn had only suffered superficial wounds, but the little boy insisted. Mike usually didn't attach himself to new people like this, but it was as if he sensed that Finn was something more than his mommy's friend.

"Why did that bad man make a bomb, Mommy?"

"He was sick, honey. In his head. A long time ago he lost his wife and his little boy, and he was missing them so much."

"Like you miss my daddy?"

"Well, sort of."

Mike had been whisked away before he could see the actual devastation. No one had died, but Mayor Svensson might very well lose an arm. The senator had a concussion.

Finn needed a few stitches on his arm and shoulders. Many people had abrasions. The elderly couple who'd been hostages were dehydrated and in shock at a nearby hospital. It could have been a deadly disaster if Finn hadn't acted so quickly.

"Are you sure Finn is okay? Are you sure he's really here? Maybe we should go in and check. Maybe he needs us ta hold his hand if he's gettin' a shot. Maybe—"

"Mike! Settle down. He'll be out soon."

He was about to argue when the inner office door opened.

"Your young man will be out soon, Lydia. We're just taking X-rays to make sure there are no internal injuries," Doc Fallon said. The gray-haired, rotund man with a jolly disposition had been her family doctor since birth. "He's a lucky man."

"Yes, I know," she said.

"So, Mikey, you wanna come back and see my ice-pop freezer?"

Mike's face brightened, but he looked to Lydia for approval.

"Sure, sweetie."

Soon after that, Finn came out, limping slightly. Dave's suit jacket was gone, the dress shirt stained with blood, with one sleeve ribbed and one pant leg ripped to gain access to his wounds. Lydia and Mike looked battered, too, but not as bad as Mr. Hero here.

He smiled at them, but his expression appeared strained. Well, why wouldn't it? He'd been through hell today. They all had.

His eyes connected with hers, and held. Something was wrong. But then he glanced at Mike. "Hey, bratling, how are you doing?"

"Okay," Mike said in a wobbly voice, then launched himself at Finn, who caught him in his arms with a wince.

"Mike," she reprimanded, "Finn is hurt."

Ignoring her, Mike buried his face in Finn's neck and locked his arms and legs around him.

With a choked laugh, Finn used one hand to hold him up, under the buttocks, and the other to tousle his hair. Then, leaning his head back, Finn inquired, "Why the headlock, little one?"

Mike had tears in his eyes. Lydia hadn't realized just how much emotion he'd bottled up since the explosion. She should have realized he was being unnaturally quiet.

"I thought you went to heaven with my daddy."

There was supposed to be a kiss, not a kiss-off . . .

Thorfinn had made some decisions in the past hour.

He sat stiffly in the passenger seat of the vehicle as they drove back to Mill Pond Farm. Mike was asleep in the back seat, the day having finally overwhelmed the little mite. Thorfinn had offered to drive; these empty country roads would have provided good practice for him, but Lydia had insisted that he was in no condition to drive with all his injuries. She had been right. Oh, these cuts and bruises were nothing for a Viking who suffered more just surviving day to day in the far Northlands, but he was off balance in other ways.

With one hand on the steering wheel, she reached over with the other and squeezed his hand. "I was so scared. Thank God you're safe."

Likewise, sweetling, he thought. *A thousand times likewise.*

He could scarce breathe for all the emotions rushing through his body, and he did not like the feeling of helplessness. Not at all. So much could have gone differently today. He felt like a warrior after a hard-won battle. "Yea, thank the gods, you and Mike are safe, too."

"Especially Mike, I'm sure. You just found Mike. To lose him would have been devastating to you."

"You, too," he said. At her look of confusion, he said, "I would have been devastated to lose you, too."

"What?" She swung her head to the right and the vehicle swerved.

"Bloody hell! Watch the road."

Once the vehicle was going straight again, she remarked, "You pick an odd moment to tell me something like that."

"Well, there are so many things that we must discuss, but I will be leaving as soon as we get to your parents' farm."

"Why the rush?"

"Magnus and his family have already departed, along with most of the SEALs. Torolf is with your parents, waiting for my return. We will go to the flying port together."

"Why?" she repeated. He could not see the tears, but he heard them in her voice.

"I have been notified of my acceptance to the BUD/S

program. They waived the written test 'til my language skills are better." When she did not respond to that, he continued, "I must needs work day and night for the next few sennights to prepare for this training ordeal." What he was saying, without words, was that he was still committed to the military. But it was more than that.

She inhaled and exhaled several times. "Mike and I can't return yet. We've got to stay another week. Spend some time with the Dentons, as originally planned."

"I understand that. 'Tis why we must settle some things afore I depart."

She drove the car over to a side road and turned off the motor. Only then did she ask, "Such as?"

"Our wedding. Can you set a date that coincides with my break afore entering the official training program in the fall?"

"I beg your pardon. I don't recall hearing a marriage proposal, let alone my acceptance."

"Will you marry me?" he asked, realizing his mistake. He had forgotten that women could be sensitive on this subject.

"I don't know. It depends."

"On what?" He was affronted that she did not immediately accept his proposal. In truth, it was the first he had ever made, his marriage to Luta having been arranged by both sets of parents.

"Do you love me, Finn?"

He groaned inwardly. "I care for you, Lydia. I just told you how strongly I felt when I feared for your safety."

"Caring is not the same as love, Finn."

"Is this about the military?"

She shook her head. "No, much as I despair of being with another military man, I concede that is what you are. But, while I can accept marriage to another SEAL, I cannot accept marriage without love."

She is like a dog with a bone. A precious dog. "When I realized that there might be a bomb behind you today, my world crashed. From that moment 'til I saw you again an hour later, I did not know if you were still alive, or injured badly. I understood then, for the first time, how strong my feelings for you are. Is that not enough?"

"No. I care about my dance studio. I care about world peace. I care about my friends. That is not love."

He put both hands to his head and pulled his own hair with frustration. "I do not even know what love is."

"Yes, you do. You love Mike, don't you?"

"You want me to love you the same way I love Miklof?"

"You are an idiot!"

"Well, we are going to wed, and that is that."

"It's not a decision you can make for me."

"I'm not letting you go."

"That's good, because I'm not letting you go, either. You can skedaddle off to California, or Timbuktu, but you won't escape me. I intend to make you fall in love with me."

Ski-dad-hull? Tim-buck-what? He smiled, he could not help himself. "Such passion! Is it possible to make a person fall in love? By the by, you never said . . . do *you* love me?"

"Of course, I love you."

"So, you intend to wage an assault on me 'til I surrender with love?"

"Exactly."

"Wage on," he said.

And she did. She released her seat belt and his, and with Miklof still asleep in the back seat, she squirmed onto his lap and kissed and kissed and kissed him. Her tongue was even in his mouth. His tongue might have crept into her mouth. For a certainty, his cock was saluting her enthusiasm.

Finally, when he was able to take her by the shoulders and set her back on her own seat, she said, "Did it work yet?"

"Nay, methinks I will need more convincing. After all, love does not come easily to a Norseman."

She grinned . . . a wicked, purely enticing grin. "Batten down the hatches, Mr. Viking, because you haven't seen anything 'til you've seen a determined *Minnesota* Viking."

Beware of women with vibrators . . .

Lydia and Mike had been back in California for two weeks, and while Finn had come to see them—or at least come to see Mike—there had been no opportunity for her to be alone with the man and try to make him fall in love with her. If that was even possible.

"I'm desperate," Lydia said on a long sigh. "Finn says he cares about me, but he doesn't love me. How can I marry a man who doesn't love me? I mean, marriage is hard enough for two people in love," she said to Kirstin, Madrene, Alison, and a newcomer to her pole-dancing class—Torolf's wife, Hilda.

They were all at the Hotel Del, enjoying a Sunday brunch, while Mike was playing video games at a neighbor's house.

"I do not see why you would even want that hard-headed, arrogant, lackwitted son of a troll," Hilda said, licking her lips and moaning with delight at the sinful strawberry and cream crepes she was devouring.

"Aren't all men like that?" Lydia laughed, especially when the other four women nodded vigorously. She'd already had a mushroom and cheese omelette with a croissant and was eyeing the fresh fruit plate on a neighboring table.

"He should be chasing you, honey. Maybe you could try making him jealous," Kirstin suggested. "It's a good thing we don't come here very often. I'd be a blimp." She and Madrene had ordered homemade waffles with blueberries and maple syrup.

"Never happen." These four women were physically fit, none overweight. She liked to think she was at least partly responsible for that.

"I think you need a very specific plan. And that means lists. Does anyone have a pen and paper?" This from Kirstin, the college professor in her coming to the fore.

"Okay, you tried telling him you loved him. Now you need to hit him where he is most sensitive," Alison said.

There was a short silence before Madrene blurted out, "His cock."

"Madrene!" the rest of them exclaimed with shock, but they were all laughing.

"His manpart, then. Same thing."

Kirstin wrote SEX on her list.

"My biggest problem is getting Finn to be alone with me. This pre-SEAL training is consuming so much of his time."

"Too bad you can't just tie him to a chair . . ." Hilda's words trailed off.

"Or a bed," Kirstin added.

"Like a sex slave," Madrene contributed.

"With chains. Naked." This from Alison.

They all smiled then, food forgotten.

And Kirstin added to her list: KIDNAP. CHAINS. SEDUCE.

They all remained silent then, pondering.

"I'm not going to do the love slave, handcuffs thing again," Lydia decided.

"Hmmm. Maybe jealousy would be the best way to make him realize how much he really loves you." This from Kirstin, who was back to picking at her strawberry and whipped cream waffle. She crossed KIDNAP and CHAINS off her list and added JEALOUSY.

"Chocolate body paint always worked for me," said Hilda.

"Where can I buy chocolate body paint?" Lydia wanted to know. At the other inquiring faces, she explained, "If I can't get him to fall in love with me by jealousy, at least I could use it as a weapon of sexual torture."

"I know where you can buy the neatest tingling body

oil to use with a special vibrating massager," Kirstin added for the "weapons" arsenal.

They all agreed to stop for one of those on the way home.

"Then there's Geek's penile wax glove, of course." Madrene had an impish gleam in her eyes. "I tried it on Ian one night, and he still gets a goofy look on his face when he puts on his dress gloves."

"Feathers would be good, too," said Hilda.

"Good heavens, when I finally get married, I am going to know so much good stuff." Kirstin actually managed a straight face with that fib; she knew plenty on her own, would be Lydia's guess.

"Listen, I have an idea that could make Finn jealous and make him realize how much he loves me all at the same time," Lydia offered tentatively. "Does anyone have a video recorder?"

"I do." Kirstin's eyebrows were raised at her in question.

"Well, I have the flesh-colored leotards and the pole." Lydia then outlined her idea.

"It might work," Madrene said.

The others smiled in agreement.

After that, they kept adding to the list of what they would need to implement Lydia's plan, laughing 'til they got dirty looks from the maître d'. When they rose to leave, they noticed a table of Navy officers behind them. They were all grinning.

Chapter 19

Was Dr. Phil ever a Navy SEAL? . . .

Thorfinn was running on the beach at Coronado with Torolf, Slick, Sly, JAM, Geek, and Cage. Amazingly, he was starting to enjoy jogging, and, for a certainty, his body was in better condition than it had ever been. He could even run and talk at the same time, which he had not been able to do in the beginning.

When they stopped at the five-mile mark to rest before the return trek, Sly looked sideways at him. "You're gonna diddle around and lose her, you know."

Navy SEALs were as bad as Vikings, Thorfinn was discovering. They minded everybody's affairs but their own.

"Close your teeth, halfbrain," he said. *Lest you want a fistful of sand clogging your throat.*

"Listen, Finnster, when I was a kid down on the bayou, my brother said he didn't like catfish. He always tossed back every catfish he ever caught. So, my MawMaw tol' Phillipe, be careful, 'cause if he didn't eat the catfish, someone else would. One day Phillipe decided he had a taste for catfish, and lo and behold, the catfish was gone. Moral of the story: Eat yer catfish when ya can, or someone else'll snatch it off yer plate, guar-an-teed."

Thorfinn snapped out his favorite Old Norse expletive.

"That means *Bite me*," Torolf told Cage.

"It does not!"

Torolf shrugged. "A rough translation."

"If I e'er meet that MawMaw of yours, if she even exists, I plan to throttle her."

"You could try. My MawMaw is one tough broad. Arnold Schwarzenegger with dentures. Talk about!"

"If you have no feelings for Lydia, would you mind if I asked her out on a date?" Slick asked. Women were drawn to this dark SEAL with his unsmiling demeanor.

I will be bloody hell damned if I just hand Lydia over to him. "Yea, I would mind. Do, and you die. And I ne'er said I had no feelings for Lydia. I merely said she does not want to wed with me 'til I am able to say I love her."

"Then say it, dammit," Torolf advised.

"I cannot lie."

"Millions of men lie about that. Besides, if you aren't already in love with her, you'll probably grow to love her," Torolf told him.

"Maybe you oughtta talk with a therapist," JAM suggested.

"A head doctor? There is naught wrong with my head." *Except it is a thousand years old.*

"Your cock, then?" Sly suggested.

"Lackwits! All of you! There is naught wrong with that body part either." *A thousand-year-old cock . . . amazing, when you think about it.* "It's my heart she wants."

They were all getting great pleasure out of his misery.

As they began running at a slow trot back to the compound, Thorfinn said, speaking to no one in particular, "What is love, anyway?"

"Wanna know what I think?" Geek asked Thorfinn.

"No."

"I think all this protesting that you're not in love with Lydia is just an excuse to cover the fact that you're scared. One woman left you high and dry, and you're afraid to give your heart to another."

"I ne'er gave my heart to Luta." *Or much else, and she gave even less in return. Pitiful, really.*

"Well, then, see," Cage drawled, "all the more reason to let the love bug into your heart."

"Love bug?" he scoffed. "If there was a love bug around me, it would probably bite me in the arse."

"Got it in one," Cage said, chuckling.

"You know, it would help if even one of you had a bit of constructive advice."

"Well, *cher*, since you asked. There's a famous Louisiana saying: Shuck Me, Suck Me, Eat Me Raw," Cage told him.

"I thought that referred to crawfish, or oysters, or somethin'," Sly said.

"Same thing," Cage countered.

Their risqué banter was giving him a headache ... that and the sap that ran in his body without release.

"Where do I find this head doctor? I think you all need him more than I do."

If all else failed, she could become a porn star ...

"This is fun," Alison said. "Can you do me when you're done doing Lydia?"

Four women giggled at her wording.

Using a rented video camera, Kirstin was filming Lydia in a flesh-colored leotard and in stilettos made up of two thin bands of black leather ... one across her toes and the other around her ankles. When she stood, her body was forced into a porn-star posture, pelvis thrust forward and butt arched back. Her hair had been curled and teased into one of those big bimbo "I Just Got Out of Bed" looks, and she wore enough lip gloss to lube a truck. She was doing some of the sexiest pole-dancing moves this side of a strip joint to the beat of "Wild Thing."

Amongst all the laughter and advice and praise, there was narration, as if Lydia were teaching moves to a class. When the video was "accidentally" shown to Finn, he would be told that it was a demo that Lydia had made for an instructional video company that might buy it.

Mike had joined Finn, Torolf, and Ian, with their kids, at some youth arcade place. Lydia had been there before and practically had to wear earplugs by the end of the evening. She hoped Finn suffered, just as he was making her suffer.

Later, up in her kitchen, where they were eating take-out Chinese, Lydia told Hilda, "Make sure no one but Finn sees this video."

"Why?" Hilda was licking soy sauce off her thumb.

"Because I would be embarrassed."

"Maybe you really should market the thing," Kirstin offered.

"Not on your life. As it is, I have fears the thing may end up on the Internet."

"Men!" Madrene said. "They do not know what they want. We have to lead them by their ears." She grinned. "Or their manparts."

"Truth to tell, I do not see what you want with the loathsome lout," Hilda remarked. "Dost know what he calls me? Hilda the Hun. I had to have Torolf explain it to me. It was not a compliment."

"I like him," Alison said. "Any man who shows such caring for a child is to be commended." When everyone turned to Alison, she blushed.

"Alison," Madrene said tentatively, "since when are you such an advocate for fatherhood? Could it be . . . ?"

"Yes!" Kirstin jumped up to kiss her sister-in-law. "You're pregnant, aren't you?"

Alison nodded, happy tears streaming down her face. Lydia knew that Alison had been pregnant before she'd married Ragnor six years or so ago, but she lost the baby. She suspected it had taken her all this time to get pregnant again.

Once all the congratulations and hugs were over, they sat down to resume eating.

"Would you like to have more children?" Lydia asked Hilda. She already knew Madrene had had a tubal ligation, and Kirstin wasn't married.

"Mayhap one more. And you?"

"I didn't think so. But now . . . I think I would. Yes, definitely."

"What I don't understand," Kirstin said, "is what caused your abrupt reversal about not being with a military man."

"Love," Madrene, Hilda, and Alison answered for her.

"Love does make a difference," Lydia conceded. *Now, if only Finn could realize that.*

"Well, let us hope that the idiot Viking takes the bait from your pole-dancing seduction," Hilda said. "I mean, lust is a given with Viking men, but that's not what you want to accomplish with this video . . . or at least not everything. Love is what you are aiming for, right? Love induced by jealousy."

Twist and shout: she twisted, he shouted . . .

Torolf was putting his bratling to bed, and Thorfinn had just showered. It had been a hard day of physical exercise, but satisfying. When he was panting for breath and his muscles screaming, he could forget about Lydia.

Liar! Lydia was on his mind, even then.

Unfortunately, there had been no opportunity these past few busy weeks for them to be alone. What little time he had was consumed with Miklof. Of course Lydia was usually there, too, but it was not the same.

Truth to tell, he had come to a surprising conclusion, especially after that talk he had had with Torolf and his comrades on the beach. He was in love with Lydia, if this constant ache in the region of his heart was an indication. Or the way he thought of nothing but her night and day. Or the way he walked about with a half-thickening at the most inappropriate times. Yea, he must be in love.

Lydia would be so happy. He could not wait to tell her. He called her number, but there was no answer, just her voice telling him to leave a message. Even he knew it would not be romantic to tell a woman for the first time that you loved her over a telephone. Mayhap on the morrow if he was able to get away from the SEAL command center.

So, it was with a smile of anticipation on his face that he walked into the solar to hear Lydia's voice. He stopped short, not having heard her arrive. But no one was there, except the shrew.

"Go away, Finn," Hilda ordered.

That of course meant he had to enter the room.

"What are you doing?" he inquired lazily as he plopped down into a soft chair. Hilda hated it when he used that lazy tone, or when he plopped onto her furniture.

"Watching an instructional video Lydia made. She's going to sell it to an Internet company."

He turned his attention to the TV box, and there Lydia was, stark naked. Nay, not naked. Wearing that skin-tight, flesh-colored garment. Not to mention tup-me-quick shoes that made a woman's body arch with the pelvis thrust forward. An invitation for sex play, if there ever was one. But, whoa, what was that dance move? It was as if she were making love to the pole. And the dreamy expression on her face! *Save me, Odin!*

As aroused as he was, instantly, he was also horrified. "Who will see this?"

"Everyone who buys it." Hilda did not even have the grace to look his way, so intent was she on watching the video.

"Men?"

"And women."

"Are you saying that strangers will pay to watch Lydia bend her . . . oh, my gods . . . did you see what she just did?"

"Yes. She *is* good, isn't she? Thousands of people will buy this video."

"Over my dead body!"

"You have no say over Lydia."

"Dost think so?"

Hilda did look at him then. "You do not love her, Finn. Why would you care?"

"I ne'er said I did not care." He could tell Hilda of his newly discovered love for Lydia and mayhap reduce her contempt, but why should he? And, really, Lydia should be the first to know. "I care too much."

"Bullshit!" Hilda was way too frank of manner and had taken on too many modern expressions, if you asked him, which nobody did.

"Coarse talk ill suits you, wench."

"Call me wench again, and I'll castrate you with that bloody sword of yours, which, incidentally, I want out of the linen closet."

Keep it up, shrew, and I will use said sword to slit your irksome tongue. "Mind your own business, Hilda." He was watching the video with his head cocked to the side. Who knew a woman could twist her body like that? He wondered what it would be like to have sex in that position. *Nay, nay, nay! I did not just think that.* Disgusted with himself, he walked up to the TV box and pressed the eject button.

"What are you doing?" she shrieked. "I need to watch that video. Lydia wants my advice on some of the moves that need work."

"I will give Lydia all the advice she needs about this wanton display." *Over my knees with her arse in the air. Betimes a good spanking is all that will do.* With that he stomped out of the room.

Smiling, Hilda listened as Thorfinn stormed up to his bedroom and slammed the door behind him. Then she called Lydia.

"It worked."

The things a woman will do for love . . .

Lydia was prepared for Finn when the doorbell rang the next night.

Mike was sleeping over at his friend's.

She was wearing a red camisole with matching tap pants, and nothing else.

Nail polish was on the coffee table, where she had presumably been painting her toenails, listening to soft rock music.

The lights were dim.

Aromatherapy candles burned on the mantel.

"Finn!" she exclaimed on opening the door. "What a surprise! But Mike isn't here."

Finn just stood frozen in place, surveying her from head to toe. She thought he murmured, "Gods help me!" before he shook his head as if to clear it and asked, "Are you alone?"

"Of course I'm alone." She was insulted that he would think she walked around like this with some man in the place. But wait . . . maybe that wasn't such a bad idea. "For now."

"Can I come in?"

Of course, said the spider to the fly. She nodded and opened the door wider for him to pass through.

"Why is it so dark in here?"

Atmosphere, honey. Atmosphere. "It's not dark. There are candles."

"Is your electricity broken?"

"No."

He went over to one of the candles and sniffed. "It smells. Like peaches. Why does your candle smell like peaches? And that one smells like lavender."

Oh, crap! Now he's obsessed with candles. "Forget the candles. Dammit."

He arched his eyebrows at her, then waved the

video in front of her face. "What in bloody hell are you thinking?"

That's right, Mr. Gullible. Take the bait. "Oh, that! It's just a little enterprise on the side to earn some extra money."

"Are you short of coin?"

"No." She sat down on the couch, put one foot on the coffee table, and began to give her toenails a second coat. He could probably see up her pant leg from where he stood. *I must have an inner bimbo gene.*

"Have you gone demented?"

"Why? Because I'm painting my toenails?" *Or because I'm chasing you like a lovesick teenager?*

"Nay, not because you are painting your toenails, though I see no sense in painting a part of the body that is covered most of the time."

"Some men think it's sexy." She looked up at him through half-mast lashes to gauge his reaction.

He thought it was sexy, all right.

"Why are you wearing such scant attire?"

To turn you on, Dunce of the Month. "It's what I sleep in."

"Not when I was here."

All these irrelevancies. Let's get on to the good stuff. "Finn, I don't sleep in the nude when I'm alone. I have a four-year-old son, after all."

"And don't you forget it, either." The lust in his eyes turned to anger as he put the tape on the floor and stomped on it. "I forbid you to sell yourself like this."

Don't hit him, Lydia. Do. Not. Hit. Him. "I beg your pardon. You're not even my . . . lover."

"I am so. I just have not had time to be with you that way these past two sennights."

"You had time to come and castigate me over a simple video."

"I was going to come tonight anyway. I have something important to—"

"Hah! It would have been nice if you had called ahead of time."

"I did, but I kept getting your bloody voice message. What I have to say to you had to be said in person."

"What? You couldn't leave a voice mail telling me you don't like my video?"

"That is not what I want to say, but since you mentioned it, let me be perfectly clear. You are the mother of my son, and for that reason, if no other, I will not allow you to entice men with your sex dancing."

"Entice? That's aerobic exercise. What century are you living in? Oops, I forgot. You *are* from a different century."

"'Tis sex and do not dare be at crosswills with me on this."

"Enough is enough!" If Mohammed wouldn't come to the mountain, she would go to him. She went over to him, stood on tiptoes, and kissed him hungrily 'til his stiff body went limp with surrender . . . except for one part that went stiffer. Then he put one hand at her nape and the other around her waist and took over the kiss, groaning into her mouth.

Her camisole was shoved to her waist and they were half on and half off the couch when he seemed to come to his senses. To her shock, he pulled her camisole back up, then shoved her away and stood. "Will you just slow down, Lydia? There is something I need to tell you first."

She put a hand to her mouth to stifle a cry. He didn't want her anymore. Not even for sex. That's what he had come to tell her. He was using the video as an excuse to dump her.

With a cry of desolation, she ran to her bedroom and locked the door after her. She soon learned that the lock was unnecessary, as she heard the front door open and close.

That was it, then.

It was over.

But she was mistaken, she realized, as she soon heard a loud pounding on her bedroom door.

Chapter 20

The best-laid plans . . .

Thorfinn was ready. All day he had been making preparations for what he was about to do, and he was not going to let Lydia change his game plan.

"Open the door, Lydia."

"Go away."

"Not 'til I tell you something."

"I've already got the message."

"I do not think so. Open the damn door, or I will break it down."

She yanked the door open and snarled, "What?"

"Ah, dearling, you have been crying." He reached for her, but she slapped his hands away.

"Don't you dare pity me, you Norse jackass."

"Pity is the last thing I feel for you." His eyes roamed

her body in the scandalous red garment, which was hardly a garment at all.

"Oh, I get it." She put her hands on her hips and glared up at him. "You want one last pity fuck, right?"

"Lydia! Such language!"

"Yeah, well, who needs you? I can get a vibrator. In fact I bought one yesterday."

"You did?" He was not sure what she had intended with a vibrator but he would surely find out later. "That is not what I meant."

"What *did* you mean? That you wanted a little more sex before you sashayed back to the Norselands or the SEAL compound or wherever the hell you intend to go next."

The only thing he could say to all she had thrown at him was, "Huh?"

"Listen, you . . . you Viking nitwit! If it's one for the road you're looking for here, forget it. No sex!"

If you think that, I have a bit of the Northlands to sell you.

"Let's get one thing straight. You made your feelings perfectly clear when you pushed me away out there in the living room. So don't think I'm going to hop in the sack with you now."

"You think I don't want you? I am a dunderhead if that is the impression I gave you." That notion was so far from his raging enthusiasm that he could hardly fathom her misreading him. "Well, that does it," he said, and began to unbutton his shirt.

"What do you think you're doing?" She was backing away from him.

"Straightening out your misconception." His shirt was gone, tossed over his shoulder, and he was toeing off his shoes. "Much as I am enjoying that wanton scrap of lace, take it off."

"No," she said, but her cheeks were now flushed with color and her eyes glued to his hands as they undid his braies and he shrugged out of them and his briefs at one time. Looking down, he saw a raging erection which impressed even him.

But Lydia stood frozen, still clothed.

Without preamble, he walked over, took the shoulder straps in each hand, then yanked them downward, pulling the entire garment to the floor, ripping it in places. She didn't seem to mind.

In fact, she seemed stunned and unsure of what was happening.

Well, he would have to show her. Picking her up by the waist, he tossed her onto the bed, followed after and over her. Rolling onto his back, he arranged her atop him, her breasts nigh riding his shoulders. He had to close his eyes for a moment, just to savor all the delicious sensations rippling through him.

She sighed.

His eyes opened, and he saw that she was already aroused. He reached a hand up to caress her cheek.

She turned her face into his palm and kissed it. "Where's your arm bracelet?" she asked, avoiding his direct gaze.

"I sold one of the arm rings."

"But you kept the star one?"

"For now. I have discovered that such jewelry is considered portable wealth. The one ring brought half a million of your American paper."

She was shocked. "Dollars?"

"Yea, dollars. Torolf helped me place it in a bank for safekeeping, though I would have much preferred keeping it on my body."

"Not that much money, honey."

"I like it when you call me honey. Even more, I like it when you move and your breasts caress my chest."

She raised herself slightly, arms now braced on either side of his head like a push-me-up, then swayed her breasts back and forth across his chest. She did it to tease him, but he could see that she was the one most excited by the friction. Her nipples were engorged already, and every sweep across the coarse chest hairs caused straight-to-the-groin erotic flames in his manpart. She moved her nether hair against his belly, and he could feel the warm wetness pooling there already.

"I should not be doing this."

"Yea, you should, my sweet."

"I don't understand. Just a short time ago you—"

"Nay, not now. The time for words will come later."

She nodded.

He watched her every reaction now. In a raw male voice, he urged, "Bring your breasts up to my mouth, sweetling."

She did. First one breast and then the other he paid homage with wet licks, hot breaths, flicks of his tongue, then deep suckling, which caused her back to arch and him to take more of her. She was keening her pleasure and reflexively undulating her hips against him. Not surprisingly, she shattered into a climax.

But he wanted to be inside her.

But wait. I'm getting ahead of my plan. "Move up farther. Methinks you are in need of laving. Bring your woman parts where I can minister to them."

"Did you say loving?"

"Nay. Laving."

She was disappointed, he could tell. "No."

"Dost say me nay? You get my longboat ready for voyage, then expect me to pull in the oars at the last second?"

"I want to know what the hell is going on here."

"We are making love."

"You know what I mean. Talk, buster. Tell me what you're thinking."

"Talk? Do not be daft. You wet my belly with your woman dew, nigh scalding me, then expect me to lie still and *talk*?"

"Yes."

He groaned.

She sat up on his waist and he tried to ignore the thrumming between his legs.

"Why do you torture yourself, sweetling?"

"You're the one torturing me with your roller-coaster moods. First you want me. Then you don't."

"Wrong, wrong, wrong. I have never stopped wanting you. Lydia! Please, for the love of all the gods, stop talking. Just sit on my cock and end this madness." He bucked his body, trying to move her downward.

She held herself in place, squeezing her knees tighter. "Not 'til we're done talking."

He groaned. "The lust sap is nigh dripping out my ears and every orifice of my body. I could not put two thoughts together if I tried."

She smiled.

"Either tup me, or get up," he demanded. When she hesitated, he took matters into his own hands. Flipping her over, he spread her legs and entered her in one long thrust that about made his eyes roll back in his head, so good did it feel.

Lydia looked equally flummoxed.

He was past the point of finesse. "Forgive me, heartling, but I cannot wait."

"Neither can I," she whispered.

Unable to hold back, he pounded into her tight sheath. With long, slow thrusts, then short and hard, he tried to show his feelings for her. Over and over he brought her to the edge of peaking, then stopped. He leaned back and flicked her woman petals with their center bud. He plunged some more. He was as out of control as she was. In fact . . . he would not admit this to anyone . . . but his knees gave out, and it was Lydia who rode him to the end when she tossed back her head and screamed. The blood drained from his scalp. His arms and hands, even his feet, tingled. His heart thundered against his chest wall. And then . . . and then he lifted his buttocks high, taking Lydia with him to a peaking that went on nigh forever. Afterward, her slick inner channels rippled around him in aftershock.

She lay splatted over him, her face buried in his neck. He was unable to move, at first. At last, he raised his head, saw that she was equally dazed, and raised his mouth to give her a quick kiss.

"This was not the way I planned this evening," he told her.

"You planned . . . ? I was the one with a plan. I mean, I don't understand."

He rolled her over onto her back and stared down at her.

"Lydia, I spent the entire day preparing. I had my hair cut, my face shaved, and I let the barber put some of this flowery water on me. All for your benefit. I even bought new clothes . . . and other things."

"I am totally confused," she replied. "I thought you left. I heard the front door slam."

"I just went outside to get something I left when I arrived earlier. Why did you flee from me, dearling?"

"Why? Why do you think, you jerk?" She shoved his chest and got up off the bed.

He laughed; he could not help himself. And stood also.

She growled and launched herself at him.

He picked her up off the ground, his arms around her waist, and hugged her tight to avoid her pounding fists.

"Lydia, I came here tonight with a purpose."

"To tell me off about the video." She was still trying to attack him with her hands and feet.

Despite their just having engaged in bedsport, he could feel his enthusiasm rising as she moved against him.

She stilled when she noticed.

"Sweetling, I came here tonight to tell you . . ." He gulped. "To tell you that I love you."

She leaned her head back to stare at him. "Liar."

He cupped her face with his hands. In a voice husky with emotion, he said, "I love you."

"What?" Her eyes blinked at him in shock.

"That is what I would have told you if you had not fled." *Or I had gathered my courage.*

"I gave you plenty of time to say . . . it."

"A man must needs pick the exact right time. I wanted to be holding you, like this, when I said the words I have ne'er said before in my life." *Who knew I had a talent for love words?*

"Say it again," she whispered.

"I love you, heartling." *It gets easier with each saying. Remarkable!*

"Oh. My."

"Is that all you can say?" He smiled against her lips. "I love you, Lydia. You have my heart."

"I love you, too, Finn. Forever."

You never know what a Viking will do . . .

Lydia was still stunned when Finn ordered her to put on a robe, and he drew on his jeans. Then he led her by the hand into the living room.

She stopped in her tracks.

All the candles had been lit and moved to the coffee table, where his sword lay, along with a shoe and a velvet box. "Good Lord. Are you planning some ritual sacrifice?

Do Vikings do that? Well, if you're expecting a virgin, you're in the wrong place, as you well know. What is this?"

"A Viking's attempt to make amends. Come." He tugged her closer, then pushed her down on the sofa.

He sat on the chair next to her.

Now, if only I can get it right. "Give me your hand, Lydia," he said. Before she could guess what he was going to do, he took the sword and ran the razor-sharp edge lightly over her wrist.

"Are you crazy?" she murmured, watching the drops of blood pool on her wrist.

You have seen nothing yet. "Of a certainty," he said.

"I know you didn't like being tied to a bed, but—"

Women can be such fools. "Who said I did not like it?"

She blinked at him. "What I meant was, there is no need for violence, just because you're irritated with me."

"Silly girling!" He chucked her under the chin.

She watched with horror as Finn made a shallow slit on his own wrist and laid the sword back down. Then he pressed his massive hand across hers so the blood mingled and their pulses merged. Looking her directly in the eye, he stated firmly, "Blood of my blood, I pledge thee my troth."

Lydia was in shock.

Oh. My. God! Heart hammering, Lydia sat frozen with shock. He really was a Viking barbarian. Then she smiled. *My Viking barbarian.*

Adjusting his hand so that their fingers twined together and folded, wrist to wrist, her wound seemed to tingle and throb with an erotic rhythm.

Oh, my!

"Now you repeat the words," he demanded raspily.

In stunned silence, her eyes locked with his. She could not speak.

"Say the words, Lydia," Thorfinn coaxed rawly.

"Blood of my blood, I pledge thee my troth," she repeated softly.

Something new and beautiful—and frightening—took root inside Lydia's chest and unfurled with exquisite intensity. She had thought she loved him before, but this was so much more. It took their love to a higher plane.

Still holding her arm fast, Finn flicked open the velvet box, one-handed, then took out a heavy, ornate gold ring in a writhing dragon motif. He slipped it on the third finger of her right hand. " 'Tis the first of my *arrha* gifts for you. At our wedding, you move it to your left hand, promising obedience to me." He chuckled. "Well, mayhap we could substitute fidelity for obedience."

Lydia admired his gift, closing her fingers to keep the huge gold band from slipping off. Looking closer, she saw that the dragon had a tiny ruby star in its mouth. "Where did you get this? It's so unusual."

"The Super Highway. And fast delivery from the FedEx man. Geek helped me. Really, Lydia, someday we must travel there. They have products from 'round the world."

She smiled. "Tell me again why you got this . . . what did you call it . . . *arrha*?"

"It means *earnest gift*. Vikings give three bridal gifts. The ring was the first." Then he handed her a pink satin ballet-type slipper. "Normally, I would have brought one of my mother's." He shrugged at the impossibility of that. "So, Wal-Mart had to suffice."

"Only one?" she asked with a laugh, pleased, despite herself, that Finn had taken the time for all these ritual items.

He grinned. "The husband swats the wife on the head with it during the marriage ceremony."

"Marriage?" she squeaked out.

"Yea, marriage. What did you think we were pledging here? Lust? Well, that, too. In the Norselands, the bride's father hands the shoe to the groom, transferring authority over his daughter. Dost think your father would do that?"

"Hah! Since I left home, my father has had no control over me. Actually, he likes you so much, he'd probably do anything if it meant bringing you into the family."

Thorfinn continued to grin. "On the wedding night, I will place the other shoe under my pillow on the marriage bed to show who is in charge."

Lydia shoved the slipper back into his hands. "Keep your slipper, but I'll keep the ring, thank you very much. Well, if that's all—"

"Nay, you forget. I mentioned there were *three* earnest gifts."

She raised an eyebrow.

"The traditional betrothal kiss." Before she could demur, he leaned forward. And he kissed her with such warmth that tears formed behind her eyelids.

He laughed then. "I give you four weeks to arrange a

wedding, but know this: my interfering family will probably insist on a Viking ceremony."

"We can do both."

He nodded. "We will be happy together. That, I promise."

"I know we will be."

He flashed her a wicked grin then. "Now, time for one more gift. I propose to reciprocate with the bed gift you gave me."

She frowned in confusion, then laughed. "Ah, the infamous intimate kiss."

"With a Viking slant to it."

"Hmmmm. Sounds . . . interesting."

That night she and Finn explored a new erotic spot, not the Viking S-Spot, or the modern G-Spot. No, this was the I-spot, thus named because all she could gasp out was, "I . . . I . . . I . . ."

It was a Viking feast fit for a king . . . uh, farmer . . .

Thorfinn Haraldsson and Lydia Denton were set to be married four weeks later under a tent at Mill Pond Farm.

Torolf Magnusson was his best man, and Kirstin Magnusson was the maid of honor, a modern designation that did not exist in his time. There were so many Vikings and SEALs in attendance that someone said they could form two football teams. So, they did, and a pickup game was held in the middle of the reception later that day.

But before that, they were married by a clergyman and then in the Norse tradition. Lydia's father led her over a white carpet . . . not an easy task on a farm. Later, people remarked that they had never heard a wedding march with a mooing backbeat. The bride walked under a canopy of swords. Viking and military dress swords. The SEALs wore white dress uniforms, often referred to as ice-cream-man attire, whatever that meant. The Viking men wore traditional garb befitting high Norse nobles, embroidered velvet and fine wool tunics over slim braies, belted with silver chains or tooled leather. Some wore fur-lined surcoats with shoulder mantles held together with ancient penannular-style brooches. Those with long hair had thin war braids framing their handsome faces. Thorfinn himself was dressed all in blue . . . a blue so dark it appeared black, from leather half-boots to braies to tunic, the darkness broken only by the gold-linked belt at his waist, and gold-embroidered stars along the edges.

Those women of Norse descent also dressed in the age-old attire of upper-class Viking women. Exquisite silk or linen *gunnas* with gold- or silver-threaded hems. Open-sided full-length aprons. And jewelry befitting a queen.

Thorfinn stood, smitten, waiting for his betrothed under the bridal canopy. He had not gone to so much fuss for his first wedding. In truth, he had married Luta by proxy. For Lydia, he wanted to do everything both new and according to the old ways.

And there she was . . . his Lydia, being led by her father and her son, both of whom wore dark suits with white *sherts* and ties. Lydia was dressed in the Norse bridal gown, which had been worn by others in his family, start-ing with Meredith, Geirolf's wife.

The undergown was a long-sleeved, collarless chemise of softest linen gauze, ankle-length in front, pleated and slightly longer in back. The wrists and circular neckline were embroidered with metallic green, gold, and white roses against a red background. The silk overgown, open-sided in the Viking style, was a deep crimson with match-ing bands of embroidery but with the colors reversed on a white background. A gold-linked belt matching his hung loose on her hips.

Torolf squeezed his arm, and they exchanged a look. 'Twas an unspoken understanding about the effect women . . . the right women . . . had on their lives.

After the Christian ceremony, Uncle Magnus, acting as loudspeaker, called out, "Hear ye, family and friends. Hear ye, Odin and all the gods. Come witness today the mar-riage of Thorfinn Haraldsson and Lydia Hartley Denton."

On a small table were placed a goblet of wine—Blue Dragon, of course—a KA-BAR knife which had be-longed to Dave, a hammer, a polished stone, and a bowl of wheat seeds.

Taking the goblet in hand, Thorfinn raised it high and said, "Odin, we thank you for this nectar of the gods . . . and the Blue Dragon Vineyard. May you bring us wisdom to deal well with each other in this marriage journey. Es-pecially give Lydia the wisdom of submission so she will bow to her husband's greater knowledge."

"Hah!" she said.

He took a sip of the wine, then pressed the goblet to her

lips. After she'd sipped the ruby liquid, he lifted the hammer. "Thor, god of thunder, I take in hand your mighty hammer, *Mjollnir*, which I just purchased at Home Depot. This I pledge: I will protect my wife from all peril. I will use the fighting skills learned at your feet to crush her enemies. Let it be known forevermore. Her foes are now my foes. My tangos are her tangos. The shield of the Yngling clan is now *our* shield." Raising the hammer, he crushed the stone with one sharp tap.

Next, Thorfinn scooped up a handful of seeds. "Frey, god of fertility and prosperity"—he sprinkled some of the seeds over her head, and then his own—"we implore fertility and the richness of love . . . and an abundance of passion." He grinned at her with those last worlds.

"Some of this ritual I am making up as I go along," he whispered to her.

"No kidding." She grinned at him.

Then he took the knife in hand.

"Oh, no. Not the cutting business again!"

"Shh." He drew blood from both of them, tied their wrists with a gold cord, and said, "As my blood melds with yours, Lydia, so shall my seed. From this day forth, you are my beloved."

And she said back to him, "With this mingling of our blood, I pledge thee my troth . . . and my everlasting love. And don't you ever cut me again."

Magnus spoke up then. "Who presents the *mundr*, or 'bride-price,' on behalf of Lydia?"

"I do," her father said, handing Thorfinn a rolled parchment.

When he opened it, Thorfinn scowled at Lydia. It was the deed to half the farm, postdated twelve years hence.

"This is my *morgen-gifu* for you, Lydia," he said, a wicked grin twitching at his lips. "This 'morning gift' is not to be opened 'til the morrow, following tonight's swi . . . uh, consummation." He could not wait to see her reaction. It was the last gift he'd had from his brother Steven . . . the polished marble harem wand. *I cannot wait to see MY reaction.*

"Who acts as witness to the *handsal*, which thus seals this wedding contract?" Magnus inquired, and five men stepped forth: Torolf, Ragnor, Geek, Cage, and Slick. It should have been six, but Thorfinn had demanded that empty space to represent his missing brother. And he was . . . sorely missed.

Torolf handed Thorfinn his sword then, and, placing a plain golden finger ring on the tip of the sword, Thorfinn offered it to Lydia, stating, "I give you this ring to mark the continuous circle of our unbreakable vows, and this sword to hold in trust for our sons."

"Did you buy that at Home Depot, too?"

"Shhh, wench." He chucked her under the chin. "Do you accept?"

She nodded, with tears filling her eyes, and repeated the ritual words with a male finger ring for her groom.

With one hand each on the hilt of the sword and their other hands joined, Magnus motioned for their witnesses to step forth. Then he said, "We declare ourselves witness that thou, Lydia of Mill Pond Farm, and thou, Thorfinn of Norstead, do bond to each other in lawful betrothal, and, with the holding of hands, dost promise one to the other love, honor, and fidelity as long as blood flows through your veins."

"Are you ready, wife?" Thorfinn asked with a wink.

"Yes, I'm ready, husband," Lydia replied, having been forewarned. With a screech of delight, she ran for the barn, lifting her gown knee-high. It was the *brudh gumareid*, or "bride-running."

Thorfinn chased after her, followed by the entire wedding party, laughing and cheering. In the end, he waited for her at the barn door, grinning, with the sword laid across the entryway. Normally, it would have been at the entrance of his keep. If she stepped over the sword, it was the final proof that she accepted her change of status, from maiden to wife.

She did, to the raucous cheers of all.

Thorfinn whacked her across the arse with a bare palm then, for all the trouble she had put him to.

She pinched his arse, for all the trouble he had put her to.

Once inside the barn, Thorfinn plunged his sword into the central beam, putting a deep scar into the supporting pillar of the barn. About a hundred cows mooed their disapproval. The depth of his cut was an indication of virility. His cut was very deep.

After that was much feasting and drinking of the honey-mead, something Vikings excelled at, as they told one and all as the day wore on. That, and something else, Thorfinn whispered to his wife when the reception seemed never-ending.

"I cannot wait," she whispered back.

"Well, why did you not say so afore?" With that, he picked up his new wife and carried her off for a private celebration.

Where was a ghost-buster when you needed one? . . .

In the secluded cabin where they would honeymoon, Thorfinn made love to his wife two times afore succumbing to sleep. It had been a long, exhausting day for both of them. Plus, he had drunk a tun of mead.

But he was awakened by the strangest dream.

A man sat on a cloud, grinning down at him. There was no doubt in his mind who it was. David Denton.

"Go away," he said, rolling over to press his face into the pillow. *It must be the alehead affecting me.*

The dream was still there.

"So, you and my wife, huh?"

He checked to make sure Lydia was still asleep. She was. "She is no longer your wife. You are dead."

"Semantics, my man. Just semantics."

He had no idea what that word meant and wasn't about to ask. "Are you here to haunt me? If so, forget about it. I am not leaving Lydia."

"Why would I haunt you? I sent you."

"Huh? Are you an angel?" *Or a jest of that joker god Loki?*

"Not yet. But know this—I was there in Baghdad when those tangos attacked you."

That is just wonderful. "Why did you not help me?"

"That's not the way it works, buddy. And I was there when the SEALs brought you back to Coronado. I was there at the Wet and Wild the night you met Lydia; in fact, I had to push you mentally to even go. And I was there the first time you made love." He paused for so long, Thorfinn thought the dream had ended. But, nay, the specter cleared his throat and spoke again. "That was hard, watching Lydia with another man, but I want her to be happy. And Mike needs a dad."

Thorfinn sat up, and the dream continued. Was he sleeping in this position now? *Please, gods, let me be sleeping.* He checked to see if he had awakened Lydia, but she slept on. "Are you saying that you approve?"

"I need to give my blessing before I can move on to the other realm."

"And do you?" *Like I care!*

David nodded and a tear slipped from his eye and slid down his almost translucent cheek. "Take care of my family, Viking. Take good care, or I will haunt you forever."

He nodded, touched beyond words. *And, yea, I do care.*

"God bless . . ."

The dream ended abruptly.

Thorfinn ran to the window. He saw one single star flicker in the sky. Then go out.

Reader Letter

Dear reader:

Well, another Viking bites the dust!

I hope you liked Thorfinn, that you smiled at his clue-lessness and felt a tug at your heartstrings when he grieved over his lost baby. I also hope you shared Lydia's pain when she lost her precious husband.

I've said it before, and will say it again: there is nothing sexier than a tormented man with a sense of humor, and that was Thorfinn, for sure. I also hope that you continue to enjoy the Viking Navy SEAL scenario; the similarities between ancient Viking warriors and modern-day SEAL operatives boggles the mind. SEALs even call themselves webfoot warriors.

But please know this: the Vikings I depict in my books

are my creation alone. I try to the best of my ability (years of research) to make the background of my books historically accurate; however, these stories are romantic humor, not historical novels. So, the Magnusson and Ericsson families are pure fantasy, based on bits and pieces of history. The ritual words are my spin on oral histories that are not always reliable. Hey, there wasn't much written word a thousand years ago; in fact, except for a few rare cases, you would have had a hard time finding a book. It is an undisputed fact, though, that the Viking men were strong, brave fighting men who had an unusual sense of humor for their times. They had an ability to laugh at themselves like no other culture. And, yes, they were reputed to be very handsome and great lovers. That bit about all Norsemen being rapers and pillagers was a figment of some monk scholars' bias . . . well, maybe not the pillaging. Vikings did relish going a-Viking, and if they picked up a few souvenirs along the way, well, those were the perks.

If this is your first taste of my Viking Navy SEALs, you may want to go back and look for others in this loosely linked series (which can be read out of order), including *Rough and Ready* and *Down and Dirty*. And look for another in 2009 . . . a contemporary woman going back to Viking times. I call it *Private Benjamin* meets *Stripes* because my heroine, after being jilted several times, finds herself in the middle of brutal training for WEALS, a female Navy SEAL program, wondering, "What was I thinking?"

Please visit my website for news, videos, genealogy charts, freebies, and a complete book list.

As always, I wish you smiles in your reading, and I thank you from the heart for all your support.

Sandra Hill
PO Box 604
State College, PA 16804
www.sandrahill.net